NEVER SAY NEVER

USA Today Bestselling Author

JENNIFER SUCEVIC

Never Say Never

Copyright© 2024 by Jennifer Sucevic

Cover Design by Mary Ruth Baloy at MR Creations

Special Edition & Animated Cover by Claudia Lymari

Editing by Evelyn Summers at Pinpoint Editing

Proofreading by Autumn Sexton at Wordsmith Publicity

Interior Formatting Silla Webb

www.jennifersucevic.com

In the darkest nights, I stumbled, couldn't see the light.
Lost in a maze, couldn't find what's right.
But deep inside, a fire burned,
refusing to fade away.
A voice inside me whispered, 'You'll find your way.'

I'm rising up, stronger now than I've ever been.
Every scar's a story, ain't letting them win.
Through the ups and downs, I'll find my truth.
In the chaos of it all, I'll find my youth.

Through every fall and every doubt, I'll stand tall.
Gonna shake off the past, gonna give it my all.
With each new day, leaving old fears behind.
Embracing every challenge, gonna free my mind.

BRITT

1

The guy hasn't said a single word yet, and already my skin is buzzing with awareness. How is it possible that his steady gaze sliding over my body feels more like a physical caress than anything else?

It doesn't make the least bit of sense.

I'm not into his brand of handsome.

He's way too attractive for his own good.

Even worse than that?

He knows it.

And uses it as a weapon of female destruction.

I'm well acquainted with his type.

And I'm not interested.

If only it were possible to stomp out the arousal that has settled at the bottom of my belly like an unmovable stone.

Ever since stepping foot on campus in August, I've been inundated with the stories that circulate regarding Colby McNichols. At this point, they're more like urban legends or Western University folklore. Tales that will be passed down for generations to come. Even if I hadn't heard about him, it would be impossible not to catch sight of all the girls that cling to the guy like baby rhesus monkeys.

And not one at a time, either.

These chicks don't care if they need to share him just to get a small taste.

Can you even imagine?

Ummm....no thanks.

In fact, I just threw up in my mouth.

Gross.

On both accounts.

Mr. Too Hot to Handle needs to move it along, because I am *definitely* not a puck bunny who'll fall onto her back and spread her legs wide. Or a groupie that'll hang on his every word, hoping to be chosen for the night. This guy eats girls up like sugary cereal in the morning before moving onto the next thirty minutes later.

I'm probably giving him way too much credit.

More like fifteen.

I bet his starfish impression is dead on.

Sadly, they love him for it.

I just can't.

"I don't think we've had the pleasure of meeting," he says, deep voice smooth and brimming with confidence as he interrupts my conversation with Carina.

I got to know the pretty blonde dancer during the fall semester and really clicked with her. She seems more like a girl's girl.

Which is refreshing.

And I enjoy her friends just as much. Juliette, Stella, Viola, and Fallyn are all great girls who have welcomed me into their tight-knit group with open arms. This is the first time in almost a decade that I can actually say I have a handful of genuine female friendships. They have no idea just how much that means to me.

Maybe if I ignore him long enough, he'll get the hint and exit stage left.

A second or two ticks by before he turns up the wattage of his smile. It makes the dimples in his cheeks pop and flash. It takes effort to stomp out the zip of electricity attempting to sizzle its way through my veins.

"What's your name, beautiful?"

Sigh.

So much for him picking up what I'm laying down.

When it becomes obvious that he isn't going to get lost until I double down on my disinterest, I flick a steely look in his direction.

One that will hopefully shrivel his balls.

"I'm not interested. So, feel free to move it along."

Dismissing him, I resume my convo with Carina.

That hard-edged tone is usually enough to cause the most obnoxious of men to deflate like a popped balloon and slink away with their tails tucked firmly between their legs.

I've spent years honing it so that it's razor sharp.

And just as deadly.

I've handled men twice my age who are execs in the biz and think that makes me fair game. So, putting this college hockey playing hottie in his place should be a piece of cake.

I wince at the unconscious descriptor.

His brows pinch as he blinks in confusion. "Excuse me?"

I'm forced to turn more fully in his direction before annunciating carefully as if talking to a two-year-old, "I said that I wasn't interested. Hockey players aren't my thing. Now, if you'll—"

The muscles in his face soften as he flashes another dazzling smile that's even more swoonworthy than the first before giving me an—*are you cray-cray* look. Confidence drips from every word. "Sweetheart, I'm everybody's thing."

Thrown off by his response, my eyes widen as a burst of laughter escapes from me. This guy really *is* full of himself.

I mean...sure, I'd heard he was, but seeing it in action firsthand is another matter entirely. All I can say is that it'll be an absolute pleasure to disabuse him of the notion that he can have any girl he wants simply by flashing his dimples. As I reach out and pat his clean-shaven cheek, another surge of desire flares to life before I douse it like an out-of-control kitchen fire.

"I'm sure that you are, pretty boy. But not mine."

Genuine interest ignites in his eyes as he invades my personal space. It's tempting to retreat a step, but I refuse to give him the satisfaction.

"Here's an idea—how about you let me buy you a shot and we'll see just how wrong you are when I roll out of your bed in the morning?"

Irritation ignites inside me.

This guy has some serious nerve.

I'm barely aware that Fallyn's jaw has become unhinged as her gaze bounces between the two of us.

Refusing to back down, I shake my head.

Now it's a matter of principle.

"No thanks." I point toward the crowded table in the back that buzzes with puck bunnies hoping to get lucky.

I slant him a cool look. "You seem to have your hands full. My advice is to stick with the groupies. You wouldn't know what to do with a girl like me."

A roguish grin slides across his face that makes him look even hotter. "Is that so?"

I lift my chin a notch. "Yup. Accept defeat gracefully while you still have the chance."

"Oh, I think we're way past that now. Don't you, firecracker?"

"Firecracker?" A gurgle of laughter escapes from me as my eyes narrow. "Do the cutesy names actually work for you? Is it so you don't have to remember someone's name in the morning?"

His blue eyes flash like lightning in a bottle.

It's almost mesmerizing.

Before the situation can escalate any further, Fallyn picks up her loaded tray and turns to Colby. "Hey, look—I have your shots. Why don't you follow me to your table?"

He continues to pin me in place with the heat of his gaze. I can't tell if he's ignoring Fallyn or if his focus is so great that her voice isn't able to penetrate it.

It's been a while since I've had anyone stare at me so intently. Even with the dim lighting in the bar, I have to force myself not to squirm beneath his scrutiny. It's the first time since stepping foot on campus that I've felt unnerved. I shake away the panic that floods my system and remind myself that I couldn't look more different.

My hair is no longer lavender in hue, and it's shoulder length. I've changed it back to its original rich, caramel color and chopped off about ten inches.

After all these months of living in plain sight, I've gradually lowered my guard.

My hand rises automatically before I realize that there isn't a ball cap to tug over the upper portion of my face. Air gets clogged in my throat as I steel myself for what will happen next.

Just as the atmosphere turns oppressive and I'm seconds away from bolting out the back door, Fallyn taps him on the shoulder to reclaim his attention. The fear holding me paralyzed dissolves when he glances at the waitress.

"Here's the shots you ordered," Fallyn presses. "Ready to head back?"

Colby's gaze returns to me. "Yup. Let's go."

With one final look that skewers me to the core, he swings away, moving through the thick press of bodies with the ease of a king walking among his loyal subjects. People scurry out of his way.

Just as a relieved breath leaks from my lungs, he twists back around and recaptures my gaze.

"This isn't over, firecracker."

Even though I'm rattled, I force a smile. "Actually, it is. You've just been hit in the head with a hockey puck too many times to realize it." With a tip of my beer bottle, I turn and dismiss him.

Taunting this guy is a terrible idea and yet, I can't seem to help myself.

It's almost a surprise when he whips around and follows Fallyn instead of making his way back to me.

The only thing I can say with absolute certainty after that explosive encounter is that avoiding Colby McNichols for the foreseeable future is now at the top of my to-do list.

2

COLBY

I throw another glance over my shoulder and stare at the girl who just shot me down in a blaze of glory. She and Carina have resumed their convo. Ford's girlfriend looks as if she's doing her best not to burst out laughing.

My guess is that she's enjoying this.

It goes without saying that I'll never hear the end of it.

Unable to help myself, my attention returns to the gorgeous girl with caramel colored hair as I silently will her to turn and meet my gaze.

She doesn't.

Her disinterest is palpable.

I nod toward the bar and fire off the question before I can think better of it. "Who's the girl?"

"Her name is Britt." Fallyn's dark brows draw together. "She transferred to Western last semester."

My gaze slices to the chick who just trampled my ego without a second thought. "Hmmm. I don't think I've seen her around. Pretty sure I'd remember if I had."

There's no two ways about it.

I would *definitely* remember.

Even though Fallyn is carrying a tray loaded down with shots, she twists around and pokes me in the chest with her finger. "Do me a favor and stay away from Britt. She's not one of your puck bunnies."

I flash a grin before nipping one of the glasses off her tray and lifting it to my lips. "Sorry, can't make any promises."

I send a little wink her way before belting back the shot. The smooth, cinnamon flavored liquor burns a fiery trail down the back of my throat. Before I can return the glass to her tray, two girls slide beneath my arms and stare up at me like I'm their long-lost god.

"Hey, Colby!" one chirps.

"We missed you!" the other adds in an equally cheerful voice.

Both shift close enough for their soft titties to press against my chest. I snake my arms around them and attempt to forget about the little firecracker who just annihilated me with one icy glare.

If there are girls who can perform just such a feat, it would be Tanya and Lindy. Not only are they sorority sisters, but they're besties who do everything together.

And I do mean *everything.*

They were both gymnasts and then cheerleaders in high school. They're bendy in ways I never dreamed possible and can always be depended on to put on a spectacular show. Their fawning is exactly the balm needed after my encounter with Fallyn and Carina's prickly friend.

Give these two honeys ten minutes and I won't even remember the previous convo. Hell, five minutes will be more than enough to forget about her light brown hair and golden colored eyes. Even in the dimness of the bar, they flashed and sparked with challenge.

Yeah...those particular thoughts aren't helping the situation at all.

When Tanya strokes nimble hands over my chest, I realize I'm staring across the bar and force my attention back to the blonde tucked against me.

She flashes a toothy grin when our gazes collide.

At least, I think it's Tanya.

It could be Lindy.

My brow furrows as I try to figure it out. I can never keep them straight.

Although, it's not like there's a reason. We're not going out. The only time we spend together takes place between the sheets. I have zero interest in getting caught up in a relationship.

Not after the crap that went down my senior year of high school. It took months to get my head on straight. Four years later, the only girls I fuck are the ones who are out for a good time and nothing more.

It keeps things easy.

Uncomplicated.

Just the way I like it.

I'm knocked from the tangle of my thoughts when one of them murmurs, "Let's get out of here." She bats her long lashes before whispering, "Lindy and I have something special planned for you tonight."

Instead of focusing on the throaty promise and the acrobatics that are sure to accompany it, my attention gets snagged by her lashes. There's no damn way they're real. They're thick and clumpy.

If I squint, they kind of remind me of hairy spiders.

Especially when she bats them.

I'm not gonna lie...it's creeping me out.

It's a definite mood killer.

Unable to stare at them a second longer without a shiver skating down my spine, I refocus on her lips. They're ridiculously plump.

It's tempting to ask if she's having an allergic reaction and in need of an EpiPen. But I'd bet my athletic scholarship they're just injected with filler.

I glance at Lindy, only to find that she's a mirror image of her bestie.

Their shirts are so low cut and tight that it wouldn't surprise me if one of their nips popped out to play peek-a-boo. And their skirts are so short that there's no way they could bend over unless they want to flash their panties.

If they're wearing any.

My gaze is reluctantly drawn to the girl on the other side of the bar. There's nothing fake about her. In fact, it's doubtful she's wearing makeup. Her outfit is basic. A simple sweater and jeans. The dark wash denim hugs her curves like a glove and the thin black sweater hints at what's hidden beneath the soft looking material. Although... one wouldn't know for certain unless they were able to get their greedy hands on her.

Fuck.

"Colby?" Lindy prompts when I remain silent. "Are we heading back to our place?"

"Sorry, ladies," I blurt. "I appreciate the offer, but I'm not feeling it tonight."

Their eyes flare as they thrust out their lower lips in matching expressions of disappointment.

"Are you sure?" Tanya cajoles. "We know exactly what you like."

It's true.

They know *exactly* what I like in the bedroom.

Under normal circumstances, that not-so-gentle reminder would be more than enough to hustle my ass out the door.

But that's not the case tonight.

I shake my head, confused as to why I'm so intent on a girl who refuses to give me the time of day.

Wait a minute...

Oh, I get it.

A relieved smile quirks the corners of my lips.

Damn, I should have realized it sooner.

This girl is playing hard to get.

I mean, duh...of course she is.

Girls don't say no to me.

This is nothing more than a chess game.

She wants me to chase her. Make her feel special. Like she's different from all the other puck bunnies and groupies.

Of course you are, firecracker.

I almost laugh as understanding slams into me with the force of a two by four. Never in my life have I worked to secure female attention. Even when I was a kid, women fussed and fawned over my big blue eyes and dimples. They melted in elementary school and wanted to be my 'girlfriend.' Sometimes I had five at the same time. One for each day of the week. I'd grin at my jealous friends while the girls buzzed around me like drunken bees.

Hey, don't hate the player.

Hate the game.

For a handful of seconds, I'd almost thought I'd lost my touch.

In an unprecedented move, I untangle myself from Lindy and Tanya. "I'll catch you two later."

The first thing I'm going to do is a bit of recon. My gaze lands on Juliette, Stella, and Viola, who are talking at one of the tables.

Perfect.

Just the people I was looking for.

Over the past fifteen minutes, I've seen all three of them give Britt a hug. So, they're obviously chummy.

A little intel will help me nail her down.

Or, more accurately, nail her.

I settle on the other side of the table across from Juliette and Viola. Riggs and Stella are chilling to my left.

My teammate lifts his chin in greeting. "Hey man. Heard you got your ass handed to you." A smug smile curls its way around his lips. "Wish someone had caught it on video. I would have loved to see it." He cranes his head and pretends to look around. "Where is she? I need to shake her hand and buy her a beer."

I give him the finger and refocus my attention on the girls. "So... your friend over there." I jerk my head toward the bar. "What's her deal?"

Juliette's brows slant together. "I assume you're talking about Britt?"

I drum my fingers against the sticky tabletop, only wanting to hasten this convo along. "Yup. That would be the one."

Just as she opens her mouth, Ryder McAdams tugs her from the chair and drops down onto it before pulling her onto his lap. This must be an everyday occurrence because she doesn't even blink at his manhandling.

This guy is so whipped.

I give Riggs a bit of side eye. He's busy nibbling away at Stella's neck. Any moment, he's going to devour her in one tasty gulp.

It's tempting to drag a hand down my face.

What the hell is going on with these guys?

They're all getting wifed up.

There must be something in the water around here.

I glance at Wolf Westerville, who's lounging at the far end of the table. His attention is locked on his newly minted girlfriend, Fallyn. Can't say I saw that one coming. It's like one day, he was all moody and surly and the next, he's in a full-on relationship with Fallyn DiMarco and totally domesticated.

A few weeks ago, I couldn't have told you a damn thing about the girl.

Even though she's seriously hot, she wasn't on my radar. Although, I'd never say either of those things to Wolf. He's liable to take me out. He's more of a strike first and ask questions later kind of dude.

It's just one of the reasons I enjoy him in goal.

I'll miss the hell out of the guy next year. He'll sign his contract with Boston, and if all goes according to plan, I'll be in Milwaukee. A couple times a year, I'll get a chance to fuck with him, but that's about it.

Juliette presses her lips together before shaking her head. "She's not your type, Colby. Sorry."

I cock a brow.

I have a type?

That's news to me.

"Oh?"

She rolls her eyes. "You know exactly what I mean."

"Nope, not a clue." I pick up my bottle of beer from earlier and bring it to my lips before waving my other hand around. "Please, enlighten me."

I take a swig.

Fuck. Talk about warm...

"Is that really necessary?" she asks with a heavy sigh.

Damn right it is.

"I'd like to hear more about my *type*."

This should be good.

She glances at her boyfriend. The asshole's shoulders are shaking. Barely is he able to keep a straight face. "Tell him what he wants to know, babe."

I narrow my eyes at my teammate. "Yeah...tell me, Little McKinnon."

"You know that I'm the older sibling, right?"

"I meant in stature."

She straightens on Ryder's lap. "Well, you like girls who have an interest in hockey."

When I lift a brow, ready to negate that factoid, she tacks on, "Players."

I don't technically have an interest in chicks who like hockey players. It just makes getting laid easier.

But I keep that little tidbit to myself.

I shrug. "Maybe."

"You especially like ones who understand you're not looking for anything long term. And, from what I've seen, more than two hours would be considered long term."

The girl's got me there.

She cocks her head. "Have you ever had a girlfriend? Maybe you'd actually enjoy it."

Ryder snorts.

When an image of Anna sneaks into my brain, I quickly shove it away.

"I'm happy being single." I take another swig of the warm beer to cover my discomfort with this line of questioning.

I've never told any of my teammates about what happened in high school, and I don't plan on rehashing it now. The lingering anxiety and anger that will sometimes wrap its icy fingers around my chest and squeeze until breathing becomes impossible is the only reminder from that time in my life. Otherwise, I try like hell not to think about it.

It's over with and I've moved on.

"Which is exactly why it won't work with Britt. She's not interested in athletes, let alone hockey players who like to hit it and quit it before moving on to the next warm body."

"It sounds suspiciously like you're trying to slut shame me. FYI—that's totally not cool. Is it really such a problem that I like to spread the love around so everyone's happy?"

She rolls her eyes. "Yeah, you're a real goodwill ambassador for Western."

"Exactly. It's important work. And someone needs to do it."

For the umpteenth time, I glance at the girl in question. I hate to admit it, but the more I hear about her, the more intrigued I become.

It's only when slender hands slide around me from behind, and a pair of soft breasts are pressed against my shoulder blades that I snap back to the convo with Juliette.

"Just the man I was looking for," a husky voice whispers in my ear.

Larsa Middleton.

I'd recognize her cloying scent anywhere.

"I was just talking to Lindy and Tanya. They said you weren't interested in having a little fun tonight. I told them that I bet a foursome would change your mind."

Fuck.

Have I jumped into bed with three girls before?

Guilty.

And I was pretty sure my dick was going to fall off afterward.

Let's just say a lot of balm was needed.

Unconsciously, my gaze meanders to the pretty girl on the other side of the bar. It feels like I'm having an out-of-body experience. Am I really going to turn down a foursome with Lara, Lindy, and Tanya?

When my gaze collides with Juliette's dark one, she raises a brow as if to say *exactly my point.*

I clear my throat and rise to my feet. "Sorry, Larsa. Tanya and Lindy were right. Not tonight."

I'm on the move before she can attempt to detain me.

The only girl I'm interested in taking home is the one with caramel-colored hair and a smartass mouth that'll look good wrapped around my dick.

Said appendage twitches at the idea.

As I cut a path in her direction, she swings away and heads toward the hallway where the restrooms are located. I watch for a moment before switching course and following from a safe distance. Culling her from the crowd and talking to her in semi-private can only work to my advantage.

Already I feel my luck with this chick changing.

When she slips into the bathroom, I park myself outside the door before leaning against the opposite wall and folding my arms across my chest as I settle in to wait.

A couple minutes later, the thick wood swings open and a few girls trickle out. They stumble to a drunken halt before their hungry gazes slide up and down my length like I'm a piece of meat.

I get the feeling the one on the left would lick me if it were socially acceptable.

"Hey, Colby," one of them says. "Can't wait to watch your next game."

"Thanks."

"We're your biggest fans!" the second one adds.

"The biggest," the third girl echoes with a slur.

"We appreciate your support." When I say nothing more, they stagger down the hallway, giggling to one another.

My attention returns to the door just as it opens for a second time. Britt's eyes widen as she stutters to a stop.

Yup...her eyes are just as mesmerizing as I remember. It wasn't a trick of the light or my imagination.

I flash a charming smile. The blinding one that makes my dimples pop in tandem. The very same one that's been known to drop panties in five seconds flat.

When she remains silent, I say, "I wanted to apologize for earlier." This is the part where I up the wattage to near dazzling. "I think we got off on the wrong foot."

Instead of melting into a puddle of goo at my feet the way I expect, her eyes narrow as she shakes her head. "Actually, I don't think we did."

There's not even a flicker of interest in her expression.

When she steps closer, swallowing up the distance between us, my breath hitches as anticipation leaps to life in my veins before flooding my system.

What the actual fuck is that about?

My breath has never hitched once in my life.

Not even before stepping onto the ice for a championship game.

I glance at her lips. They're plump and shiny. But not oversized like the blonde sorority chicks who were trying to have their wicked way with me.

It takes effort to force my gaze back to hers, where it stays fastened. There's an intensity within her golden depths that makes me feel like I'm drowning.

It's the strangest sensation.

One I don't understand.

She tilts her chin to maintain eye contact. "Spoiler alert—I'm not going to sleep with you."

That's unfortunate.

"You sure about that?" I rasp.

She presses close enough for me to feel the softness of her breasts through the thin sweater she's wearing. I can't help but flex my chest, desperate for more contact.

"Yeah, I am. I will *never* sleep with you." Seconds tick by as she carefully searches my gaze. "The girls that were just hanging all over you are the ones you should take home."

The edges of my lips quirk upwards. "Ahhh...so you were watching. Good to know."

She snorts. "My point is that they would be easy. More your speed. You should stick with that."

"Maybe I don't want easy," I blurt.

The throaty chuckle that escapes from her breaks the thick tension building between us.

"Of course you do. You like the thrill of the chase."

Her smile is like a gut punch.

When I remain silent, unsure what to say, she continues. "Please. Easy is what you're used to."

"Interesting. I didn't realize we knew each other so well."

"I don't have to know you personally to know your type. I've seen it a million times before. Trust me when I say that I'm not what you're looking for."

Before I can fire back another response, she says, "I was just about to take off. But it was nice *not* meeting you." She cocks her head. "Let's keep it that way, shall we?"

I...

Have no words.

I'm pretty sure that my mouth is gaping wide like a smallmouth bass.

With that, she takes a step in retreat. Air rushes between us, making me miss the warmth of her smaller body pressed against mine.

It's only when she swings away and is no longer staring at me that I find my tongue. "Never say never, firecracker."

She throws a glance over her shoulder. Our eyes lock for a heart-beat before she walks away, leaving me alone in the dark hallway with only my chaotic thoughts for company.

IN THE DARKEST NIGHTS, I STUMBLED, COULDN'T SEE THE LIGHT.
LOST IN A MAZE, COULDN'T FIND WHAT'S RIGHT.
BUT DEEP INSIDE, A FIRE BURNED,
REFUSING TO FADE AWAY.
A VOICE INSIDE ME WHISPERED, 'YOU'LL FIND YOUR WAY.'

I'M RISING UP, STRONGER NOW THAN I'VE EVER BEEN.
EVERY SCAR'S A STORY, AIN'T LETTING THEM WIN.
THROUGH THE UPS AND DOWNS, I'LL FIND MY TRUTH.
IN THE CHAOS OF IT ALL, I'LL FIND MY YOUTH.

THROUGH EVERY FALL AND EVERY DOUBT, I'LL STAND TALL.
GONNA SHAKE OFF THE PAST, GONNA GIVE IT MY ALL.
WITH EACH NEW DAY, LEAVING OLD FEARS BEHIND.
EMBRACING EVERY CHALLENGE, GONNA FREE MY MIND.

BRITT

I strum a few chords on the acoustic guitar cradled in my arms. It's the same one I've had since I was twelve years old and wrote my first song. For just a moment, memories of a simpler time press in at the edges. A decade ago, all I could dream about was making music and getting offered a record deal by a label. It's what I spent every spare minute running toward.

Now, I'm doing everything in my power to escape from it.

A puff of air leaks from me.

It's funny how life works.

Or maybe a better word would be ironic. Sometimes you get exactly what you asked for, but it's a twisted version you could have never imagined.

It's only when I realize that my thoughts have become mired in the past that I shake them away and refocus on the chords, listening to the notes as they vibrate throughout the silence of the apartment. I close my eyes and repeat the movement, allowing them to wash over me for a second time.

When the lyrics accompanying the notes appear in my mind, I snag the pencil tucked behind my ear to jot them down. Then I repeat the chords and sing the verse to see how it sounds.

> "In the darkest nights, I stumbled, couldn't see the light. Lost in a maze, couldn't find what's right. But deep inside, a fire burned, refusing to fade away. A voice inside me whispered, 'You'll find your way.'"

Pleasure rushes through me. There were times throughout the years that I wondered if I'd ever feel inspired to create more music.

It might have taken six months, but it's finally coming back to me.

This is all I ever wanted to do.

I never asked for the other bullshit that came along with it.

The reality show.

The online haters that watch my every single move, waiting for a fuckup so they can rip it to shreds frame by frame.

So they can rip *me* to shreds.

That's the hardest part and what took me the longest to wrap my brain around. As much as they love you, they hate you and want to see you fail.

Even when I tried to close myself off to the criticism, it still managed to invade my brain, contaminating it like a virus, rotting it from the inside out.

Until I started wondering where the truth really lies.

Was I just another one-hit wonder?

Were my fifteen minutes of fame long gone?

Was I now one of those celebrities famous for being famous?

I never realized how easily other people's hatred and jealousy could be soaked up like a sponge until even the most confident individuals couldn't help but question themselves and their talent.

If so many people held the same opinion, then it had to be true, right?

Maybe if I'd understood just how much life would change until it became almost unrecognizable, I never would've signed that first contract.

But you don't know what you don't know.

Especially when you're a kid.

All I could daydream about was being famous and getting the chance to play my music in front of a real audience. Not one made up of family and friends.

Then again, I was thirteen. There was no way my parents would have turned down that kind of life-changing opportunity or money.

They barely read through the legal document before signing on the dotted line.

The past eight years have been spent in front of a camera before finally getting fed up enough to walk away. After wrapping the final episode of *All Day Long with Bebe*, I'd slipped from the celebration, packed a bag, and taken off.

It didn't matter if my family or the producers understood.

I needed a break.

From the show.

From them.

From the life we'd created.

I needed time to figure out who I was and what I wanted my future to look like. I was no longer sure if it was long days of filming and a never-ending string of LA parties.

So, I escaped to the one place I knew I was welcome.

My aunt and uncle's house.

Uncle Sully mentioned that the fall term at Western would start soon and reminded me that I'd always wanted to attend college. It was all the incentive I needed to fill out an application and look for an apartment.

With one semester under my belt, I was even more confused about what I wanted out of life. Every day that passed, California felt less like reality and Western felt more like home.

I pluck the strings again, dispelling those thoughts and refocusing my attention on the music. Another line comes as I harmonize with the tune.

Just as I reach for the pencil, there's a knock on the door.

I shoot a frown at the entryway.

Since moving into my apartment, I haven't gone out of my way to make friends with my neighbors. At first, it felt safer to keep my distance. I was afraid someone might recognize me and blow my cover. The longer I've been absent from LA, the more speculation has brewed as to why I haven't been seen out with my family.

Or Axel.

When there's another, more impatient rap of knuckles against the thick wood, I set my guitar down and pad across the carpet before peering through the peephole.

It's probably Lance, my neighbor. We've studied together half a dozen times or so. He's a sweet kid. A couple days ago, he asked me out.

I told him that I'd think it over.

My eyes widen and my brows pinch together as I press closer to the door.

No.

Fucking.

Way.

What the hell is Colby McNichols doing here?

I thought I'd nipped his interest in the bud the other night at Slap Shotz.

This guy really can't take no for an answer, can he?

Unable to help myself, I peer through the tiny hole for a second time, only to find him pressed against it on the other side.

All I see is the blue of his iris that rings the black pupil.

With a squeak, I fall back a step. My hand flies to my chest as my heart thrums an unsteady beat.

Did he see me?

I really hope not.

I freeze, not wanting to make any noise that will give me away.

If I'm lucky, he'll—

There's another, more insistent knock. "I know you're in there. I can hear you breathing."

Well, hell.

With a huff, I straighten my shoulders and open the door. "What are you doing here?"

He thrusts a tall to-go cup toward me. "Just thought you might like a peace offering in the form of dark roasted beans."

I tilt my head and narrow my eyes. "And you know where I live how?"

Even though he shrugs as if it's no big deal, there's nothing casual about the intensity that fills his eyes. "Oh, you know...asked around. Turns out that a couple of my teammates live on the second floor."

"How unfortunate."

He pretends to wince. "Ouch."

Or maybe he's not pretending at all.

My gaze settles on the coffee as the rich aroma wraps around me, tantalizing my senses. I'm operating on fumes and could really use a midafternoon pick-me-up. I chew my bottom lip before reluctantly reaching for the cup. My fingers brush against his, and a zip of electricity sizzles across my skin.

I jerk away, but not before wrapping my hand around the warm container and taking it with me. Unsure what to say, I bring the coffee to my lips and take a sip. My eyelids feather close as a tiny sigh escapes from me before I can reel it back in.

It's like crack in the form of coffee.

I take another taste before inspecting the tan and white container. "What's in here?"

The smile that spreads across his face makes his dimples pop. "The Roasted Bean has a McNichols special on the menu. Sorry, I'm not at liberty to tell you what the ingredients are." He winks. "It's top secret."

My mouth falls open. "You're joking."

"'Fraid not." He steps closer and drops his voice. "If I told you, I'd have to tie you up and—"

I roll my eyes and shove him back a pace or two. "I meant that the coffee shop on campus has a drink named after you."

When his grin intensifies, it becomes necessary to stomp out the arousal attempting to bloom to life in my core. This is *exactly* how he slides into bed with so many girls. A killer smile coupled with a charming personality—which he has—can work wonders on the female species.

But not me.

I'm the exception to the rule.

"It's delicious, isn't it?"

I force my gaze to the to-go cup and grumble, "Yeah, it is." There's a beat of silence before I clear my throat, strangely tempted to take another sip.

I give in to the urge.

Damn him.

It really is amazing.

I clear my throat and force myself to remember that I don't like this guy.

"Well, it seems like your objective has been achieved. You rather creepily found out where I live and delivered your peace offering." I raise the cup. "Thank you and good day."

As I take a step in retreat, ready to slam the door in his face, his hand springs out, the palm smacking against the wood.

With a frown, I glance at it and then him.

"I thought we could chill together. Maybe get to know one another a little better."

Spend time with Colby McNichols?

No way.

I have zero desire to spend another second in his company.

All right...maybe that's not one hundred percent true, but being alone with this guy would be a mistake. It's disturbing to realize that I'm not as immune to his charms as I'd originally thought.

"You realize that it's super stalker-like to just show up at my door, right?"

His face scrunches for a second or two as if seriously pondering the question. "I think what you meant to say is that it's super romantic I took the time from my busy schedule to track you down and make my interest known."

Laughter gurgles up in my throat as I shake my head. "Nice reframe, bro. But no."

He cocks his head. "Did you just call me bro?"

I smirk. "Guess I did."

"Huh. Is it weird that I kind of liked it?"

The corners of my lips tremble before I flatten them.

Ugh. This guy is completely dangerous.

He needs to go before I cave.

"So...like I told you the other night, I'm not interested. Even with this tasty coffee, my opinion hasn't changed."

He flashes another high-wattage smile. "I figured that you couldn't possibly mean it."

"Actually, I've never been more certain about anything in my life. I am most definitely *not* interested in you."

"Wow. It's a good thing I have such high self-esteem or that might actually hurt."

"Oh, I think your self-esteem will be just fine. You can find someone else to kiss your fragile ego."

"I'd much rather you kiss—"

"Hey, Britt!"

I drag my attention away from Colby, only to find Lance standing beside him. I try not to notice how my neighbor is both shorter and less muscular in comparison to the brawny hockey player.

With a frown, Lance looks Colby up and down before dismissing him.

His expression brightens as he turns his attention back to me. "Have you given any more thought to getting together this afternoon?"

Unsure what he's talking about, I rack my brain. "Getting together?"

"Yeah. We talked about making plans last week while studying."

"Oh, right." I nod, remembering that he floated the idea after I'd picked up my guitar and played the song I've been working on. From everything Lance told me, he wasn't into pop culture and didn't watch reality TV.

I'd become so absorbed in the music that I'd forgotten he was sitting across from me until he clapped and whistled, asking for an encore. He'd gone on to say that I was good enough to play professionally. That's when I shut down the convo.

"When were you thinking?"

Lance looks at his watch. "I'm free if you are."

"Ummm." I give Colby a bit of side eye. This would certainly be the easiest way to get rid of him. "Yeah, sure. That works."

"Great!" Lance beams before pumping his fist in the air. "This is going to be epic!"

I wouldn't go that far.

But at least I won't have to spend time—

"Hey, would you mind if I tag along?"

Lance blinks at Colby.

Say no.

Say no.

Say no.

"Sure! The more, the merrier I always say."

Well, shit.

"I'm sure you're super busy with hockey and..." My voice trails off.

Screwing groupies?

He grins. Almost like he can hear the thoughts running rampant through my head. "Nope, I'm all yours for the next couple hours."

My shoulders sink as I frown. "Lucky me."

"I know, right?" Laughter dances in his eyes. "Isn't it amazing when everything falls neatly into place?"

I press my lips into a tight line and glare. "When that actually happens, I'll let you know."

Before I can think of an excuse to wiggle out of this impromptu date, Colby says, "You know what? I have a great idea." He flashes another smile. "Make sure you dress warm."

Did this girl really think she could evade me so easily?

Yeah, not happening.

The proof is that she's sitting beside me in my black Cadillac Escalade.

And she's none too happy about it, either.

I glance at Britt as she stares straight out the windshield. She hasn't given me more than one-worded responses since sliding into the truck.

Lance, on the other hand, has been doing enough talking for the three of us.

He seems like a nice enough dude. Wicked smart, from what I can tell.

Another observation?

He has a thing for his hot neighbor.

The way he stares at her as if she hung the moon and stars in the sky hasn't gone unnoticed by yours truly. As far as I can tell, Britt is either oblivious to his crush or she doesn't return his feelings. I'm leaning toward door number two.

"This is a really nice truck," Lance says, positioning himself between us so he can check out the dash. "It's the top-of-the-line package, right?"

"Yup."

He strokes his hand over the leather. "This right here is the dream."

"Oh?"

"Yeah. I've already got a cyber security job lined up after graduation this spring. With the salary they're paying me, I should be able to buy one of these babies within eight months for straight-up cash. Then, a year later, I'll buy a starter home. Hopefully the interest rates will still be low. The plan is to live there for about five years before turning the property into a rental."

"Wow." My brows draw together as I take a left at the light. "You've really got it all figured out."

"You have to." He pushes his glasses up the bridge of his nose. "Can't just leave things to chance."

"That's really fantastic," Britt adds. "It's important to have a road map of where you want to go in life."

"Exactly," he says with a nod.

I didn't think it was possible for Lance's smile to broaden, but I was wrong. He's practically preening from the compliment.

The only future I've contemplated involves hockey. From a young age, it was a given that I'd follow in my father's illustrious footsteps. Coaches, parents, and other players always made a fuss over me because I was Gray McNichols' son. His NHL career spans more than a dozen years before he landed a plum sportscasting gig on ESPN.

I've worked hard to live up to his legend and have lost track of all the hours spent on the ice. There have been private coaching sessions that cost an arm and leg. Along with the highest-level triple A travel teams and summer camps.

You name it, I did it.

As important as hockey is, Mom always made sure I understood my education came first. Even when I had the opportunity to play juniors after high school. She wanted me to attend college and graduate with a degree.

It goes without saying that I would have preferred to play for a minor team these past four years, but it all worked out in the end. I'll graduate with a degree in communications, just like my old man. If I'm lucky, my career will have a similar trajectory. I'll play in the pros for at least a decade before landing a broadcasting job.

Or maybe I'll go in a different direction and try my hand at college coaching instead.

So...yeah. Maybe Lance isn't the only one with a mental roadmap in place.

Mine just isn't as finely detailed.

I swing into the gravel parking lot.

"We're ice skating?" Lance asks, head still positioned between the seats like a labrador as he stares at the outdoor rink near the center of town.

"Yup. I thought it would be fun." I glance at Britt to get a read on her thoughts.

She looks...intrigued.

Which is way better than the irritation that's been wafting off her in suffocating waves.

"I don't know," Lance mumbles with a frown. "I haven't skated since I was a kid. I'm not sure if I'll be any good."

I give him an awkward pat on the shoulder. "It's just like riding a bike."

"Yeah...I think it might be a little more challenging than that." He swivels toward Britt before rallying. "But I'm game if you are."

She flashes him an encouraging smile. "Sure, it looks fun. We can give it a whirl and see what happens."

"Great, let's go." I pop the trunk where I keep an extra pair of skates. Like hell I'm using my hockey ones. This ice would totally fuck up the blades.

We exit the SUV and I grab my Bauers before we stop at the little wooden shack and pick up a pair of rentals for Britt and Lance. Then the three of us settle on a long stretch of bench, slip off our shoes, and slide our feet into the boots. After mine have been laced up tight, I straighten to my full height.

Britt and Lance do the same.

Even though it's later in the afternoon, there's a smattering of people gliding across the ice. Couples along with a handful of children with pinkened cheeks. A few teenagers chase after each other. Everyone is bundled up in jackets, hats, mittens, and scarves.

I nod toward the oval. "Ready to get out there?"

Lance casts another dubious glance at the ice. "Maybe?"

I wave a hand. "Trust me, you'll be fine."

I hope.

When he takes a tentative step and wobbles, Britt loops her arm through his. "Come on. We'll do this together. I haven't skated since I was a kid. Colby's right. Once we get out there, it'll all come back to us."

Her encouragement does the impossible and transforms his face until he's beaming.

I can't stop the smile that curves my lips. This girl is a lot softer with him than with me. It only makes me want to work harder to secure her attention.

That thought nearly stops me in my proverbial tracks.

When the hell has that ever happened?

I rack my brain but come up empty.

With narrowed eyes, I watch as they make their way across the thick black mats to the edge of the rink.

All I can say is that it's slow going. Lance is like a newborn foal who can barely keep his legs under him.

And he hasn't even hit the ice yet.

It doesn't bode well.

Britt is the first one to step onto the smooth surface. Lance follows, clinging to her like she's his lifeline.

"You need to loosen up," I tell him. "Bend your knees a little. Trust me, it'll help."

His brows slam together as he takes a few tentative bounces. His tongue peeks out from between his teeth as he concentrates on staying vertical. He looks like he's trying to solve the Riemann hypothesis.

"Like this?"

Ummm...

"Yeah. Just like that."

The guy looks like he's been cut from a piece of cardboard.

"You ever play any sports as a kid?" I ask.

He flicks a glance in my direction. "Does robotics club count?"

"No."

"Then I didn't."

"I would have never guessed."

He releases a shaky puff of air as his muscles loosen. His shoulders no longer look like they're swallowing up his ears.

"That's it," I say, praising him.

He nods. "It's not so ha—"

The last word isn't even out of his mouth when he hits a rough patch and goes down in a tangle of limbs, taking Britt with him.

"Oh shit." I rush across the ice before reaching down and dragging Britt up.

She wobbles a bit on her skates. With my arms wrapped around her, the front of our bodies press together.

A smile springs to my lips. "I knew it wouldn't be long until I had you in my arms."

With our faces scant inches apart, I'm able to see the way her pupils dilate and her breathing hitches.

Interesting.

This girl isn't nearly as indifferent as she'd like me to believe.

I'll just tuck that tidbit away for later.

"A little help down here," Lance mutters with a groan, still sprawled at our feet.

That's all it takes for Britt to shove out of my arms before leaning down and trying to hoist Lance up, but she's not strong enough to do it on her own. If anything, she'll only get pulled down.

Again.

I secure my grip around Lance's hand before lifting him to his skates. When he wobbles, looking like he'll end up on his ass for a second time, his arms fly out in an attempt to steady himself.

Britt holds onto him.

"I'm pretty sure that's going to leave a mark," he mutters.

"Consider it a rite of passage," I tell him.

We spend the next thirty minutes trying to teach Lance how to skate. If they'd had one of those PVC pipe chairs that little kids use when learning the basics, I would have grabbed one. It would have been easier.

This is almost painful to watch.

Scratch that—it's excruciating.

And the guy is right—he's going to be covered in bruises tomorrow morning. I'll say this about him, he's determined. I can't help but admire his attitude. Although, I suspect he enjoys clinging to Britt. He's soaking up her attention like a sponge.

After the dozenth fall, Lance points to a bench near the firepit. "I'm going to take a break before I actually break something."

Britt frowns. "Maybe we should head home."

"Nah. You two skate. I just want to sit for a few minutes and warm up. I can't feel my toes."

As soon as his blades hit the rubber mats, a relieved sigh escapes from him. "I never thought I'd be so happy to be back on land."

"Technically, you were never off it," I point out.

"Tell that to my backside," he grumbles.

With a wince, we watch as he drags himself to the red bench. He has the looks of a man who has just returned from a hard-fought war. One who has been changed by the experience.

And not for the better.

I'll just refrain from telling him that he'll probably feel twice as bad when he wakes up tomorrow morning.

"I hope he'll be all right," Britt murmurs, concern lacing her voice.

Unwilling to waste another second we have to ourselves, I wrap my fingers around hers and tug her into motion.

"He'll be fine. I'll send over some of the bruise cream I have. The guy should take ibuprofen for the next twenty-four hours. It'll help with the inflammation."

"We probably should have done something less physical." With a frown, she shoots me a glare. "Or nothing at all."

"How can you say that? Then we would have missed all this fun."

She snorts as we glide across the ice. Now that Lance is gone, it only takes a few minutes for us to make a complete circle. By the end of the second loop, her muscles have loosened, and a smile quirks the corners of her lips.

The happiness that lights up her face is like a kick in the balls. The expression isn't even aimed in my direction, and I feel it to the tips of my toes.

As pretty as I thought she was at the bar, it's nothing compared to the way she looks with the bright winter sunlight streaming down, making the reddish highlights in her hair pop along with the rosiness of her cheeks from the cool breeze that slides over us.

If I didn't fully acknowledge it before, I do now.

This girl is a knockout.

"Is this where you take all your dates in an effort to lure them into bed?"

A chuckle escapes from me. "Nope. Never."

She glances at me with narrowed eyes. "Should I consider myself lucky?"

"Extremely. But you already realized that, right?"

With a shake of her head, she slants another look my way. "You're kind of incorrigible."

"I try my best."

"You don't have to try so hard."

"Now you sound like my mother."

"Smart woman."

"Damn right, she is."

She gives me another considering look. "Huh. You didn't strike me as a momma's boy."

"Loud and proud. That woman is an absolute saint. There's nothing I wouldn't do for her." No matter what happens in my life, Mom has always been in my corner.

Britt turns, studying me more intently. "Are you close to your parents?"

"Yup. They're the best. How about you?"

It would be impossible not to notice the way she tenses. Instead of pushing, I drop the topic and keep it light. I want to get to know her better and will take whatever crumbs she's willing to throw my way.

When it comes down to it, I'm no different from Lance.

"You're pretty good at this," I say, only wanting to keep the conversation flowing.

With a shrug, her gaze flickers to mine before focusing straight ahead. "I used to skate all the time at a pond near our house when I was a kid. It was cheap entertainment."

"That's usually the best kind." I waggle my brows. "Wouldn't you agree?"

She shakes her head as if annoyed, but there's a tiny quirk of her lips that tells me otherwise. "You really are incorrigible."

"Noted."

We make it a quarter of the way around the oval before she says, "Sometimes I really miss that, you know?" Her lips purse and a faraway look comes into her eyes. "The simple stuff."

"Yeah, the memories I cherish the most and think about often are the ones we did as a family that didn't cost a dime. Ice skating on a pond in the winter with my dad, sitting around a campfire and roasting marshmallows, Saturday night movie marathons in the family room with butter-soaked popcorn."

A soft smile lights up her face and I'd bet money she's thinking about her own happy childhood memories. A comfortable silence falls over us as we circle the ice at least half a dozen times. There's something nice about spending time with Britt.

Almost like we've been doing it for years instead of just having met.

Even stranger than that, I'm pretty sure I could get used to this.

And it has everything to do with the girl at my side.

The one that doesn't necessarily want to be there.

When Anna tries to creep into my brain, I wait for the anger and sadness to take hold and choke the life out of me from the inside out.

It's a surprise when it doesn't happen.

I draw a lungful of frigid air into my body and hold it captive before gradually releasing it back into the atmosphere.

As we skate past Lance, I realize that he's no longer alone. A girl with two dark braids and a pink pom-pom knit hat tugged over the tips of her ears is seated next to him.

I nod toward her neighbor. "Well, well, well...would you look who found a friend?"

Britt's gaze fastens onto the couple.

"Our little boy is finally growing up. Do you think one of us should have the birds and bees talk with him before things progress any further?"

The edges of Britt's lips quirk before she attempts to suppress it. "I'll leave that to you."

"Coward. We should do it together. Give him both of our perspectives."

Her attention stays pinned to the couple as we make our way around the ice again.

"Please don't tell me that you're upset that your admirer has found someone else to admire."

Her surprised gaze slices to me. "Of course not. Lance is a great guy. He deserves a girl who will appreciate him for all his amazing qualities."

"You're one hundred percent right about that. And he does seem like a perfectly nice guy," I agree. "But not for you."

It's adorable the way her face scrunches. "Excuse me?"

"Pretty sure you heard me the first time."

She bristles. "I don't think you know me well enough to make that kind of assessment." Before I can respond, she adds, "You have no idea what I like or am into."

Maybe not.

But I intend to find out.

Call it my new mission in life.

A lazy smile spreads across my face as I jerk my head toward the bench. "Were you interested in him? If so, I'll do the noble thing and step aside. Far be it for me to stand in the way of true love."

In answer, she presses her lips into a thin, tight line.

I grin and lean close enough for her floral scented perfume to tease my senses. "That's what I thought."

Instead of continuing the convo, she says in a clipped tone, "I'm cold. Are you ready to go?"

Not really, but...

"Sure."

Britt pulls away, leaving me in her dust. By the time I make it to the bench, Lance is already introducing his new friend.

"This is Maddie. We have a data analytics class together this semester."

"Hi," Britt says easily. "It's nice to meet you."

"You, too." With a shy smile, she glances at Lance and blushes.

If I had to guess, I'd say that someone has a little crush.

Good for him. The girl is a real cutie.

I wholeheartedly approve of the match.

He clears his throat. "You guys wouldn't mind if I catch a ride back to campus with Maddie, would you?"

"Not at all." Britt smiles, gaze shifting between the two of them. She certainly doesn't look jealous or upset about this new development.

His attention settles on me. "You'll make sure that Britt gets back to the apartment safely, right?"

Even though I don't take offense to the question, I straighten to my full height. "Of course I will."

I like that Britt's neighbor is concerned about her and apparently not afraid to let me know it. It only reconfirms that Lance is a good dude. Maybe he's not someone I would have befriended on my own, but I'm glad we got the chance to spend time together.

It's only when the couple heads to the wooden shack to turn in their brown rentals that we're left to our own devices.

"And then there were two." That's when I realize I'm not ready to let her go just yet. "Any interest in grabbing something to eat?"

As she opens her mouth to no doubt shoot down the idea, her belly lets loose a loud grumble.

"Excellent. I know the perfect place."

In the darkest nights, I stumbled, couldn't see the light.
Lost in a maze, couldn't find what's right.
But deep inside, a fire burned,
Refusing to fade away.
A voice inside me whispered, 'You'll find your way.'

I'm rising up, stronger now than I've ever been.
Every scar's a story, ain't letting them win.
Through the ups and downs, I'll find my truth.
In the chaos of it all, I'll find my youth.

Through every fall and every doubt, I'll stand tall.
Gonna shake off the past, gonna give it my all.
With each new day, leaving old fears behind.
Embracing every challenge, gonna free my mind.

BRITT

I 'm still trying to figure out how I got stuck having dinner alone with Colby McNichols as he pulls his massive black truck into a crowded parking lot.

The first thing I realize is that it's a diner.

A brightly lit, retro fifties one.

Harvey's Eats and Treats.

This isn't one of the restaurants located near campus. Instead, it's on the outskirts of town.

Even though I don't ask, he says, "A teammate mentioned that they have the best burgers here. So, I thought we could give it a try." When he pats his toned belly, my gaze dips to the movement. "I really worked up an appetite after all that skating."

"I'm sure you work much harder during practices."

"You're right about that. Coach is kind of a hardass when it comes to conditioning, but I can't say we're not in the best shape of our lives. So, it's working." He slants a look my way as we exit the vehicle. "Have you checked out one of our games yet this season?"

I shake my head. "Nope. I don't really like hockey."

Lie.

The last thing I need is this guy thinking I'm a fan. As painful as it is to admit, the Western Wildcats hockey team is a pretty big deal around here. You can't step foot on campus without hearing people talk about them.

Especially number ninety-seven.

Colby McNichols.

"Maybe I'll be able to change that."

"I wouldn't bet the farm on it."

He flashes his trademark smile. The one that makes his dimples pop. It's the very same one that makes most girls go a little stupid in the head.

Except...I'm not like most girls.

"Challenge accepted."

This guy is so damn cocky and confident.

It should be a complete turn-off.

So...why isn't it?

Once we reach the glass door, he holds it open. A little bell tinkles overhead as my gaze darts to his before I force myself to study the place.

My first impression wasn't wrong.

Walking inside the restaurant is like taking a step back in time.

The floor is made up of black and white checkered tiles while the ceiling is covered with shiny silver tin. Framed photographs of old Hollywood stars are interspersed with Coca-Cola memorabilia that decorate the walls. An equal number of tables and booths fill the space. The latter are upholstered with red vinyl while gleaming white linoleum tops glow under the bright lights. Music from decades ago pours through the speakers from a jukebox at the far end of the restaurant.

Just as I take a step, a familiar face snags my attention. "Ava?"

With a smile, she waves.

"Speak of the devil," Colby whispers. "That's Coach Philips."

"And his daughter, Ava."

My new friend flicks a glance at Colby before her brows rise. Humor simmers in her eyes as they refasten onto mine.

Looks like I'll have some explaining to do.

Like me, Ava is new to Western University. Her father is Reed Philips, head coach for the Wildcats hockey team. We met in one of our general education classes this past fall and bonded over the fact that we're both older freshmen. Instead of attending college after graduating high school, Ava's been focused on her figure skating career. From what I've been able to gather, something happened last year, which is why she's taking a break from the circuit to train and take a few classes.

Her father rises to his feet. He's a handsome man with blond hair and blue-green colored eyes. It's easy to see where Ava gets her looks from. She's the spitting image of him. Except where he's big and broad, she's petite.

"Hey, Coach," Colby greets. "Looks like the cat is out of the bag regarding this place."

The older man smiles. "Yup, one of the assistant coaches mentioned it the other day and I thought we'd give it a try." A soft look fills his eyes as he glances around. "Reminds me of a restaurant I used to eat at in college."

Ava tilts her head. "Didn't Mom work at a place like this?"

The grin that lights up his face makes him look even more handsome. "She sure did. Stella's Diner. Had the best Salisbury steak and mashed potatoes I've ever eaten."

His daughter's eyes twinkle with mischief. "I'll be sure to tell Mom that."

"Better not." Coach glances at his sports watch. "Well, we should get moving. I still have a few hours of film to squeeze in tonight."

"Don't worry, Coach. We got the game in the bag."

"I'll relax after the final buzzer rings." He glances at his daughter. "I'll take care of the bill and meet you at the car."

She nods before turning to me. "Sorry about not texting back yesterday. Between practice and classes, I'm a little overwhelmed this week."

I nod. "Don't worry about it, but let's find time to get together. Even if it's only to study at the library for a few hours."

"That sounds good."

She pulls me in for a quick hug before whispering, "Colby McNichols? Really?"

"It's not what you think," I grumble.

"Actually, it's exactly what she's thinking," he interjects with a smile.

Ava chuckles before taking off with a quick wave. And then she's out the door, leaving me alone with Colby.

Precisely where I don't want to be.

A waitress wearing a hot pink retro uniform flashes a friendly smile as we slide into a booth. There's a mix of people dining here. Older couples, families enjoying a rare night out, and groups of teenagers laughing and flirting with each other.

It's exactly what I imagined it would be like to hang out with friends in high school. It's not something I have any experience with. As soon as I was discovered, we packed up and moved to sunny California where dreams are made.

Or crushed beneath someone's wingtip.

Instead of enrolling in a public high school, I was homeschooled. My parents and agent felt that it would give me more time to write music. The show followed shortly after.

At first, it was all exciting and new. I didn't miss my boring classes on subjects I had zero interest in. Or an endless string of homework, tests, and quizzes. Or the social pressures that went hand in hand with it.

Fast forward three years and I longed for the ordinariness of high school and my peers. I missed out on all the monumental firsts that get experienced during that time. Homecoming. Prom. First dates and boyfriends. Friday night football games under the stadium lights. Slumber parties and shopping with your besties at the mall.

I never had a chance to experience any of it.

With all the time spent on set, friends were a distant memory.

"What can I get for you, hon?" the waitress asks, pencil poised over a small pad of paper.

I blink out of the memories tangling around me only to stare at the plastic menu. "Oh, um...I'll have a chicken salad."

"A salad?" Colby echoes in disbelief. "Absolutely not. Friends don't allow friends to order salads at a burger joint. Get one of those. I promise you won't be sorry."

I chew my lower lip as I consider his suggestion.

Truth be told, I've spent the past six months deprogramming myself and changing my eating habits. Up until I took off, my mother was still watching what I ate like a hawk.

I'll never forget the summer I gained eight pounds after turning fifteen. The producer of the show pulled my agent and mother aside and said that I needed to lose it. ASAP. They all put their heads together and decided that the season would revolve around my weight loss journey. They figured that the fans would relate to my struggle.

Instead, I was picked apart all over social media.

The memes were out of control.

It was a mentally scarring experience.

After that, I was careful not to deviate more than a pound from what they deemed an acceptable weight.

But that was then.

And this is now.

I no longer have to worry about being filmed and what I looked like on camera.

I get to make my own decisions.

Even if it's something small like ordering a burger that most people wouldn't think twice about.

"What's it gonna be?" the waitress asks, tapping her pen against the pad.

"Okay, sure. I'll try the burger."

"Load it with the works," Colby adds.

"You want fries with that?"

Just as I'm about to shake my head, Colby cuts in. "You can't eat a burger without fries. I think it might be illegal in some states."

The older woman points to Colby. "The kid knows what he's talking about. You should listen to him."

It's tempting to roll my eyes. "Fine. I'll have a burger and fries."

"Excellent choice," Colby says with a smirk. "I'll, um, have a salad."

When my mouth tumbles open, he laughs. "Just kidding. I'll have the same. Thanks."

"And to drink?"

"Two Cokes?" he says, raising his brows in silent inquiry.

"Diet, please," I cut in.

"No problem. Your order will be up shortly." She takes off, beelining toward a family with young kids who look to be on the verge of a meltdown.

Colby glances around, studying the restaurant. "This place has a great vibe."

"Is this your first time here?"

"Yup. Wolf mentioned it a few times, so I thought we could check it out."

As he falls silent, I can't help but wonder if this guy really thinks a cheeseburger and diet soda will seal the deal.

If so, he's in for disappointment.

Unable to hold back my thoughts, I blurt, "Just so we're clear, I have zero intention of being hustled into your bed."

His eyes crinkle at the corners as he smiles. "I think we both know I don't have to hustle chicks anywhere. They come willingly."

There's that cockiness again.

I shake my head. "Remember when I mentioned earlier that you were incorrigible? I'm standing firmly behind that statement."

When his smile intensifies, something unwanted pings at the bottom of my belly. It takes more effort than before to stomp it out.

What bothers me most is that I'm not as immune to his charms as I'd hoped. And the more time we spend together, the harder it becomes to resist him.

"Why else would you bring me here?"

With his eyes fastened onto mine, the arrogance fades from his expression as he leans forward, closing the space between us. "Guess I wanted the chance to get to know you better. Is there something wrong with that?"

The waitress sets our drinks down before zipping off and leaving us alone again.

Only now do I realize how dangerous it is to have all of Colby's attention focused on me.

I feel strangely alive in his presence.

Confusion circles around in my brain as I tear the wrapper from my straw and drop the slender tube into the fizzy fountain soda before bringing it to my lips and taking a sip.

Colby's attention dips to my mouth and heat flares to life in his eyes before he slants them upward again. "You never answered the question."

My brows rise. "There was a question?"

One side of his mouth hitches. "Is there a problem with me wanting to know you better?"

A burst of nerves scampers across my flesh as I rip my gaze away. "I'm not sure. I've got a lot going on right now. I really don't have time for any...*new friends.*"

It's not a total lie.

But it's not necessarily the truth either.

It never occurred to me when I packed up and took off that I might create a whole new life for myself. And that it would become necessary to hide the old one. I didn't realize how lonely it would be to keep those two worlds separate.

There've been a handful of times when I've gotten together with the girls and it's been so tempting to blurt out the truth. Especially after a few drinks.

Fear is what ultimately kept me silent. As much as I like Fallyn, Carina, Juliette, Stella, and Viola, I don't know them well enough to trust them implicitly with my secrets.

Other than my aunt and uncle, there's no one I can talk to.

You confide in the wrong person and suddenly your private life is plastered all over social media. If that were to happen, the ordinary existence I've created for myself would disappear in the blink of an eye and I'd be forced to return to LA and a career I'm no longer sure I want.

Until I figure out that piece of it, I need to keep my mouth shut.

"That's too bad. I think we could all use a few new friends."

I pop my shoulders and try to remain unaffected. "I'm good with the ones I have."

He cocks his head, eyes sifting through mine until it's tempting to squirm on the red vinyl. Energy intensifies before crackling in the air like lightning.

"Here you go!" The waitress sets both plates down in front of us. "Enjoy!"

That's all it takes for the thick tension to dissipate. I force my attention to the mountain of shoestring French fries alongside a burger that's stacked with lettuce, tomato, pickles, and onion. Unsure where to start with this monstrosity, I set aside the onion as Colby does the same.

My belly rumbles as the tantalizing scent inundates my senses and makes my mouth water. Without further ado, Colby picks up his burger and takes a gigantic bite. It takes two hands to hold the massive sandwich.

When I don't make a move toward my meal, he sets his down before pointing to my plate.

"Wolf was right. It's fucking delicious. Go ahead and try it. Don't be shy now."

I'm still trying to figure out if I should use a knife and fork.

"If you don't eat it, I'll be forced to take it home and give it to the jackals I live with. Trust me, it'll be a fight to the death." A small smile quirks his lips. "Can't say it wouldn't be amusing to watch."

"It kind of sounds like you're a sadist," I joke.

"Not at all. I'm all about the pleasure." He gives me a flirty little wink. "Play your cards right and you'll find out firsthand."

And there he is again—cocky Colby.

Or, as he's known around campus, the baby-faced assassin.

"It would appear that your nickname has been well earned."

His shoulders shake with silent laughter. "Oh, firecracker...you haven't seen anything yet."

That's precisely what I'm afraid of.

Colby chows both his burger and fries in a matter of minutes. I've never seen anyone demolish a meal with so much gusto. It's like a car accident I can't look away from.

When my belly grumbles for a second time, I wrap my hands around the burger before bringing it to my mouth. The butter-seared bun, perfectly seasoned meat, and toppings practically melt in my mouth.

Holy crap is this good.

My eyelids drift shut as I chew and swallow. It's only when I go for a second bite that my eyes pop open, and I find him staring at me with a heated expression.

"Watching you eat shouldn't be so sexy."

Warmth floods my cheeks at the thought of him staring at me so intently. I clear my throat and try to lighten the mood. "Don't worry, watching you wasn't. I was afraid you might choke and then I'd be forced to jump in and save you."

Instead of being offended, he bursts out laughing.

"I have two brothers and a sister. It was always a fight to grab what you wanted and eat it as fast as you could so you could go back for seconds."

"Sounds like you come from a large family." It's reluctantly that I admit, "I guess we have that in common."

His eyes widen comically as his hand lands in the middle of his chest. "No! We have something in common?"

I roll my eyes as a smile simmers around the corners of my lips. "I have three sisters and a brother."

As soon as the comment is out of my mouth, I realize my mistake and wish I could snatch it out of the air.

"So where are you in the lineup?"

"Oldest."

"Gasp! Another thing we have in common. It's almost like we're twinsies."

"Please." I pop a fry into my mouth. It's delicious.

"Are you guys close?"

I draw in a deep breath before releasing it gradually back into the atmosphere. "We are, but our family dynamic is...complicated."

That would be the nicest way to put it.

My sister, Cheyenne, and I were super close while growing up, but we've drifted apart over the years. She's resentful that the show has been built around me. From what I've seen online and on TV, she's the only one who's delighted by my disappearance and is doing her damnedest to take advantage of the opportunity.

"Aren't most families complicated?"

Probably. But I feel like mine is more tangled than others. We have the added layer of fame to contend with.

But I keep that to myself.

Even if there's a teeny tiny piece inside that wants to purge all the secrets from my system.

"You're right, they probably are," I murmur, hoping we can drop the subject and move on to more surface-level conversation.

"My parents met in college." His eyes spark with both love and humor as he continues. "The way Mom likes to tell it, she couldn't stand my dad. They started fake dating because his mother was seeing her father."

Huh?

I raise my hand to pause the convo. "Hold up now. Let me get this straight. Your Mother's *father* got together with your father's *mother*. Which means that your *grandparents* were at one point, dating each other?"

All right...so maybe his family *is* complicated.

"Yup. They tied the knot in the Bahamas and are still married to this day. For their twentieth wedding anniversary, they flew everyone out for a recommitment ceremony."

This sounds more like an episode of one of those daytime TV talk shows where they reveal cheating scandals and paternity results.

"Your grandparents from different sides are married to each other?"

He chuckles. "Yup."

"Wow." That's insane.

And a story I'd love to hear in more detail.

"At first, my parents didn't want them together, so they pretended to be an item in order to break them up."

My mouth drops open. "Get out of here!"

"Nope, it's all true. Guess my grandparents were *pissed* when they finally found out about it."

"I can't even imagine. Obviously, their scheming didn't work."

"If it had, I wouldn't be here." With a tilt of his head, he grins. "And wouldn't that be a real shame for you."

I snort out a laugh and realize just how easy it is to be with Colby.

"Admit it, you're having a good time." He leans closer and drops his voice. "Despite your best efforts, I'm growing on you."

I press my lips together, refusing to smile. It'll only encourage him, and that's the last thing I want to do. I'm already in over my head with this guy.

"Kind of like a wart. One that'll have to be frozen off in the not-so-distant future."

It's a relief when the waitress stops by to drop off our check.

After Colby pays the bill, we head back to campus.

Music filters through the speakers of the truck. Even though being with him shouldn't feel so comfortable, it does. When he parks in the lot, my fingers wrap around the handle, ready to jump out and make a quick getaway.

What I've discovered from this little excursion is that I like Colby more than I thought possible. He's easy to be around, and it wouldn't take much coaxing on his part for me to lower my defenses. Which is exactly why I need to end this budding friendship before it can bloom into something more.

"Thanks for taking me skating and then to dinner. It was actually fun."

He swivels toward me. "You don't have to sound so surprised."

Unable to resist, my lips bow. "More like shocked."

"Just know that I'm full of surprises."

I have little doubt.

I also know that I won't be sticking around to find out.

Before he can even think about making contact, I pop the handle and roll from the Cadillac. Graceful, it is not. "See you around."

"Hold on and I'll walk you to your door." With that, he exits the SUV.

Argh.

"Oh, no." I wave my hand and consider taking off at a dead run. "That's not necessary."

"I promised Lance that I'd make sure you got home safely. And that's exactly what I'm going to do."

I t only takes a handful of seconds to catch up to Britt on the walkway. As soon as we reach the apartment complex, she hits the code on the keypad and the door buzzes, allowing us entrance inside the building. There's a small group of girls chatting in the lobby. They flick disinterested glances at us as we walk by.

As soon as recognition sets in, their eyes widen with excitement.

"Hey, Colby!" one of them calls out.

I wave as Britt presses the elevator button and taps her foot impatiently. The last thing I want to do is give these chicks the green light to proceed. The pretty auburn-haired girl will latch onto the flimsiest of excuses to escape my evil clutches.

I'm bound and determined not to give her any.

Just as one breaks free from the pack and saunters over, the elevator dings and the metal doors slide open. I hustle Britt into the car before the chick can reach us.

Crisis averted.

A second later, we're closed inside the car together.

She leans against the far wall and stares at me. "You could have stayed downstairs and talked to your friends."

"They're not friends. I don't even know them."

With a jerk of her brow, she gives me a disbelieving look.

"It's true."

"It doesn't really matter."

Before I have a chance to respond, the car doors are sliding open and dumping us on the third floor. Britt slips out as I trail behind her. It feels as if all the painstaking progress I made earlier has been wiped away.

What can't be denied is that the more this girl holds me at a distance, the more I want to break down her walls and discover what makes her tick. I've barely scratched the surface and already I know that she's unlike anyone I've ever met.

I'm so lost in thought that I nearly crash into her when she grinds to a halt in the middle of the hallway.

"What the—"

My voice trails off when I get a good look at the couple making googly eyes at one another outside the apartment next to Britt's.

"It's official. You've been replaced," I whisper against her ear, seizing upon any reason to invade her personal space.

She twists her head just enough to meet my gaze. "It would seem so."

Without breaking eye contact with Maddie, Lance pops open his apartment door before ushering her inside.

"Well, damn. Looks like we won't be having that little chat," I say with a heavy sigh.

"I think he'll be fine. Lance has a good head on his shoulders."

"With a forty-year plan that includes APRs and becoming a land baron? I suspect you're right about that."

A chuckle slips free from her. "If anyone will achieve his goals, it'll be Lance. We'll be reading about him in Western's alumni magazine ten years from now."

"True that."

Britt stops in front of her door before swinging around and pinning me in place with her steady golden eyes. "This is me."

My gaze stays locked on hers. I couldn't look away even if I tried. "From all my previous stalking, I've already surmised that."

A chuckle escapes from her as she shakes her head. "Creepy."

"Romantic," I correct.

She clears her throat. "I'll make sure to tell Lance the next time I see him that I arrived home safe and sound."

"Excellent." When I step closer, challenge sparks in her honey-colored depths as she tilts her chin just a bit to maintain eye contact. Britt is tall for a girl, but I still have a good six inches on her. "I had fun this afternoon."

There's a beat of silence.

Then another.

She flinches when I slip my fingers beneath her chin and angle it upward. "This would be the part where you agree."

Tension fills her muscles. "Is it?"

"Pretty sure."

It takes a moment or so before she reluctantly admits, "I had a good time."

My lips lift into a genuine smile. "Was that really so difficult?"

"You have no idea."

"Oh, I can imagine, firecracker. You're dead set on fighting this."

"And what exactly would *this* be?"

"You and me getting to know each other better."

I draw closer until I'm able to feel the warmth of her breath feather across my lips. The sensation is dizzying. It takes effort to keep from devouring her the way every instinct is clamoring for me to do.

"It's a bad idea," she whispers.

"You think so?" My cock stiffens as I consider closing the distance between us just enough for my lips to drift over her cupid's bow of a mouth.

"One hundred percent."

Her breath turns labored as I ghost over her lips, never quite touching them. It's so tempting to take her the way I want, but this needs to be her decision.

I've never forced a girl to do anything, and I refuse to start now.

I press against her softness, caging her in against the door.

Britt is slender but curvy.

It's a wicked combination.

The most surprising part is that I don't think I've ever been more turned on than I am at this moment.

And we haven't even kissed.

Yet.

We're so damn close.

There's only a millimeter of space to separate us.

My body goes on high alert, waiting for the slightest signal to take this further.

I have the sneaking suspicion that I could explore her mouth for hours and it wouldn't be nearly enough.

Just as I lose my internal battle, her apartment door springs open, and she staggers backward across the threshold. We stare from across the space that now separates us.

Shock colors her expression as her shaking fingers rise to her lips. "I should go."

The magnetic pull between us is almost too much to bear. I want to leap forward and detain her. The last thing I want is for her to disappear inside the apartment. Instead, I force myself to remain frozen in place.

It's one of the hardest things I've ever had to do.

"All right." My voice comes out sounding more like a feral growl.

She takes a tentative step in retreat. It's as if I'm a wild beast she needs to tread carefully with.

"Night, Colby."

Before I can force out a response, the door is slammed in my face. For a second or two—hell, it could even be longer—I stare at the thick wood, silently willing her to open it again and let me in.

That doesn't happen.

I haven't even tasted this girl yet, and already, I know that one kiss won't be nearly enough to satiate the deep well of need that now churns within.

I want more.

I want everything she's willing to give.

IN THE DARKEST NIGHTS, I STUMBLED, COULDN'T SEE THE LIGHT.
LOST IN A MAZE, COULDN'T FIND WHAT'S RIGHT.
BUT DEEP INSIDE, A FIRE BURNED,
REFUSING TO FADE AWAY.
A VOICE INSIDE ME WHISPERED, 'YOU'LL FIND YOUR WAY.'

I'M RISING UP, STRONGER NOW THAN I'VE EVER BEEN.
EVERY SCAR'S A STORY, AIN'T LETTING THEM WIN.
THROUGH THE UPS AND DOWNS, I'LL FIND MY TRUTH.
IN THE CHAOS OF IT ALL, I'LL FIND MY YOUTH.

THROUGH EVERY FALL AND EVERY DOUBT, I'LL STAND TALL.
GONNA SHAKE OFF THE PAST, GONNA GIVE IT MY ALL.
WITH EACH NEW DAY, LEAVING OLD FEARS BEHIND.
EMBRACING EVERY CHALLENGE, GONNA FREE MY MIND.

BRITT

"**I**'m fine, Dad. Really," I repeat into the cell, trooping across campus.

My eleven o'clock psychology 101 class just let out for the day. The plan is to stop by the Union and pick up a protein bar for lunch before heading to the library for a few hours. I love studying at the apartment, but the temptation to pick up my guitar and work on my music is too great. I don't know what's going on lately, but my creative juices are flowing.

And I love it.

The heavy sigh he huffs out comes across loud and clear over the line. "I still don't understand why it was necessary for you to take off the way you did, B."

When a guy walking toward me snags my attention and smiles, I tug the black ball cap I'm wearing a little lower over my eyes, shielding them from view, and glance away.

"You know why I left." This isn't the first time we've had this conversation. More like the hundredth. It would be nice if my parents could accept that I might not want to return to the life we created.

I'm ready for a change.

Even if they aren't.

"You've been gone for more than six months. Linc is getting fed up with the excuses. He wants you back home now. He's threatening to pull the plug on the show." There's an uncomfortable pause as his voice dips, becoming more hushed. "No one wants that to happen."

A heavy stone settles at the bottom of my belly as I stare at the massive brick and glass building that looms on the horizon. Sometimes, I think all our lives would be better without the show. It's become toxic. I feel trapped and stifled by a world of my own making.

But I don't bother admitting that to my father.

He wouldn't understand.

And even if he did, he wouldn't take a stand against my mother.

I love my dad, but he's content to allow Mom to make all the hard decisions that affect our lives. It's bizarre that at twenty-two, I don't have freedom over my own choices and need to wrestle control away from her.

When I think about packing up my life here and returning to LA, my chest constricts and my throat closes, making it impossible to breathe.

I've spent the last nine years working fifty hours a week with barely a day off.

At this point, I'm burnt out and tired.

There aren't many who can say that they have a platform on the world's stage. Sometimes I feel like a spoiled and ungrateful brat wishing it all away when there are millions of people who would kill for the opportunities I've been given.

I'd assumed a few months away from the bright glare of the spotlight would help quiet the restlessness that has been growing inside me. Instead, all it's done is give me a taste of the freedom I can't have in LA with my family.

I pull the phone closer to my mouth and drop my voice. "We've been doing the show for eight years. Aren't you tired of it?"

I've grown to hate the cameras that follow my every move, documenting every misstep. Every embarrassment. Every ridiculous argument.

The worst part is that after a while, you become so used to them that you forget they're there. You say and do things you never would if you weren't so desensitized to the production staff. If it didn't feel so normal. And when you plead with them to cut out a part, they look at you like you're the crazy one.

"It's our life," he says simply. "The younger kids grew up on the show. It's all they know. It'll be easier to launch Cheyenne's music career with the network backing it."

There are times when it feels like our lives no longer belong to us.

We're living them for the show.

Not the other way around.

So much of it is scripted.

I mean...who wants to watch the seven of us sitting around the living room, picking our noses all day?

I snort at that image.

"What's so funny?"

My good humor melts away, leaving discontent to fill the void. "Nothing."

"The right thing to do would be to come home and discuss the situation with your mother."

"I'm more than happy to have a convo with her over the phone, but she refuses."

"That's because she wants to see your face. She wants to sit down with you in person like grown adults. Isn't that what you claim to be?"

Ouch.

"She misses you, B," he continues, attempting to soften the previous blow.

Unlikely.

What she wants is to manipulate me into falling in line.

And that's easier to accomplish in person.

Sharon Benson is a formidable woman.

Even the producers are terrified of her.

Let that sink in.

"Plus, there's Axel to consider. You just took off and left him hanging. He's concerned about you. I actually feel bad for the guy. He says that you won't even answer his calls or respond to his texts."

An avalanche of guilt attempts to bury me alive.

Axel is an entirely different problem.

One I try not to dwell on.

Just as I'm contemplating a response, a brawny arm is thrown around my shoulders and I'm hauled against a hard body before being inundated by a woodsy scent. My eyes collide with bright blue ones as a spark of electricity charges the chilled air that swirls around us.

"B? Are you still there?"

My attention stays locked on Colby. "Yeah, I'm here." Even though I have zero intention of doing it, I say, "I'll think about everything we talked about and get back to you later, all right?"

"Sounds good, honey. I love you."

"Love you, too." When Colby's brows shoot up and the laughter brimming in his eyes fades, I blurt, "Dad."

Ending the call, I slip my phone into the pocket of my black puffy jacket.

"Fancy meeting you here," he says in greeting.

My visceral reaction to him takes me by surprise.

Maybe after the other night, it shouldn't.

"Yeah...what are the odds of running into each other on a campus we both attend?" I slant a look his way. "Probably astronomical, right?"

There's a flash of white teeth in the sunlight. "You're hilarious."

"I'm not trying to be," I mutter, hating the way my heartbeat picks up tempo with his proximity.

He hauls me closer before whispering, "I know. That's what makes it so damn funny."

Before I can think of a pithy retort, he changes the subject. "Are you headed to the Union for lunch?"

"Umm..." It's so tempting to lie, but part of me is exhausted by how often I'm forced to fabricate pieces of my life. As much as I want to dismiss Colby and walk away without a second thought, that's no longer possible. Somehow, he's managed to crawl beneath my skin when I wasn't looking. "Yeah, but only to grab something before heading to the library."

"How about you eat lunch with me instead?"

Air gets clogged in my chest. "Eat with you? Again?"

"Yup. We'll just call this date number two."

"Ahhh—"

"A bunch of the guys will be there. And probably a few of your friends as well."

I chew my lower lip as he propels us closer to the brick building.

It's a terrible idea. My life is maxed out in the complication department. The last thing I should do is add Colby to the mix.

He turns his head until his warm breath can ghost across my skin. "What do you say, firecracker? Have lunch with me?"

The huskiness of his voice coupled with the way he squeezes me against him is enough to send a cascade of shivers careening down my spine. Before I can decline the offer, he ushers me through the glass doors and into the warm building. After the bite of the breeze, the heat feels good. My breath catches when he pulls me close enough to feel the hard lines of his muscular body.

"Are you cold?"

"A little."

"Lucky for you, I have a few ideas on how we could warm up," he murmurs, wickedness dripping from his gravelly tone.

"No, thanks." I shove my way out of his arms because it's the right thing to do. Not necessarily because it's what I want. In fact, I've never been more tempted to snuggle up against someone than I am now.

And that includes the man who asked me to marry him.

"Long time no see, McNichols. Where have you been hiding yourself?"

The interruption seems timely.

Colby grins at the dark-haired guy before they bump fists like only bros can.

"At the hockey arena. You should stop by and catch a game sometime."

As they continue talking, Colby reaches into his pocket and pulls out his cell before tapping the miniature keyboard. It's tempting to peek at the screen to see who he's messaging, but I resist the urge.

A few more texts fly back and forth.

If there's a twinge of jealousy, I stomp it out.

"Nah. But thanks for the offer. I enjoy watching winners. Not sure if you know what those are."

"Is that so?"

"Yup."

Colby shifts and his teasing tone disappears. "Hey, congrats on bringing home a national title. It's pretty fucking amazing what you guys accomplished this season."

The other guy jerks his head toward a table packed with people. "There's no doubt about it—I'm gonna miss playing with them next year."

I can't help but look in that direction. From their size and musculature, I'm guessing they're all athletes.

"I know exactly what you mean." Colby clears his throat and glances at me. "Brayden, this is Britt."

His eyes fill with speculation as his manner turns joking again. "Please tell me you're not actually with this loser. If you're interested in dating a real man, I'll introduce you to one of the football players. There are still some single ones."

Colby's grip tightens as if he's afraid I might try to make a run for it. "Don't listen to a damn word this meathead has to say."

"Nope, we're just friends," I tell him.

And maybe myself as well.

It seems like I need the reminder.

"Interesting." Brayden's expression turns thoughtful. It would be difficult not to notice how handsome he is. "I wasn't aware that the baby-faced assassin had any friends of the female persuasion."

Colby cranes his neck and glances toward the crowded table of football players. "Hey, looks like some guy is hitting on Sydney. You should probably run him off before he steals her from beneath your nose. I mean, it wouldn't be that difficult to do."

A snort escapes from Brayden as he glances over his shoulder, only to see that Colby is telling the truth. Some dude is talking with his girlfriend.

Brayden's brows snap together. "Well, it was nice running into you, McNichols. Good luck with the season."

After a quick clap on the shoulder, he takes off, cutting a direct path to the blonde before slipping his arm around her waist and hauling her close.

"Yeah, I was pretty sure that would do the trick," Colby says with a laugh. "The guy is head over heels in love with his girlfriend. Can't say I saw that one coming. You've heard of the Campus Heartthrob competition, right?"

I rack my brain. "Maybe."

Colby nods toward Brayden. "He's won the title three years and counting."

I can't help but stare as the handsome football player wraps his arms around the athletic-looking blonde and lays one on her in front of everyone. The entire table breaks out into loud applause and catcalls.

"Have you two been friends for a while?"

Even though the interaction had been brief, they had an easy camaraderie that only comes from knowing someone well.

"His father played in the NFL and was repped by the same agent as my dad. So, we've known each other since we were kids."

"They make a cute couple."

"Sydney plays soccer for Western's women's team. She's probably the only girl on campus who could put that guy in his place."

Even from here, it's easy to see that the blonde is feisty.

After that, he steers us toward a table packed with both hockey players and their girlfriends.

Juliette perks up and waves when she catches sight of me. I can't help but return the welcoming gesture. She's such a sweetie. Next to her is Ryder McAdams. He's big and blond with a fan club of groupies that he doesn't seem to care about.

How could he when the guy can barely take his eyes off his girlfriend?

When we reach the table, Carina pops to her feet before pulling me in for a quick hug. "Are you eating lunch with us?"

I shouldn't...

"Yup," Colby cuts in before I can respond. "She decided to sit with the cool kids today."

"How does that make sense when she's here with you?"

Colby glares at the blonde dancer. "Hamilton, come get your girl-friend. She's annoying me."

"Then she's doing her job," Ford calls back.

Carina grins before glancing at me again with raised brows. "You and Colby? Now this is an interesting story I need to hear. And don't leave out any of the juicy parts."

The kiss we almost shared nudges its way into my brain before I shove it away.

Heat stings my cheeks when I glance around and realize how much attention we seem to be garnering.

Crap.

I should have listened to my intuition when alarm bells were going off in my head and declined his invitation.

Stella locks her fingers around my wrist and tugs me down beside her. "OMG, tell me the truth—did you sleep with Colby?"

"Of course not," I gasp. "We ran into each other on the way over. We were together for about five minutes. That's it."

Colby squeezes in beside me before saying, "Are you seriously trying to downplay our relationship, firecracker? I picked you up and we went ice skating and then out to dinner last night. Pretty sure most people would consider that a date."

"You're not most people," I snap as more of his friends and team-mates turn and stare like we're an exhibit at the zoo.

Viola's eyes widen before she gives her head a little shake as if totally thrown off guard. "I'm sorry...did I just hear this correctly? You and Colby are *dating*?"

"What? Of course not!" I shoot a scowl at Colby, who's laughing his ass off.

It's so tempting to elbow him in the ribs.

Hard.

Except we're packed in so tight there's barely room to maneuver.

"Oh, girl...I have *so many* questions," Fallyn adds with a smile.

I force out a steady breath and attempt to keep my cool.

It's no easy feat.

Hayes and another teammate, Steele, return with loaded-down trays. There's an array of items—soups, sandwiches, chips, and a few salads.

Hayes glances at Colby. "You wanted a roast beef and Swiss?"

"Yup." He holds up his hands as Hayes tosses the wrapped sandwich to him along with a bag of chips. All the other items get passed out until a cup of soup and half a sandwich are placed in front of me.

"Thanks, but I didn't order anything," I say to the good-looking center who settles at the far end of the table next to Steele. He's a junior and Bridger's cousin. Now that I know they're related, I can see the family resemblance. They both have mahogany colored hair and dark blue eyes.

Now that I'm hanging out with the girls more, they've been explaining who all the guys on the team are. There's sixty of them, and it's not easy to keep everyone straight. Especially the ones who don't get ice time.

Steele nods toward Colby. "He ordered it for you."

With a frown, I glance at him. We're close enough for me to feel the warmth of his breath ghosting across my lips. It's a little dizzying.

It shouldn't be.

In fact, he shouldn't affect me at all.

"When did you do this?"

"While we were talking with Brayden. I saw them in line and shot Hayes a text."

"The plan was to grab a protein bar and run," I mumble while staring at the soup and sandwich. It's almost a surprise how touched I am by the gesture. But instead of softening everything inside me, it reinforces how imperative it is to keep my distance.

Not only physically, but emotionally as well.

This guy will steadily chip away at my defenses if I let him.

"It's chicken and wild rice." Unaware of the thoughts circling around in my head, he nudges my shoulder with his broader one.

"It'll help warm you up since you seemed so opposed to my previous suggestion."

I huff out a chuckle as some of my growing tension dissolves.

"It's a good mix of carbs and protein," he adds when I don't make a move toward my lunch. "Exactly what you need to power through the rest of your day."

"Thank you."

"Not a problem. Now eat up before your soup gets cold. Otherwise, I'll be forced to warm you up myself."

"I don't want that," I blurt before I can stop myself.

"I didn't think so." His eyes spark with challenge. "At least, not yet."

He rips off the wrapper of his sandwich and digs in. Just like last night, he attacks his food with gusto as if he hasn't been fed in days. I glance around the table and realize his teammates are doing the same.

It must be an athlete thing.

Or maybe a hockey thing.

It's certainly not a guy thing. The ones I know in LA are just as health conscious as the women.

As I lift the plastic cover, steam rises from the bowl and the scent of wild rice and chicken hits me, making my mouth water.

"Looks good," he says, eyeing the container between bites.

"Actually, it does." Even though I've been on campus since August, I rarely stop and sit down to eat with friends. I'll grab a bar or a piece of fruit. Maybe a sandwich to chow down on the run if I'm really hungry.

I dip the utensil into the bowl before lifting it to my lips and blowing on it for a second or two. The first spoonful proves to be just as delicious as its aroma suggests. After a few bites, I realize that it's doing exactly what Colby said and warming me up from the inside out.

I glance around the table and reluctantly admit that this is nice. The camaraderie and friendships. The easy banter back and forth.

It's exactly what I spent years secretly longing for.

Midway through my meal, Stella poses a question to the table. "Does anyone watch *All Day Long with Bebe*?"

Those eight little words are enough to kill my appetite. I freeze, spoon poised midway to my mouth.

She glances at Juliette, Carina, and Viola before her gaze fastens onto mine. I give my head a little shake as my fingers tremble. It's carefully that I place my utensil back in the bowl before any soup can spill onto the table. The last thing I want to do is draw any further attention to myself.

"You're such an addict when it comes to reality TV," Fallyn says with a laugh.

"Isn't that the show about the singer who went viral when she was a teenager?" Juliette asks.

I swipe my damp palms against the sides of my jeans as the conversation swirls around me, picking up steam. I had no idea any of them watched the show.

No one's ever mentioned it before.

Maverick groans. "Please tell me that you're joking. Reality TV is such garbage."

Stella sticks out her tongue. "Don't judge. It's a guilty pleasure. Like cotton candy for the brain."

"If you say so," he mutters, clearly not understanding the attraction.

When I started hanging around with the girls, Stella explained that she, Juliette, and Maverick were related. Their father, Brody McKinnon, is her older half-brother, which technically makes her their aunt.

But they're more like cousins and super close.

Riggs presses a kiss against Stella's cheek. "You're adorable. I'd never judge you."

Hayes makes a few gagging noises before coughing out the word, "Simp."

Unoffended, Riggs fires back, "I've finally got to this place with the girl I've always wanted, just let me enjoy it."

"I've watched it a few times. The last season left off on a major cliffy," Fallyn chimes in while eating her chicken sandwich.

"I'm dying to know if she said yes to Axel's proposal. I've scoured the internet and haven't been able to find anything about it. In fact, it seems like Bebe dropped off the face of the earth."

A lump forms in my throat, making it impossible to swallow.

"I heard that she's in rehab or resting, or something like that," Carina adds.

Ford raises his brows. "Wait a minute...you watch the show, too?"

With a smile, she shrugs. "You don't know everything about me."

"Bet?" The heat that ignites in his eyes gives him more of a predatory look. "Pretty sure I know you inside and out."

She knocks her shoulder into his. "Shut up."

"I really hope she tells him to take a hike." Stella scrunches her nose as she pops a fry into her mouth. "I don't like the guy at all. He seems like a douche."

Surprised by her comment and the distaste woven through it, the question shoots out before I can stop it. "You really think so?"

She nods as if they're personally acquainted. "Definitely. He's *so* arrogant."

A smirk settles on Maverick's lips as he jerks his head toward Colby. "So is that guy, but I wouldn't call him a douche." There's a pause. "Most of the time."

"You're hilarious, McKinnon," Colby responds good-naturedly. "Watch yourself on the ice. You never know when you're going to get knocked on your ass."

Maverick flashes a dazzling smile. "I'll dust you every time, old man."

Colby snorts before snagging a fry from Bridger's plate and tossing it at the younger player.

"Hey, I was going to eat that," Bridger complains. "Grab someone else's food."

"Anyway..." Stella glares at the guys who interrupted our conversation. "I think she can do way better. Axel seems more concerned with how he looks and the labels he's wearing than with her."

The comment hits me like a punch to the gut. I've secretly thought the same thing before but when I mentioned my suspicions to Mom, she waved them away. She'd tell me that people loved us together and that I shouldn't mess with a good thing.

"When does the next season of the show start?" Viola asks. "I'll have to check it out."

"We should have a girls' night in and binge the last season," Juliette says. "It would be kind of nice to chill out. We can order pizza and make spicy margaritas."

"Ohhh, that sounds good," Carina says, warming to the idea. "I'm definitely down for that."

I can't imagine what it would be like to watch the show with them. Even though I've altered my appearance, I'd be sitting on pins and needles the entire time.

It's a nightmare scenario.

"What about you, Britt?" Stella asks with a tilt of her head. "Are you in?"

I shift, wishing there was a way to skirt the issue. The last thing I want to do is push them away or make them think I'm not interested in getting to know them on a deeper level. "Oh. Um...I'll have to check my schedule and get back to you."

Colby turns and stares at me. I can practically feel the heat of his gaze singeing my flesh.

"No time to hang with the girls?"

"I'm not saying that. I just need to check and see what's going on." I force a tight smile.

It's a relief when Wolf clears his throat, and everyone turns their attention to the tatted-up goalie. "Fallyn and I were thinking of flying to Vegas for the weekend." The expression on his face belies the casualness of the comment.

"Why?" Hayes says with a laugh. "Have you two decided to get hitched by Elvis?"

The couple glances at each other before exchanging secret smiles.

Silence crashes over the table as Bridger exclaims, "Holy shit, you're getting *married*?"

"No fucking way!" Steele says.

"Fallyn?" Carina gasps, looking wide-eyed. "Is that what's going on? Are you two eloping?"

A grin spreads across Fallyn's face, making it look like she's glowing from the inside out as Wolf tugs her close, wrapping her up in his brawny arms.

"That's the plan."

A dozen voices erupt around us. Questions and comments are fired off furiously.

Wolf's gaze stays locked on Fallyn. "I've been waiting for this girl to get with the program for years. Now that she has, I'm unwilling to wait another minute before making her my wife."

Viola is the first to jump up and throw her arms around her cousin. Carina, Juliette, and Stella all follow suit, congratulating the couple.

I can't help but watch Wolf as he stares at his wife-to-be. I've never seen any man look at his girlfriend the way he does. Although, the other guys aren't far behind. But there's something about Wolf...

He's totally obsessed with Fallyn.

I don't think there's anything he wouldn't do for her.

That kind of all-consuming love makes my heart happy. It only confirms that walking away from Axel was the right decision. I can't imagine him watching me with that kind of love brimming in his eyes.

Because, at the end of the day, that's what I want.

Someone who'd be willing to move heaven and earth for me.

Someone who can't imagine their life without me by their side.

And I want the same.

Once the girls are done congratulating Fallyn, I pop to my feet. I'm thrilled for her.

All right...maybe I'm a little jealous.

But only in the best way.

"Congrats, girl! I can't wait to hear all the details. Make sure you post lots of pics of the big day."

"Well...that's the thing," she says. "We were kind of hoping everyone would come with us. It's winter break and there isn't a hockey game this weekend, so it's the perfect time to do it. Then we can all celebrate together."

Excitement bursts from around the table as everyone agrees to check out flights and hotels.

Stella's gaze fastens onto mine. "You'll come with us, right?"

I squirm as everyone turns my way. "Oh, I'd just thought it was for—"

Fallyn shakes her head. "No, we want all our friends there, and that's exactly what you've become, Britt. It would mean a lot to me if you came with us to help celebrate."

Colby nudges my shoulder. "Yeah, you gotta come. It wouldn't be the same without you."

I chew my lower lip as indecision spirals through me.

Of course I'd love to see Fallyn and Wolf tie the knot. Their story is like a fairytale. Or maybe more like Romeo and Juliet. Except with a happy ending.

I'm just not sure it's a good idea to get so wrapped up in their lives when I'm not being honest about my own. When it comes down to it, I'm lying to them about who I really am.

Colby slants a look my way. "So, what's it going to be, firecracker? You coming to Vegas or not?"

After shoving my duffle bag in the overhead bin, I drop down beside Britt in the aisle seat. "Fancy meeting you here."

She gives me a bit of side eye, looking none too happy by my presence. "Please tell me we're not sitting next to each other for the duration of this flight.

The widening of my smile is response enough.

"I want to see your ticket," she grumbles, holding out her hand. "There's no way in hell we got seated next to each other by chance."

I show her the boarding pass on my phone to prove my innocence. What I won't mention are the strings I pulled to arrange it.

"Damn. Talk about shitty luck."

"What I think you meant to say is that you're thrilled by this turn of events."

Her lips and brows flatten. "Nope. Pretty sure I meant what I said."

"How disappointing. I'd thought we moved past all this and were now the best of friends." I stow my backpack beneath the seat in front of me before fumbling with the latch on the seatbelt.

She turns her head just enough to skewer me with a look. "I hate to be the one to break this to you, but we weren't meant to be besties."

Unable to help myself, I lean closer and whisper, "Never say never, Britt. It'll get you in trouble every single time."

Our gazes stay locked in a silent battle of wills.

It's only when the flight attendant walks by that the connection is severed.

"Ma'am, you need to fasten your belt in preparation for takeoff."

Britt glances at him before flashing a smile. Even though the expression is in no way meant for me, it still hits me like a freight train. I need to figure out what it is about this girl that has me so fixated.

Until I do that, I'm not sure if I'll be able to move on.

Fifteen minutes later and the plane is in line and waiting for the green light from control tower to taxi down the runway. I double and then triple check my belt, making sure it's secured before pulling out a stick of gum and popping it into my mouth.

I nudge Britt and offer one.

"Are you trying to tell me something?" she asks while flipping through a magazine.

She's cool as a cucumber, as if she flies all the time and this is nothing new.

It only makes me want to poke around in her past and find out more.

"Yeah, that your ears will be popping in a few minutes. I'm trying to help with that."

She stares at the silver-wrapped stick for a handful of silent seconds before finally reaching out and taking it. "Thanks."

"No problemo." I lean back in my seat and screw my eyelids tightly shut. My hands settle on the armrests on either side of the seat before my fingers curl into the cool metal.

Know what I hate more than flying?

Abso-fucking-lutely nothing.

Unfortunately, my dislike of airplanes has only grown over the years. As tempting as it was to sit this one out, there was no way I could miss Wolf's wedding. Even if it meant forcing myself onto a tin can with wings that propelled itself into the sky, defying gravity.

As a kid, flying was always a fun adventure. We'd take family vacations or travel to the cities where my father was playing.

It was awesome.

Until I was eleven years old, and we hit a rough patch of turbulence. I was so scared that I almost pissed my sweatpants. The overhead compartments burst open, and the bags stowed inside came flying out. Then oxygen masks dropped from the ceiling.

I'm not joking when I say that I'd thought we were all going to die.

It was the worst five minutes of my life.

It doesn't matter if that incident happened more than a decade ago and I've flown dozens of times since, I've never been able to shake off the terror of that experience. It replays through my mind with a disturbing vividness that makes it feel like it was yesterday.

I startle when the engines fire up and the plane rolls down the runway.

I'm not very spiritual, but in this moment?

I'm praying like my damn life depends on it.

Hell, I might even throw in a few Hail Marys if it'll help tip the odds in my favor.

My fingers bite into the smooth metal as my jaw locks.

A warm palm settles over my clenched hand. "Are you all right? You look like you're about to be sick."

"I hate flying. Is it obvious?"

"Just a little. If you hate this so much, why are you doing it?"

I crack open an eyelid only to find Britt staring at me. Concern is etched across her features. "Wolf isn't just a teammate, he's one of my best friends. There's no way I'd miss his wedding. No matter where I had to go or what I had to do to get there."

Her expression softens as she squeezes my fingers. "You're a good friend. I'm sure he appreciates it."

"The fucker better," I grumble.

The engines roar as the plane lifts from the asphalt, taking flight, nose tipped toward the sky.

Fuck.

Fuck.

Fuck.

"It's going to be fine," she says in a soothing tone. It's probably the same one she'd use when speaking with an out-of-sorts toddler. "I've flown a bazillion times and have never had any problems."

"Yeah, I know. But that's the thing about fear—it's not exactly rational, is it?"

She's silent for a moment. "I'm sorry. You're absolutely right. Is there anything I can do to help or make it better?" There's a beat of silence before she adds in a teasing voice, "Besides join the mile-high club with you?"

My lips twitch. "It's almost like you can read my mind."

"Guess now that we've spent a little time together, I've gotten to know you."

"Don't leave me hanging. What do you think so far?" Before she has a chance to respond, I add, "If you had to rate me on Yelp, what would it be? 'Five stars and loving every minute of it?'"

She rolls her eyes as a smile simmers at the corners of her lips. "I'd give you two stars, at the most, along with a 'would definitely *not* recommend.'"

"Ouch. That hurts."

"Well, you did ask," she points out.

"You're right about that," I agree. "I did."

There's a beat of silence.

"Do you want the truth?"

"That depends. Are you going to hurt my feelings?"

Her lips tremble as if she's fighting back a smile. "Here's what I think so far—you're turning out to be different than I expected."

I'm not altogether sure that's a compliment. "Is that good or bad?"

She ponders the question for a handful of seconds. "A mix of both, I suppose."

Ironically, this is the first girl I've actually *wanted* to like me. All the ones that came before her haven't meant a damn thing. I have the sneaking suspicion that whatever this is with Brit could turn out to be something more.

If I let it.

And if she gives me a chance.

I swivel toward her as much as the seat and belt will allow. "You sound disappointed by the revelation."

She rips her gaze from mine before I have the chance to study it. "You should probably know that I'm not interested in getting involved."

"In general, or with me specifically?"

My heart constricts as she contemplates the question.

"With anyone."

I tamp down the disappointment that tries to bloom at the bottom of my belly and lighten my tone, wanting to keep the conversation playful. "All right, I hear what you're saying. So...what are we talking about here? Just a one-night stand? Because I'm totally down for that."

A reluctant smile springs to her lips as she shakes her head. "Have I mentioned lately that you're incorrigible?"

"Possibly."

"It might not seem like it from the outside, but my life is...*complicated*. And it wouldn't be smart to make it more so."

Instead of deterring me, all she's making me want to do is demolish every wall she's attempting to throw up between us.

"I'm curious as to what's so complicated about it. You're a college student. Are you secretly married or is there a fiancé tucked away somewhere?"

Panic leaps into her golden eyes before it's quickly concealed. "Don't be silly," she whispers.

I lean closer and drop my voice. "Let me guess, you're a criminal on the run."

"No."

"Okay. You're undercover and you've been relocated to Western to blend in with the locals?"

"Ridiculous," she mumbles before shifting in her seat.

It doesn't escape me that she stares straight ahead, refusing to meet my gaze, the entire time I rapid fire questions.

I'm not sure what to make of that.

It might be something.

Or it could be nothing.

I don't know Britt well enough yet. What I've discovered is that she likes to keep both her thoughts and feelings to herself.

She's controlled.

Reserved.

Unflappable.

It makes me wonder what it would be like to unravel her.

And make her come undone.

I bet it would be fucking spectacular.

Like fireworks.

"Then tell me what's so complicated about your life."

Just as she's about to respond, the plane jolts. Within seconds, the red and white seatbelt lights flash throughout the cabin.

Good thing I never took mine off.

"Sorry about that, folks," the captain says, coming over the loudspeaker. "Seems like we've hit a patch of rough air. The flight attendants will be returning to their seats. But don't worry, it shouldn't last long."

"I really fucking hate this," I grit through clenched teeth. Any second, they'll shatter into a million pieces.

"It'll be fine," she soothes, squeezing my fingers.

When we hit another pocket of turbulence, I'm pretty sure it's game over for all of us and we're seconds away from plummeting to our deaths.

It was nice knowing you, world.

It's a surprise when Britt leans closer and sings,

> *"In the darkest nights, I stumbled, couldn't see the light.*
> *Lost in a maze, couldn't find what's right. But deep*
> *inside, a fire burned, refusing to fade away. A voice*
> *inside me whispered, "'You'll find your way.'"*

I squeeze my eyes tight as her soothing voice washes over me like a gentle wave.

If I'm going to die, this wouldn't be the worst way to go.

When the lyrics fade, I mutter, "Don't stop." I gulp down the icy cold tendrils of panic that are trying their damnedest to wrap around my heart. *"Please."*

> *"I'm rising up, stronger now than I've ever been. Every scar's a story, ain't letting them win. Through the ups and downs, I'll find my truth. In the chaos of it all, I'll find my youth."*

Her voice rises ever so slightly as she sings the chorus. Gradually, my fear recedes and my muscles lose their rigidity. I focus on her voice and the lyrics instead of what's happening around us.

> *"Through every fall and every doubt, I'll stand tall. Gonna shake off the past, gonna give it my all. With each new day, leaving old fears behind, embracing every challenge, gonna free my mind."*

By the time her voice fades, I realize the turbulence has passed, and the seatbelt signs are no longer illuminated. My heart doesn't feel like it's being crushed in a vise, and I can suck a lungful of air into my body. The adrenalin rushing through my veins recedes.

My gaze stays pinned to hers. "Thanks for that. It really helped."

Our faces are scant inches apart. It would be all too easy to close the distance between us and sweep my lips over hers. I've been jonesing for another taste ever since I walked her to her apartment after our impromptu date.

"It wasn't a problem."

She doesn't move a muscle as everything around us falls away.

It's like we're the only two people on this plane.

"You have a beautiful voice."

The corners of her mouth tilt upward at the compliment.

I rack my brain, trying to remember if I've heard that song before. There's something familiar about it.

I think.

Maybe.

"What's the name of the song?" Because now I need to find it on Spotify.

Her breath catches and her eyes flare slightly as she withdraws her hand from mine so that we're no longer touching. The sudden loss after the intimacy we just experienced feels sharp and painful.

Strangely devastating.

"I don't remember."

"Really?" My brows pull together. "You knew every word."

She jerks her shoulders and shifts in her seat. "Muscle memory, I guess."

That's a bummer.

Even now the melody continues to churn through my brain.

"Well, thanks again. You saved me from a total freak-out. Had that happened, the pilot would have diverted and made an emergency landing in Tulsa." I wave toward the rows of passengers that surround us. "What you did was a public service to all those aboard flight 7809."

She snorts. "I think you would have managed to hold it together."

Now it's my turn to shrug as the corners of my lips bow. "Maybe. Maybe not. Guess the world will never know." Which is for the best.

We fall into a comfortable silence as she stares out the window at the cloud-filled sky.

How is it possible that after only a handful of minutes, I already miss her touch?

Unable to help myself, I reach over and wrap my fingers around her slender ones. Her gaze falls to our clasped hands before she lifts them.

I flash a smile. The one that makes my dimples pop.

Although, from what I've been able to suss out, they have zero effect on this girl.

But...it never hurts to try, right?

Sometimes you gotta bring out the big guns.

"You don't mind if I hold your hand for the rest of the flight, do you? It helps with my anxiety."

There's a second or two of hesitation before she huffs out a long-suffering sigh. "If it'll save you from making a total spectacle of yourself, then I suppose there's no other choice but to suck it up and take one for the team. I speak for all the other passengers on board when I say that no one wants to reroute to Tulsa for an emergency landing."

I can't help but grin. "We'll just call you the Colby whisperer."

"Not only is it a job I never applied for, I'm pretty sure it's one I don't want."

"Too late, firecracker. It's already yours."

"Damn. I was afraid you were going to say that."

In the darkest nights, I stumbled, couldn't see the light.
Lost in a maze, couldn't find what's right.
But deep inside, a fire burned,
Refusing to fade away.
A voice inside me whispered, 'You'll find your way.'

I'm rising up, stronger now than I've ever been.
Every scar's a story, ain't letting them win.
Through the ups and downs, I'll find my truth.
In the chaos of it all, I'll find my youth.

Through every fall and every doubt, I'll stand tall.
Gonna shake off the past, gonna give it my all.
With each new day, leaving old fears behind.
Embracing every challenge, gonna free my mind.

BRITT

By the time we're dropped off at the hotel, all I want to do is stand under the spray of a nice hot shower. Unlike Colby, I enjoy traveling. I've been flying all over the country for years. The time I've spent at Western is the longest I've stayed in one place in almost a decade. Once discovered, I rocketed into the public eye. And then the show made our family a household name.

As I make my way to the reception desk, it occurs to me that I don't really miss the constant hustle and bustle. The crazy schedules.

The group stares around them while oohing and aahing over the grandness of the lobby. Crystal chandeliers drip from high above, casting kaleidoscopic constellations across the gleaming marble floors. You can't help but feel the anticipation as it hums in the air.

This isn't my first trip to Vegas. I'm usually here a couple times a year for parties that the studio hosts.

It's all part of the gig.

I tug at my jacket. It had been freezing when we boarded the plane early this morning but in Vegas, the temperature is in the low sixties. It'll be nice to shed some of my outerwear for the weekend and soak up some sunshine. The seasonal weather is probably the only thing I miss about California.

Wolf and Fallyn are the first in line to secure their room. Next is Juliette and Ryder. And then Carina and Ford. Stella and Riggs along with Viola and Madden check in and are handed room keys. Only now does it occur to me that I'm the lone girl on this trip. I probably should have realized it earlier. Maverick, Hayes, Bridger and Colby booked a suite together.

On the plane, Colby waggled his brows as he offered to let me bunk with him so I wouldn't be all by my lonesome.

I shot down that idea before it was fully out of his mouth.

When it's my turn, I step up to the long stretch of counter and give my name. The woman standing behind it smiles and taps a few keys before securing my credit card.

Since the guys are checking in next to me, I can't help but overhear their conversation.

"I'm sorry, sir," the receptionist says to Bridger. "There appears to be a problem with your reservation. The only room we have available for the weekend is one with two twin beds."

Hayes stares in dismay at Maverick, who pinches the bridge of his nose. "I'm not sleeping on the floor, dude. You can forget that idea right now."

"There's nothing else available?" Colby asks the employee. "We were supposed to have a four-bedroom suite."

The man assisting them makes a big show of striking the keys on his computer before shaking his head. "I'm afraid not." His expression brightens. "But we can bring a rollaway to your room free of charge."

Maverick, Colby, Bridger, and Hayes glance at each other and frown. I can almost see them doing the mental math and figuring out that it doesn't add up.

"That's only three beds for four of us," Bridger says. "Is it possible to add a second rollaway?"

The clerk shakes his head. "Sorry, no. There isn't enough square footage. It's against code—fire hazard. Perhaps there's someone else in your party who wouldn't mind sharing their room?"

"There's no way in hell I'm bunking with my sister and Ryder," Maverick grumbles. "I'd rather fly back home than listen to them get it on. It would be psychologically damaging for all concerned."

"I don't know, man. I wouldn't mind it," Hayes says with a grin.

Maverick punches him in the arm.

"Fuck, dude. That hurt," the blond attackman says with a laugh.

"Good."

"Hey, Britt—"

Before Colby can even get the rest out, I shake my head. I see where this is going from a mile away and want no part of it.

"Absolutely not."

"It would solve the problem," he cajoles, jerking a thumb at his three teammates. "They can share a room, and I'll shack up with you."

"There's only a king," I tell him. "And we're not sleeping in the same bed."

Mr. Helpful behind the counter types away while staring at the computer screen. "Actually, that room comes with a pullout couch."

I glare. "Thanks for sharing."

He beams, clearly not comprehending sarcasm when he hears it. "No problem. It's important that all our guests are happy."

"Then you've failed miserably," I grumble.

Colby steeples his hands before giving me sad puppy dog eyes. "Please, Britt. I'll sleep on the couch and stay out of your way. You won't even know I'm there."

Ha!

"That's doubtful."

All he has to do is enter a room and I'm hyperaware of his presence.

It's a problem.

"Listen," Maverick cuts in, jerking a thumb in his teammate's direction. "If you don't want to bunk with this guy, I'll sleep on your couch."

Colby shoots him a death glare as a hard edge creeps into his tone. It's not one I've heard from him before. "Wanna bet, McKinnon?"

Juliette's brother flashes a grin as his expression turns downright giddy. "Actually, I think the decision is up to Britt. Not you."

When Colby narrows his eyes and takes a step toward the younger player, I slap my palm against his chest to hold him at bay. A shiver of awareness slides through me at the steely muscles that bunch beneath his sweatshirt.

"Fine," I mutter. "You can stay in my room."

Deep down inside, I know it's a decision I'll end up regretting.

Hell, it's only been thirty seconds and I already wish I'd kept my mouth shut.

The thick tension vibrating off him in suffocating waves dissipates as his gaze shifts to mine. "Are you sure?"

Nope. Not even a little.

"Is there really a choice in the matter?" I fire back.

One side of his mouth quirks. "Of course there is. You can do anything other than share a room with one of these guys."

Instead of responding, I turn to the clerk who had been assisting me. "Can I get another keycard for the room, please?"

"Absolutely," she says.

"And I'll have a bottle of our best champagne brought up for your trouble," the man helping the guys adds as if that will make the situation better.

"Great."

After everyone in our group is checked in, we pile into the elevators to our assigned floors. None of them are the same—some are even in different towers. We agree to meet downstairs in two hours to grab dinner and enjoy the nightlife.

As soon as we step inside the room, Colby releases a low whistle.

All right...so maybe it's not just a room. More of a king suite with eight hundred square feet of living space.

His gaze bounces around the beautifully decorated interior. "Damn...this is really nice."

"It was the only thing available when we booked," I mumble.

"Must have cost a pretty penny." He slants a speculative look in my direction as he strolls further inside the suite. "I have to admit—I'm having a tough time figuring you out, Britt."

The nonchalant comment has a boulder the size of Rhode Island taking up residence at the bottom of my belly. It's the last thing I want him to do.

I gravitate toward the floor-to-ceiling windows that overlook the Strip. At night, it'll be a million-dollar view of the city spread out before us.

"There's nothing to figure out." It takes effort to keep the quiver from my voice.

Air gets clogged in my lungs as I hold my breath, waiting to see if he'll press the issue and dig for answers.

"You mind if I jump in the shower? I feel gross after that plane ride."

Relief floods through me, nearly weakening my knees. Even though I'd been thinking the same thing, I have no problem waiting if it means putting an end to this uncomfortable convo.

"Be my guest."

It's the whisper of shed clothing that has me whipping around to find a bare-chested Colby standing in front of me. As much as I don't want to stare, my gaze roves over him, dipping to his chiseled pecs.

Holy hell.

The man looks more like he was carved from marble than is made up of flesh and bone. I've been with my fair share of male models as well as professional athletes over the years, and he puts them all to shame.

It's so tempting to close the distance between us and stroke my hands over all those rigidly held muscles.

And his abs...

If I'm counting correctly, he has an eight pack.

My eyes widen when his hands settle at the waistband of his joggers.

"Don't—"

Too late.

The gray fabric gets shoved down powerful thighs and well-defined calves before he kicks it away. And then he's standing in nothing more than a pair of form-fitting black boxer briefs that hug every sinewy muscle.

Did I say holy hell already?

Well, I'm saying it again.

Holy hell.

No man should look this good.

My gaze rises from his legs that would give tree trunks a run for their money until it settles on his package. That's all it takes for my mouth to turn bone dry until swallowing becomes an impossibility.

He's, um...big.

Like, *really* big.

Fun fact—the longer I stare, the more of a rise I get out of him.

Pun intended.

Heat crawls up my cheeks as arousal pools in my core like warmed honey. It takes effort to drag my gaze away and stare out the window. The spectacular view does nothing for me. In fact, I don't even see it.

All I see is Colby.

"You should take that shower so I can do the same." As unaffected as I want to sound, nothing could be further from the truth. Even I can hear the thick tension vibrating in my voice like a live wire.

"Or," he says conversationally, "we could conserve both time and water by showering together."

I give him a bit of side eye. It seems like the safest option considering that I just went a little stupid when looking directly at him.

I keep my tone clipped. "No thanks."

He shrugs before rifling through his duffle. "You sure there's no way I can convince you to do your part and help save the planet?"

"I'm good."

"Your loss."

Probably.

With that, he swings around, sauntering into the bathroom like he doesn't have a care in the world. As soon as he turns away, my head whips around to watch him. And yeah, his backside is just as firm and fine as the front. I wilt as soon as the lock on the bathroom door clicks into place.

How the hell am I going to share space with this guy for the entire weekend?

I squeeze my eyes shut and repeat my new mantra.

I will not complicate my life.
I will not complicate my life.
I will not complicate my life.
Because that's exactly what Colby McNichols is.
A complication.

IN THE DARKEST NIGHTS, I STUMBLED, COULDN'T SEE THE LIGHT.
LOST IN A MAZE, COULDN'T FIND WHAT'S RIGHT.
BUT DEEP INSIDE, A FIRE BURNED,
REFUSING TO FADE AWAY.
A VOICE INSIDE ME WHISPERED, 'YOU'LL FIND YOUR WAY.'

I'M RISING UP, STRONGER NOW THAN I'VE EVER BEEN.
EVERY SCAR'S A STORY, AIN'T LETTING THEM WIN.
THROUGH THE UPS AND DOWNS, I'LL FIND MY TRUTH.
IN THE CHAOS OF IT ALL, I'LL FIND MY YOUTH.

THROUGH EVERY FALL AND EVERY DOUBT, I'LL STAND TALL.
GONNA SHAKE OFF THE PAST, GONNA GIVE IT MY ALL.
WITH EACH NEW DAY, LEAVING OLD FEARS BEHIND.
EMBRACING EVERY CHALLENGE, GONNA FREE MY MIND.

BRITT

An hour later and I feel a ton better. The shower has managed to work wonders. It's like I'm a new person. One who's more than capable of resisting the baby-faced assassin who I've been forced to shack up with for the weekend.

Let him do his worst.

I can handle it.

No problem.

I give myself one final perusal in the mirror, swiveling one way and then the other as the television drones in the background. The strapless silvery dress hugs my curves and hits mid-thigh. This is the first time since walking away from my life in LA that I've bothered to make an effort with my appearance. Even when the girls and I danced the night away at Blue Vibe, I kept everything lowkey.

Another first for me—applying my own makeup and styling my own hair. There's always been a glam squad to take care of it. Even for the casual shoots when I was working out at the gym it was full glam, although more subtle to make it seem like I wasn't wearing anything at all.

Fun fact—filming a reality show isn't about filming reality.

But that doesn't matter. People still eat it up and want more.

Just like Stella claimed, it's cotton candy for the brain. It's a mindless way to escape what's happening in the world for an hour or so.

I can't help but silently study the person reflected back at me.

It's taken six months and a lot of soul searching to realize that Bebe is nothing more than a persona.

A studio creation.

Deep down inside, it's not who I am.

Or want to be.

It finally feels like the shackles of the past are being broken and falling away.

I feel freer than I have in a long time.

The sound of a low whistle is what drags my thoughts from the past. Even though I'm fairly confident that Colby doesn't have a clue as to who Bebe is, my muscles constrict, and air gets trapped at the back of my throat as I send a cautious look over my bare shoulder to meet his gaze.

"You look gorgeous." His voice is low and gravelly as if it's been dredged from the bottom of the ocean. The deep timbre of it does funny things to my insides.

Heat seeps into my cheeks. "Thank you."

I hate that the compliment means so much more coming from him.

My gaze roves over his length. I'm used to seeing Colby in joggers or jeans and a sweatshirt. The unofficial uniform of the college athlete.

Or maybe just college dudes in general.

It's a campus epidemic.

Tonight, he's wearing a light pink button-down that showcases his broad shoulders and gray slacks that fit him to perfection. A punch of arousal hits me deep in my core.

"Good enough to eat," he adds with a sly wink.

I roll my eyes.

That comment dissolves the growing tension that had sprung up between us.

Before I can think of a comeback, a chipper voice catches my attention.

"Give us all the deets, Sharon! Where's Bebe? Why hasn't anyone seen her in months? Has she gone into hiding? Did she and Axel elope and they're off living their very best lives away from the cameras?"

My head snaps toward the large screen TV so fast that I nearly give myself whiplash. A plastic-looking blonde has a microphone shoved in my mother's smiling face. All four siblings are crowded behind her, looking glammed up. Cheyenne whips her long, golden hair over one shoulder and beams at the camera. They must be attending an opening. There's always a ton of them in L.A. One every night of the week.

I can only stare in shock as my heart thumps a painful tattoo against my ribcage.

"You're *so* bad, Maryanne." My mother wags a glossy manicured finger at the interviewer. "Of course, Bebe isn't in hiding. She's taking a well-deserved break. The poor girl hasn't had one in years, and this seemed like the perfect opportunity to indulge." Mom flashes a practiced smile at the camera. "What I will say is that she's been working on new music."

"Ohhh, is Axel with her? Has she made a decision yet?"

Mom shakes her head and makes a locking motion with one hand in front of her lips. "You know that I'd love to tell you, but I've been sworn to secrecy."

The interviewer sidles closer before pressing the microphone more firmly to my mother's mouth. "Our viewers would just love an exclusive scoop."

Mom looks directly at the camera, and an icy shiver skates down the length of my spine. It's like she's staring straight into my soul.

Talking directly to me.

"We'll be shooting the show soon, and then everyone will find out if Bebe and Axel will be planning a wedding next season. In the meantime, Cheyenne will be performing—"

Colby clicks off the television with the remote before my mother can finish her sentence.

It takes a second or two to shake myself out of the stupor that has fallen over me. Even the thought of returning to my old life has a sick knot settling in the pit of my belly. I draw a deep breath into my lungs before holding it captive for a heartbeat. Then two. Only then do I release it back into the atmosphere.

"Is that the show Stella was talking about the other day?"

Well, shit.

My gaze reluctantly skitters to him as a burst of nerves rush through my veins. "Umm, yeah. I mean, I think so."

He shakes his head as his upper lip curls with distaste. "The only thing those people are famous for is being famous. They don't actually *do* anything. It's kind of pathetic, the way that woman whores out her kids to get ahead in life."

My eyes widen as my mouth falls open.

His comments are like a slap in the face.

It's not like I haven't thought the same thing a million times before. But, for some reason, it's different coming from him.

Colby is an outsider who doesn't know anything about my family.

He has no idea how hard my mom works. She's the one who manages all our schedules and negotiates deals and sets up gigs, shows, and interviews. We're able to live the kind of life we do because of her tenacity and strength. I've never doubted that she'd walk barefoot to the ends of the earth if it meant that her kids would have every opportunity for success. No matter how I feel at the moment, I've always been grateful and appreciative.

I draw myself up to my full height. "That's a little harsh."

"Just calling it like I see it." He jerks his shoulders. "Tell me, am I wrong?"

My tongue darts out to moisten my lips. For some reason, it feels like I'm walking a tightrope. "There's more to that family than the show. Bebe isn't just a reality star. She's a musician. The show just allows a glimpse into the process." Is there anything more bizarre than talking about yourself in the third person? "I, um, read an article a while back about how they were barely scraping by." I point to the television. "That woman was working twelve-hour shifts as a nurse at the hospital before her daughter was discovered. She made the decision to uproot them all and move to a place where they didn't have any family or friends. And then she busted her ass to make sure all her kids would have an opportunity to live out their dreams, no matter what they were. So, tell me...how does that make her a terrible mother?" My heart thrashes beneath my breast. "Were you ever at the point where your family didn't have enough money to pay the bills?"

From what I know about his famous hockey-playing father, my guess is that the opposite is true.

His brows pinch together. "I..."

An uncomfortable silence falls over us.

In the short time I've been around Colby, not once have I ever seen him at a loss for words.

With a tilt of his head, he studies me more carefully. It's difficult to hold steady beneath the heavy scrutiny.

"No, I haven't," he finally acknowledges in a softer voice. I'm trapped within his probing stare and the questions that dance in his eyes. "But my guess is that you have?"

"A long time ago," I admit.

"Sorry, I didn't mean to hit a nerve or offend you."

I nip my lip with my teeth. It's tempting to tell him that he hasn't, but that would be a lie, and we both know it.

My muscles loosen as he glances around the lavish suite.

"It would seem like times have changed for the better."

I release a steady breath and realize that we're creeping dangerously into a territory that'll be difficult to navigate my way out of.

And I'm tired of the lies.

My entire existence feels built upon them.

"Yes, they have." Before he can ask any more questions I won't want to answer, I change the subject. "Are you ready to go? Everyone's probably waiting for us downstairs."

The strain of moments ago dissolves. "Yup."

I slip into heels and grab my purse off the credenza as we leave the suite behind and head to the elevator down the hall. Colby's gaze stays fastened to mine the entire ride to the lobby. It takes everything I have inside to tamp down my body's reaction to him. It's a relief when the doors slide open and noise pours inside the elevator. The fresh air cuts through the growing tension.

He holds open the door as I step into the corridor and search for our friends.

That thought is almost enough to stop me in my tracks, because over the past months, that's exactly what they've become.

My friends.

Warmth bubbles up inside me before spreading outward at the realization.

One nudge from Colby and I'm brought back to the moment at hand. "Hey, isn't that the dude from the action movie that released last summer?"

I glance at the guy in question. He's swarmed by both his entourage and fans. "Yeah, it is. Want an autograph?"

He snorts as his face scrunches. "Hell, no. He can ask for mine instead. *Maybe* I'll give it to him."

From all the gossip floating around campus, it sounds like Colby will end up taking the NHL by storm. If people don't know him because he plays professional hockey, they'll recognize him from all the endorsement deals his agent secures for him.

In a couple years, Colby McNichols will be a household name. He's too hot, talented, and charming not to be.

That combination is a magical trifecta.

We recognize half a dozen famous faces as we move through the crowded lobby before noticing Carina and Ford along with several others.

The blonde dancer waves as she spots us. Her gaze travels up and down my length. "Well, hello there, hot mama!"

I flash a smile. "Thanks. You're looking pretty amazing yourself."

She flips her high ponytail over one shoulder. "Thanks."

Juliette and Ryder stroll through the lobby hand in hand, looking happy. In fact, she just might be glowing. We won't go into any in-depth reasons for that. Both are dressed to kill. Ryder's arm is wrapped possessively around his girlfriend. They're the perfect match.

Maverick, Hayes, and Bridger trail after them. The three of them are laughing and jostling one another like kids. Heads swivel in their direction as they pass by. They're good-looking guys. Tall, muscular, and handsome. Even if you didn't know they were athletes, you'd suspect it from the easy way they move.

Ford glances around the group. "I think the only ones missing are the bride and groom."

"I can just imagine what's keeping them," Hayes says with a laugh.

Bridger elbows him in the ribs, which only makes him chuckle harder. Even though Hayes seems chill and is always smiling, I get the feeling there's more to him than meets the eye. Almost as if he puts on a façade for his friends.

Probably because I do the same.

Like recognizes like.

He's just as good looking as the other guys with dirty blond hair that's long on top and has a tendency to flop over his eyes.

"Here they are," Maverick says. "Guess we're ready to get this party started."

"And where exactly are we doing that?" Bridger asks, raking a hand through his mahogany-colored hair.

I'm used to seeing him with a ballcap. This is probably the first time I've caught sight of him without one. Like everyone else at Western, I've read the mass messages that have been sent to both staff and students and understand that he's trying to keep a low profile. It's obvious that someone has an ax to grind with him.

"We're gonna grab something to eat at a place down the street—the concierge made reservations. And then we'll hit the clubs to shake our asses," Stella says.

"Sounds good to me," Carina agrees. "I'm always down for a little dirty dancing."

"The only dirty dancing you do is for me, baby," Ford laughs, pulling her close and brushing a kiss against her lips.

"Sounds like we have a plan," Wolf says. "Let's hit it."

Our evening starts out at a restaurant that a reality star owns. I don't mention it, but I've been here before as her guest. The food is delicious, and the drinks flow freely. Everyone has a good time. It's so easy to see that this group is tight knit and comfortable with one another. It's moments like this that I'm grateful the girls were so welcoming and made room for me.

Once the bill is paid, we head to a nearby club and find a long line snaking down the block. Colby talks to the security manning the door, and within a matter of minutes, the burly man in a suit waves us inside as if we're VIPs. People at the front of the line grumble when we skip ahead.

I can't resist asking, "What did you say to him?"

Colby throws his arm around my shoulders and tugs me close before whispering, "Stick with me, kid. I'll take you places and show you things you've never seen before."

A reluctant smile quirks my lips as I shake my head.

This guy...

He's so damn full of himself.

It shouldn't be sexy.

It really shouldn't...

But I can't deny that it is.

The space is shadowy and frenetic with unspent energy. Colored lights cut swaths through the darkness. It's wall to wall people packed inside. Perched high above the dance floor sits a DJ who mixes music. Neon lights flicker at the far end of the club, illuminating a long stretch of sleek and sexy bar.

Even though the temperature outside has dropped about ten degrees, I'm glad I didn't wear a wrap. We might have just arrived, but already I can feel the heat from the mass of gyrating bodies.

We all stick together, cutting a path to the bar. Ryder orders a round of shots for the group. Then Carina buys another. After that, Stella pulls me to the dance floor and all the girls follow until we've carved out a small space for ourselves.

Techno thumps a steady rhythmic beat until I'm able to feel it deep in my bones. It doesn't take long for my eyelids to drift shut as I raise my arms and allow the music to pour over me. All I want to do is forget about everything that nags at my subconscious.

All the pressure I feel to return to LA.

And my family...

I love them, but I no longer want the responsibility of carrying us anymore. I want the freedom to walk away without it affecting the business we've built over the past decade.

Is that even possible?

It's the question that gnaws away at me in the darkness and keeps me up at night.

One song bleeds into the next until it feels like I'm floating. I'm not sure if it's the alcohol coursing through my veins, the music, or the party atmosphere, but I never want this moment to end.

It's only when strong arms slip around my ribcage and pull me against a hard chest that I come back to myself. Without turning, I know exactly who's holding me tight. I'd recognize his woodsy scent anywhere.

If I were thinking clearly, I'd untangle myself from Colby and put some distance between us.

Instead, I burrow against his brawny strength as he tightens his hold. It's been a long time since I felt this safe or protected.

I'm tired of fighting this attraction.

"The way you move is so damn sexy," he growls as his hands drift over my curves.

I turn my head just enough for our gazes to become ensnared. Even in the darkness of the club, his eyes glow with heat and arousal. The longer we stare, the more everything else fades away.

Air stalls in my lungs as his face looms closer.

That's when I realize it wouldn't take much to fall for this guy.

That thought is like a bucket of cold water dumped over my head, and I wake from my dream-like state with a jolt.

"I need to use the restroom," I murmur, untangling myself and stepping away. As soon as I do, the thick haze clouding my brain clears enough for rational thought to once again prevail.

After everything I've done and been through, it takes a lot to unnerve me.

But that's exactly how I feel at this moment.

"Want me to come with you?"

With a shake of my head, I take another step away from him. "No, I'll be back."

Maybe.

Before he can respond, I slip through the mass of gyrating bodies to the other side of the spacious area where the bathrooms are located. And just like the rest of the place, they're ridiculously over the top and fancy. After taking care of business, I detour to the bar for a much-needed bottle of water.

As I wait for a server to take my order, my gaze roves over the glamorous crowd before getting snagged by the roped-off VIP section. I've partied here dozens of times, and that's always where we sat, away from the mob where there's more breathing room—along with personal waitstaff that caters to your every whim.

The tiny hairs at the back of my neck rise as my attention lands on a guy with inky black hair and pale blue eyes who's lounging on a plush velvet couch. There's a drink in his hand to go along with the look of boredom etched across his face.

It's one I'm intimately acquainted with.

Unless we're shooting the show.

Then he's all boyish charm and charisma.

An act meant for the cameras and the millions of people who tune in every week.

When his idle gaze collides with mine, electricity snakes through me, robbing the air from my lungs, making it impossible to breathe.

With a frown, he straightens.

Fuck.

That's all it takes for me to bolt.

COLBY

I trail after Britt from a distance as she slips through the crowd and down the hallway to where the restrooms are located. Maybe she didn't want me to come with her, but I have a younger sister and I'd never want her walking around alone at a place like this.

It takes about ten minutes before she returns. I straighten to my full height as she beelines to the sleek bar instead of heading back to the dance floor where everyone is busy busting a move.

It's so damn tempting to eat up the distance that separates us and pull her back into the warm circle of my arms where she belongs. I almost shake my head as that thought coalesces in my brain. The mix of emotions pumping through me are strange and new. Unlike anything I've experienced before. Instead of shutting them down and backing away, they only make me want to dig deeper and figure out what it all means.

Even though it goes against every instinct, I force myself to hang back and observe. I'm curious if she'll return to the dance floor.

To me.

She loiters near the bar, trying to catch someone's attention. But the bartenders are busy and the customers are at least two deep. My muscles tense when a few guys pause to check out her ass. I'm like a racehorse straining at its bit. If any of these dickheads even attempt to shoot their shot, I'm moving in.

I'm itching to mark her as my own, so these jokers understand that she's taken.

Except...that's not the case.

Britt doesn't belong to me.

Hell, I'm not even sure we're friends.

Oblivious to the attention she's drawing, she glances at the VIP section. I follow her line of sight and find a dark-haired guy. He's lounging on a sumptuous couch as the well-dressed people who surround him laugh and drink.

There's something familiar about him. Although that's not altogether surprising. I've caught sight of a ton of celebrities since we walked into the hotel. From movie and television stars to athletes and world-renowned chefs.

Vegas is a playground for the rich and famous.

Britt's attention stays pinned to him. Under the colorful lights that flash and flicker, her body stiffens. She reminds me of a deer caught in the bright glare of headlights.

Frozen in place.

Does she know him?

I study the guy more carefully, only to find him staring back at her. His expression shifts to one of surprise as he snaps to attention like a bird dog who's just spotted fresh quarry.

When my gaze cuts to Britt, it's a shock to find that she's disappeared. I catch a flash of silver moving through the mass of bodies and take off. After a couple of steps, I throw a glance over my shoulder, wanting to make sure the dude in question doesn't plan on following. A frown mars his face as he rises to his feet and searches the darkness.

Unwilling to lose her for a second time this evening, I twist around and hasten my pace. I'm tall enough to see over most of the crowd packed into the club and catch sight of her again as she slips through the exit.

My heart jackhammers an unsteady beat as I give chase. It takes less than a minute for me to pull up alongside her.

She startles, fear flickering across her expression as her head whips around and her gaze collides with mine.

"Colby." Her voice is unsteady.

Breathless.

"Hey."

Relief floods her features before it's quickly shuttered behind a mask of indifference as she continues to stride purposefully toward our hotel in the distance.

I wait a beat.

Then another, hoping she'll give me an explanation for her sudden departure.

After a handful of seconds, it becomes clear that she isn't going to bother.

"What happened back there?"

She stares straight ahead. "Nothing. I just got a little overheated and decided to head back to the hotel."

Overheated?

That's her justification for taking off like a bat out of hell?

"And you weren't going to tell anyone? Don't you think your friends would have been concerned that you just dipped without a word?"

She stutters to a stop and stares at me. Emotion flickers across her face. "You're right." She fishes her phone out of the sparkly purse that matches her tiny excuse for a dress before firing off a text. Then she holds up the sleek rose gold device. "All taken care of. I sent a text to the group chat letting them know that I'm headed back to the hotel."

Since she's not going to address her reason for leaving the club, I decide to take the bull by the horns.

"Who was the guy?"

There's a flash of panic in her golden eyes before it disappears. "What guy?"

"The one in the VIP lounge. The one you were staring at." There's a beat of uncomfortable silence before I add, "The one who was staring back like he knew you."

Her teeth scrape across her lower lip as she glances away. "I have no idea."

I tilt my head and study her under the neon flashing lights of the restaurants, casinos, and hotels. "Are you sure about that? Because the way you looked at each other says otherwise."

Her brows pinch together as she fires off a question of her own. "Were you watching me?"

Sure, I could lie...

But what would be the point?

"Yeah, I was."

Her eyes widen. "Why?"

I step closer, eating up the space between us before reaching out and stroking my fingers along the curve of her jaw. "I think that should be more than obvious." When she remains silent, I add, "Don't you?"

"Colby..."

She blinks as her face fills with indecision.

Instead of pushing for more, I allow my hand to fall away before slipping it around her waist and tugging her close. There's something about her warm weight anchored against my body that settles everything rampaging within me.

"Come on, let's head back to the hotel."

"You don't have to cut your night short. There are a ton of people out walking the streets. I'm perfectly safe."

Like hell I'd let her walk back alone.

Maybe I don't always act like a gentleman, but buried deep down, that's exactly what I am.

In fact, my motto has always been 'ladies first.'

And if that doesn't say it all, I don't know what does.

I shrug. "I'm more than ready to call it a night."

It's a relief when her muscles loosen, and we resume walking in companionable silence.

For the first time in my life, I'm locked on one girl.

I assume that once we sleep together, my interest will wane, and

I'll be able to move on. A little voice inside my head wonders what will happen if that doesn't turn out to be the case.

I quash that thought before it can burrow into my brain and cause irreparable damage.

Because there's no way in hell that's going to happen.

IN THE DARKEST NIGHTS, I STUMBLED, COULDN'T SEE THE LIGHT.
LOST IN A MAZE, COULDN'T FIND WHAT'S RIGHT.
BUT DEEP INSIDE, A FIRE BURNED,
REFUSING TO FADE AWAY.
A VOICE INSIDE ME WHISPERED, 'YOU'LL FIND YOUR WAY.'

I'M RISING UP, STRONGER NOW THAN I'VE EVER BEEN.
EVERY SCAR'S A STORY, AIN'T LETTING THEM WIN.
THROUGH THE UPS AND DOWNS, I'LL FIND MY TRUTH.
IN THE CHAOS OF IT ALL, I'LL FIND MY YOUTH.

THROUGH EVERY FALL AND EVERY DOUBT, I'LL STAND TALL.
GONNA SHAKE OFF THE PAST, GONNA GIVE IT MY ALL.
WITH EACH NEW DAY, LEAVING OLD FEARS BEHIND.
EMBRACING EVERY CHALLENGE, GONNA FREE MY MIND.

BRITT

12

Colby's arm stays wrapped around me as we walk through the hotel and step inside the mirrored elevator before rising to the twenty-fifth floor. There's something comforting about his presence and the way he holds me anchored against him as if we've been doing this for years.

I have to continually remind myself that this guy is a player.

This is what he does.

He charms girls into bed.

And they're thrilled with the opportunity. From everything I've heard, they're just as cheerful in the morning when he boots their asses to the curb. Now that he's focused solely on me, I understand just how heady his full attention can be.

What doesn't make sense is that I've dealt with my fair share of slick dudes and am pretty good at figuring out what's hidden beneath the shiny exterior. It was never a problem walking away without a second glance.

But Colby is proving himself to be different.

The woodsy scent of his aftershave slyly weaves around me, making it impossible to keep him at a firm distance. By the time he swipes the keycard against the lock, I realize exactly how tonight will play out. After spotting Axel at the club, I'm out of sorts and not thinking clearly. My life at Western feels like a sandcastle that will crumble with the first wave, and that's terrifying.

Silence fills the suite as he flicks on the lights and a warm glow illuminates the space. I gravitate to the floor-to-ceiling windows and the bright lights of the city that are spread out below us. The Strip is filled with so many iconic resorts and casinos that glitter against the velvety darkness.

It's gaudy and over the top.

But also magical.

I don't realize that Colby has snuck up behind me until his hands settle on my bare shoulders and he draws me against the solid strength of his chest.

"It's beautiful, isn't it?" I whisper.

"Gorgeous."

His hand rises to sweep my hair away from the side of my face before the tip of his nose drifts along the curve of my cheek. A shiver of desire dances down the length of my spine as his warm breath ghosts across my flesh. When his fingers bite into my bare skin, a sharp punch of arousal settles low in my belly.

Even though I'm entranced by the sight spread out before me, my eyelids feather closed as he nips my earlobe.

It's been a long time since anyone has turned me on to this degree.

Years.

I swivel in his arms until I can search his face.

Sparks fly from his heated gaze. "Tell me what's going through your head."

"That I don't understand what this is between us."

It feels good to finally admit the truth out loud.

His lips quirk. "Attraction. Need. What more is there to understand?"

He's right, of course. That's all this is.

A little bit of physical attraction that refuses to be doused.

His fingers slip beneath my chin. "The question now is—what are you going to do about it?"

Maybe the real question is—*what do I want to do about it?*

I've spent half a year holding myself at a distance because I was frightened of getting too close. Scared someone might ferret out my secret.

It's been exhausting.

For one night, I want to pretend that my life in LA doesn't exist and I'm exactly who I portray myself to be. I want to give in to the attraction rushing through my veins and dampening my panties where this man is concerned.

Just for tonight.

A few hours of meaningless fucking.

And Vegas is the perfect place to do it. We can get it out of our systems and then fly back to school and go our separate ways. If there's any truth to what I've heard about Colby, that's exactly what he has in mind.

It'll work out perfectly.

Decision made, I tangle my arms around his neck and stretch on the tips of my toes before brushing my mouth against his. A groan rumbles up from deep within his chest as he nips at my lower lip and tugs it with sharp teeth. That's all it takes for a tidal wave of arousal to crash over me, threatening to drag me to the bottom of the ocean.

When a whimper of need breaks free, the velvety softness of his tongue slips inside my mouth to tangle with my own. He takes full command of the kiss as his hands slide around my hips to cup my backside and palm the rounded flesh. He presses me closer until I can feel the thick length of his erection dig into my lower abdomen. Need pools in my core.

With a groan, he pulls away before resting his forehead against mine and staring into my eyes.

"I don't want this to go any further unless you're fully on board. Do you understand?"

I nod, amazed that he can pump the brakes when all I want is to feel his lips sliding over mine, making me forget everything that eats away at me in the darkness.

"Yes," I whisper. "I want this. I want *you*."

For tonight.

Maybe even tomorrow.

But nothing more.

His gaze sifts through mine for a handful of seconds before he jerks his head into a tight nod and takes a step in retreat. Before I can protest the distance, his hands land on my shoulders as he swivels me around until my backside is turned toward him.

"Lift your hair, sweet girl. As hot as you look in this dress, it needs to go."

My hands tremble as I gather up the thick strands and hold them away from my neck. The grind of metal teeth is the only sound that breaks the heavy silence of the suite. My heart picks up tempo as the slinky material slips down my body like a waterfall until it puddles around the three-inch silver heels.

The only piece of clothing I'm wearing is a thong that barely covers anything.

"Fuck."

I didn't bother with a bra, since the dress is strapless and has a built-in shelf.

When I attempt to lower my arms, a guttural groan escapes from him. "No. Stay just like that. I'm not nearly done admiring you."

My belly dips at the appreciative tone that floods his voice.

"You're so damn beautiful, you know that?"

I twist just enough to glance over my shoulder and meet his heavy-lidded eyes. The heat that fills them almost scorches me alive.

"Are you going to stare at me all night or fuck me?"

A predatory expression darkens his features. "Oh, I plan on fucking you all night long."

His wicked promise has an explosion of butterflies winging their way to life deep in my core.

One long-legged stride is all it takes to swallow up the distance between us until he's close enough to align himself with my spine. His hands slide around my ribcage to cup my naked breasts with his palms. He squeezes the softness as if testing the weight before rolling my nipples between his thumbs and forefingers. Pleasure shoots through me, electrifying my insides.

My head falls back until it can rest against his chest. That's when I realize he's still dressed in his slacks and crisp pink button-down while I'm practically naked.

I have no idea why that mental image is so erotic.

That thought disintegrates when he tweaks the tightly puckered buds.

A gasp escapes from me. There's a bite of pain before pleasure rushes in to drown it.

"You like that, sweet girl?"

His teeth scrape against the curve of my jaw as he repeats the movement.

A tortured groan is the only response I'm capable of giving.

"If I slip my hand into that shameless excuse for underwear, am I going to find your little pussy soaking wet and sobbing for me?"

Oh god...

I didn't expect him to have such a dirty mouth.

A rush of heat fills my thong.

"Hmmm?" He nips my ear as he pinches me again. "You didn't answer the question."

That's because I've been rendered speechless. My brain is short-circuiting, and I'm unable to string together a passable answer. If I open my mouth, all that will come out is gibberish.

He's barely touched me and I'm already dancing on the precipice.

If this is any indication of what the night will bring, I totally understand why girls leave his bed with a smile and nothing but praise.

"Guess I'll have to figure it out myself."

One hand drifts from my breast, along my ribcage and belly before delving past the elastic band of my thong. His fingers brush over my throbbing clit and then the seam of my lips before gliding through the slick folds. Two fingers slip inside my pussy until he's buried knuckle deep. He holds them firmly in place as his lips graze the outer shell of my ear.

"Mmmm...drenched." He pumps them in and out. The movement is unhurried as if he has all the time in the world to explore my body. "I hope you're going to let me lick up all that cream." He groans when another burst of arousal floods my core. "You like a little dirty talk, don't you?"

I cry out in protest when he slips the digits from my body. "Yes!"

"Good girl," he praises, dragging them upward until he's able to rub my clit with lazy circles that force me to the brink.

My hand locks around his until my nails sink into his flesh.

"I don't mind a few scratches. You want to mark me as your own? I don't have a problem with it."

My body tightens as he continues to stroke my flesh, drawing out every ounce of pleasure until I want to scream.

"Please," I whimper, unable to hold back. I've never begged anyone for anything in my life.

But I can't stop the word from tumbling free.

His body crowds mine until it feels like I'm surrounded on all sides by his masculine presence. He pinches my nipple with one hand while grinding against my clit with the other. My spine arches and my muscles constrict as I go off like a firework. A scream tears from my throat and fills the air.

"Open your eyes, sweet girl."

Even though it's the last thing I want to do, I force them open until the colorful lights of the Strip fill my vision. My breath catches at the back of my throat as wave after wave of pleasure crashes over me. My knees weaken as he plays my body like a fine instrument.

It only draws out my orgasm.

By the time the final wave of pleasure floods my system, I'm limp as a noodle. His fingers continue to caress me as he holds me pinned against him. My gaze locks on his reflection in the window.

"You're beautiful when you come undone."

Heat floods my cheeks as he slips his hand from my thong. With his gaze locked on mine, he lifts his fingers to his lips and licks away the cream before sucking them into his mouth.

Air stalls in my lungs as my eyes widen.

I couldn't look away even if I wanted to.

Have I ever seen anything as sexy in my life?

"Fucking delicious."

The same hand drifts down to my thong before slipping beneath the band and dipping inside me for a second time. Only now do I realize how soaked I am. It's almost embarrassing how quickly he was able to make me come.

What's worse is that I'm still turned on and hungry for more.

He pumps his fingers deep inside me. With each languid movement, more arousal gathers in my core.

Of course, I've had sex before.

Sometimes I would come. Other times it would remain elusive, and I'd finish myself off afterward. Unless it was really bad...

Then I didn't bother.

Axel was selfish. He preferred to receive but didn't always want to return the favor.

Colby's behavior has totally thrown me. I figured he'd be like all the other handsome guys from my past. I blink away those thoughts as another orgasm begins to build. Before I can give myself over to the sensation, his hand slips free and a tortured moan escapes from me.

My head falls back, resting against the steely strength of his chest as my heavy-lidded gaze stays pinned to our reflection in the window.

A smile quirks his lips. "Greedy, aren't you?"

That's the thing...I never have been before.

His fingers rise until they can trace my mouth, painting them with my own arousal. It's only after my lips have been coated that he presses his fingers against them. His hot gaze stays pinned to our reflection.

"Open wide. Show me exactly how you're going to choke on my big cock."

That command shouldn't turn me on, but it does.

So much that it almost defies logic.

It never occurs to me not to follow the directive. I open and wait for what will happen next.

Even though he smirks as if pleased by my acquiescence, arousal burns so brightly in his eyes that they practically glow with blue fire.

"Such a good girl."

My gaze stays pinned to the erotic image in the glass as he lazily circles my lips. The other hand palms my breast as his fingers pluck and torment my nipple.

"Stick out your tongue."

Again, I do as he commands.

My heartbeat thuds painfully beneath my ribcage as a handful of seconds tick by.

Just as I grow impatient, he presses the digits against me.

He turns his face until it's buried in my hair. "Do you taste that?"

With a moan, I shift against him.

"Do you taste how excited your pussy gets when I play with it?"

Another whimper works its way free from me.

His warm breath feathers across my flesh. "Close your mouth around my fingers and draw them deep inside."

It's not even a question of whether I'll follow the instructions. There's something strangely freeing about relinquishing all control. It's the first time in years—maybe even a decade—that I've allowed myself to do it. I can almost feel the shackles of my past loosening before dropping to the floor.

All the pressure that normally weighs me down, choking the life out of me.

I've never felt so light.

Like I'm floating.

It's almost as addictive as the mind-blowing orgasm he just gave me and the one that's already brewing deep within my core like an impending storm, waiting to explode at his slightest command.

"Mmmm, that's so good. Can you take me a little deeper, sweet girl?"

His fingers slide to the back of my throat. There's a strange concoction of both pleasure and pain.

"Now swallow."

The muscles of my throat constrict around the foreign intrusion.

"You're going to take my cock so nicely, aren't you?"

In response, I repeat the movement, only wanting to please him.

His lips drift along the side of my face as he tweaks one puckered bud. "I'll take that as a yes."

He presses just a bit deeper until tears sting my eyes.

"So fucking good," he murmurs before dragging them out. The arm snaked around me falls away. "Turn around."

My body vibrates like a live wire as I spin on my high heels. I expect a smirk to lift the corners of his lips. After all, he's gotten me to do what he wanted with a ridiculous amount of ease. Instead, his expression smolders. There's so much pent-up arousal etched across his features.

Almost as if he's in pain.

That's when I remember that I might have found my release, but he hasn't.

My gaze drops to the fly of his dress slacks and the way they're tented in the front.

"Pop the button and unzip me."

My fingers tremble as I follow the instructions until the black cotton peaks out from the fly.

"Take out my cock so you can play with it," he says, voice strung tight with need.

That's all the impetus I need to delve inside his boxers and wrap my fingers around his hot length before slipping it free from its confines.

Just as I suspected, his dick is thick and long.

More arousal floods my core.

"On your knees, sweet girl."

I flick a glance upward before lowering myself to the carpet until I'm eye level with his erection. One of his hands tangles in my hair as the other strokes my lower lip with his thumb. They're soft, sweeping caresses that leave me aching for more.

"The only way you'd look more beautiful is if your mouth was stuffed full of cock."

Another punch of desire nearly steals my breath away.

"Open wide and take me inside your mouth. I want you to deep throat me just like you did with my fingers."

My tongue darts out to moisten my lips as I draw his crown inside me. His fingers tighten around my scalp as if to hold me in place as a groan rumbles up from his chest and I suck his hard length deeper.

"That feels so damn good," he groans.

Moisture pricks my eyes as he hits the back of my throat. With a gentle touch, he thumbs away the wetness.

Concern cuts through the look of utter bliss etched across his handsome face. "Am I hurting you?"

I give my head a little shake.

"Good. There's a fine line between pleasure and pain. I'd never want to cross it. Only give you enough to make your body come alive and sing for me."

He presses closer until the wiry hair at his groin tickles my nose and my lips are forced to stretch wider around his girth.

When my wet lashes flutter closed, he says, "Eyes on me, sweet girl."

I force them open until my gaze can fasten on him. Just when I think he'll come, he pulls away. As soon as his cock slips free, I drag a lungful of air into my body. In one smooth motion, he reaches down and slips his arms around my ribcage before hauling me to my feet and pressing his lips against mine. His tongue delves inside my mouth to tangle with my own.

"You taste just like me," he growls. "I love it. Are you ready to get fucked?"

So ready.

I can't imagine what it'll feel like to have his thick length filling me so completely, but I'm desperate to find out.

My thong is so soaked that I could probably wring it out.

He spins me around and walks us to the floor-to-ceiling windows that span the wall. A gasp escapes from me as I'm pressed against the cool glass. My bare breasts and belly flatten against it. With his hands locked around mine, he drags them above my head until I'm stretched out completely. I turn my head until one cheek can rest against the smooth surface. If anyone were to look up or across the street from another building, they would see my naked form.

That thought only turns me on more.

"Don't move or I'll spank that gorgeous ass."

When I remain silent, he whacks one cheek. The sound of flesh striking flesh fills the suite.

"Understand?"

"Yes," I gasp as more heat gathers in my core.

My heart beats a steady tattoo against my chest as a rip of paper catches my attention.

A condom.

He's opening the wrapper of a condom.

Thank fuck he's thinking about protection because I certainly wasn't. Even though I have an IUD, I'd still want him to use something.

And then his hard body covers mine, surrounding me until he blots out the world around us.

His thick length presses against my backside. He cants his hips before flexing them so that his cock slides against the cleft that separates my cheeks. I arch, offering myself up.

"Tell me...is that greedy little pussy in need of a hard dick?"

"Yes," I sob, unable to help myself.

Even though a chuckle slips free from him, it's tinged around the edges with tension as he yanks the thin string to the side and slides deep inside my body with one smooth stroke.

"I'm going to make you feel so good."

I can only groan as he fills me completely. I don't think I've ever been stretched this tight. The pleasure and pain of it is exquisite. I'm so turned on that I won't last long. Even after coming no more than fifteen minutes ago, I'm ready to go off like a shot.

A groan slips free from me as he pulls out before sliding back inside. Every time he flexes his hips, another wave of pleasure crashes over me. His fingers wrap around mine as he fucks me against the glass. No more than a dozen strokes later, I shatter. As soon as my inner muscles clench, he follows me over the edge and into oblivion.

I'm pretty sure I scream out his name—maybe even chant it—as he pummels me with his cock.

The only coherent thought I'm able to grasp hold of is that nothing I've experienced up to this point has ever felt so incredible.

It's also what scares me the most.

"To the bride and groom!" Ford toasts as he raises his shot.

The fifteen of us follow his lead. Small glasses are clinked together before everyone brings the fiery liquid to their lips and downs it in one fell swoop.

A few cough and sputter as their eyes water.

Amateurs.

My gaze settles on Britt. She's standing with Stella, Juliette, Viola, and Carina as they gather around Fallyn. My attention shifts to Wolf as he stares at his new wife with a besotted expression plastered across his ugly mug. The man is definitely one smitten kitten.

It's nice to see.

It's obvious from the way she returns his heated looks that the feeling is mutual. I can't imagine what it would be like to move through life with someone steadfast by my side.

I glance at Britt again. She's a fucking knockout in a black dress that hugs all her delectable curves.

Curves I ran my hands over last night before pressing them against the glass. Then I fucked her until we were both sated. Afterward, we tumbled onto the king-sized bed and fell asleep. I'd woken up this morning with her wrapped up tight in my arms.

Can't say that I didn't enjoy every minute of it.

And I'd slept better than I had in months.

I don't know what it is about the girl. She's like a burr under my skin. An itch I can't quite scratch.

I'd expected to wake up this morning and find the insatiable need I've felt for her since she snagged my interest at Slap Shotz to have dissipated.

At least a little.

Instead, morning wood and the need to fuck had greeted me.

So, that's exactly what we did.

Twice.

We were about to go for round three when Carina called to tell us that we were late for breakfast. Afterward, the girls left for their appointments at the spa. And the guys headed to a golf course to play nine holes.

At three o'clock, we loaded into a limo and took off for one of the nearby chapels. Even though I tried to convince Wolf to let Elvis preside over the service, he nixed that idea. Thirty minutes later, the happy couple was hitched. Now we're at a bar, celebrating the newlyweds.

It's probably the best damn wedding I've ever been invited to.

Britt flashes a smile at Fallyn before wrapping her arms around the inky-haired bride and giving her a warm embrace.

Since she's unaware of my perusal, I allow my gaze to rake over her from head to toe. For the life of me, I can't figure out why I'm so obsess—

Woah.

Correction. I am not *obsessed*.

I'm...

I don't know what the fuck I am anymore.

Whatever it is, I need to work it out of my system.

Fast.

I'm jerked from those thoughts when someone knocks into my shoulder. I swing around and find Hayes.

Before I can say anything, he nods toward the group of girls. "What's up with you and Britt?"

I don't bother to pretend that I'm clueless as to what he's talking about. Everywhere that girl goes, I find myself following. It's like there's an invisible string connecting us to one another.

All I have to say is that it's a fucking first.

I shrug before raising a finger and signaling the bartender for another bottle of beer. "We're just having a little bit of fun."

He grins like a Cheshire cat.

"Let me guess—what happens in Vegas stays in Vegas?"

"Yeah. Something along those lines," I mutter, not liking the sound of that at all even though it's exactly what I'd tried convincing myself of this morning after we showered together.

It's nothing more than sex.

Normally, that assurance would bring me a modicum of comfort.

This time, it leaves me feeling vaguely dissatisfied.

It has to be the wedding atmosphere that's putting all these strange thoughts in my head. People get all mushy and sentimental when they watch their friends get married. Then they start entertaining ideas they have no business thinking about.

"She's definitely a gorgeous girl." He glances at Britt and cocks his head. "If you're not going to make a play for her, maybe I will."

My head snaps in his direction as a growl rumbles up from my chest. "What the fuck did you just say?"

With a grin, he slaps my back and laughs, "Bit of fun, my ass. You're totally screwed."

When the bartender returns with my beer, Hayes snags her attention. "I'd like to order a round of Fireballs."

"You got it," the pretty girl behind the stretch of counter says with a wink.

Once the shots have been poured, Hayes carries the tray to our friends. Right before he takes off, I nab two small glasses and trail behind him. I circle the group before sliding in next to Britt and passing one over.

A smile lights up her face as color rides high on her cheeks. It only makes her golden eyes shine even more brightly. I'm struck all over again by just how gorgeous she is. Normally, when I see her around, she's lowkey in jeans and a sweater with a ball cap pulled low over her eyes.

Don't get me wrong, the girl is beautiful no matter what.

But dressed like this?

I'm definitely feeling a little tongue tied.

Her attention settles on the liquor in her hand. "I probably shouldn't. I've already had way too much."

There's a slight slur to her voice.

Unfortunately for me, I haven't had nearly enough to dampen the arousal careening through my veins or the wicked ideas that fill my head.

With my eyes fastened to hers, I lift my glass. "To the happy couple. May the love they feel for one another last until the end of time."

Her expression softens. "Aww, that's shockingly beautiful."

Before I can ask if she wants me to drink hers, she tosses it back like a champ.

It's only after she sets the glass down on the table that she swipes the back of her hand across her mouth. "That was such a bad idea."

My gaze dips to her pink-slicked lips.

Lips that had been wrapped around my dick last night while I'd deep throated her. That's all it takes for my cock to stiffen right up.

The question is out of my mouth before I can stop it. "Any interest in another bad idea?"

With a tilt of her head, she raises her brows. "That depends...is it something I'll regret in the morning?"

"Probably."

"Hmmm." Her expression turns pensive. As pensive as one can look three sheets to the wind. "Should we take another shot?"

"Definitely."

IN THE DARKEST NIGHTS, I STUMBLED, COULDN'T SEE THE LIGHT.
LOST IN A MAZE, COULDN'T FIND WHAT'S RIGHT.
BUT DEEP INSIDE, A FIRE BURNED,
REFUSING TO FADE AWAY.
A VOICE INSIDE ME WHISPERED, 'YOU'LL FIND YOUR WAY.'

I'M RISING UP, STRONGER NOW THAN I'VE EVER BEEN.
EVERY SCAR'S A STORY, AIN'T LETTING THEM WIN.
THROUGH THE UPS AND DOWNS, I'LL FIND MY TRUTH.
IN THE CHAOS OF IT ALL, I'LL FIND MY YOUTH.

THROUGH EVERY FALL AND EVERY DOUBT, I'LL STAND TALL.
GONNA SHAKE OFF THE PAST, GONNA GIVE IT MY ALL.
WITH EACH NEW DAY, LEAVING OLD FEARS BEHIND.
EMBRACING EVERY CHALLENGE, GONNA FREE MY MIND.

BRITT

A tortured groan escapes from me as I surface from a deep sleep. My head throbs a painful beat until it's questionable if there's a drumline inside my brain. I crack open one eye, thankful it's dark inside the suite.

We'll just consider that a small blessing.

Holy crap...

What the hell happened last night?

I search my mind, disturbed that I don't remember returning to my room after the wedding.

What I do recall is downing a bunch of shots.

Damn. I *knew* that was a mistake.

I never overindulge in alcohol. One glass of wine or whatever the hip new drink in LA is.

That's it.

But we'd all been having such a good time and had ended up celebrating late into the night.

Or maybe it would be more accurate to say the wee hours of the morning.

One shift against the high thread count sheets and I realize that I'm not wearing a stitch of clothing. Before I can investigate that further, a slight snore cuts through the silence of the bedroom.

With a turn of my head, I find Colby sacked out next to me.

The pounding in my skull isn't enough to dampen the arousal that pools in my core.

A few fuzzy memories flicker in my brain of stumbling through the hotel door last night.

There'd been laughter.

And long, deep kisses that left my head spinning.

Along with Colby's hands all over my body.

Working me over.

Not to mention his mouth.

Damn but he knows exactly what to do with it.

My gaze roves over his naked chest.

He really does have a nice one.

It's a shame I don't remember more of the details so I can lock them away for later and take them out when I'm lonely. I'm sure that whatever happened was just as hot as the first night.

What are the chances that I'll be able to talk him into another sweaty bout of sex before heading down to meet everyone for breakfast?

My guess is high.

Although it's doubtful we'll see Fallyn and Wolf. If I were them, I'd be enjoying my newly minted married status.

In bed.

Afterward, we'll have to pack up and catch a ride to the airport for our flight that leaves later this afternoon.

I raise my arms above my head to stretch.

The first thing I need are painkillers and a cup of—

Every muscle locks up and my movements freeze as I stare at the giant rock on my finger.

I blink and squint.

There's no damn way I'm seeing this.

Except, there's not just a giant diamond adorning my ring finger, but an actual silver band wrapped around it.

My heart skips an uncomfortable beat before pumping into overdrive as I drag my hand closer to my face. More snippets from last night roll through my brain, but there's a hazy quality to them.

Dreamlike.

Except...

Oh fuck.

Colby's left arm is thrown haphazardly over his eyes. Even though it's painful, I scoot up and attempt to catch a glimpse of his hand. The silky sheet pools around my waist as I lean across his hard body. That's when I see it—a matching silver band around his ring finger.

Everything inside me plummets as another groan breaks free.

How could I have allowed something like this to happen?

Exactly how drunk was I?

Stupid question.

"Mmmm, now that's an awfully nice sight to wake up to."

The low timbre of his voice vibrates through every cell in my body before settling deep in my core as he palms my breasts. He rolls onto his side and sucks one nipple between his lips. A hiss of air escapes from me and every panicked thought swirling through my brain leaks out of my ears as pleasure flares to life.

No doubt about it—the man has magic lips and hands.

Not to mention a pretty amazing cock.

No, don't think about that.

It's how you got into this mess in the first place.

It takes a herculean effort to rip myself away from him.

As soon as I put a little distance between us, his brows pinch together. "What'd you do that for?"

It's rarely that I've seen Colby frown. But that's exactly what he's doing now. It's tempting to lean down and kiss away—

Argh.

I was right about this guy being dangerous.

He's a hazard to the female species.

And stupid me fell for it hook, line, and sinker.

I hold up my shaking hand now adorned with rings. "Because of this!"

He stares at them for a silent moment before meeting my eyes. "Who'd you marry?"

"You!" I shriek. "I married *you!*"

Does he seriously not remember?

Guess that makes two of us.

I lean over his body before wrapping my fingers around his hand and yanking it in front of his face.

My heart hitches as he stares at it. "Well, I'll be damned."

A curious quality fills his voice as if this is happening to someone else and he's merely an observer.

Air rushes from my lungs as I flop against the pillows and blow a few tendrils of hair out of my eyes. "If you haven't already realized it, those shots were a mistake."

His hand slides over mine before he entwines our fingers and lifts them closer to his face to inspect the rings. "At least I bought you a nice matching set. Definitely not cheap."

I twist my head to stare at him.

No matter what kind of reaction I was expecting, this wasn't it.

"That's all you have to say?"

He shrugs, looking unperturbed by our current predicament. "Would you rather I was upset?"

I blink, not understanding this man at all. "Yeah, kind of."

"What good will that do?"

I open my mouth to fire back with a scathing response, but not a sound escapes. Everything inside me deflates as I shake my head, my brain spinning out of control. Or maybe it's short circuiting. It's difficult to tell in my hungover condition.

"I don't know."

He shifts onto his side before smacking a kiss against my lips. His hand rises to toy with my breast again. "I certainly hope we consummated the marriage."

I release a shaky breath, fairly confident that we did.

When I fail to respond, he growls, "I've always wondered what married pussy would feel like."

He rolls on top of me and with one swift motion, his cock slides deep inside my body, filling me to the brim. There's something so delicious about the stretch.

I couldn't hold back the moan that escapes from me if I tried.

This man is so insistent about teasing out every bit of pleasure so that nothing gets left behind.

"Damn, Britt," he growls. His voice is all deep and gravelly. "There's nothing on the face of this earth that compares to being inside you. You're so wet, hot, and tight. And the way your pussy clenches around my cock...it's like we were made for each other. The perfect fucking fit."

When a groan reverberates throughout his chest, I feel it deep in my bones.

"It's so good," I say with a gasp when he shifts his hips before grinding them with more force.

Even though he just slid inside me, I'm already primed and ready to go. One nudge will send me crashing over the edge. Unlike the other guys I've been with, there's no chasing an elusive orgasm, hoping I can find it.

Nope.

It's already there, threatening to crash over me.

"Condom," he says between gritted teeth.

Oh, god. He's right.

Before I can gather my thoughts, he pulls out and rolls toward the nightstand before grabbing a rubber and sheathing himself with it. And then he's back, sinking inside me.

Our eyes stay fastened as he grinds against my pelvis. No more than two dozen strokes later and I come. Stars explode behind my eyes in a sunburst of bright color. My release sets off a chain reaction and he follows me over the edge as if we're perfectly in sync.

After his muscles loosen, he braces himself on his elbows and rests his forehead against mine before staring deep into my eyes. It wouldn't take much to drown within their deep blue depths.

It would be like diving into the ocean and never surfacing again.

I blink away those strange thoughts when he says, "If this is what married life is like, I could definitely get used to it."

Oh, shit.

How could I have forgotten that we're married?

"The look on your face is priceless, firecracker," he says with a chuckle.

He rolls to the side and then off the mattress before popping to his feet.

My mouth turns cottony, making it impossible to swallow.

He's naked.

And gorgeous.

Not to mention completely unconcerned about his own nudity.

I can't help but stare. It's only after a handful of seconds that I realize he hasn't moved a muscle. He's standing still. Even though he just came, his cock is still semi-aroused. I've never been the kind of girl to think that a dick could be beautiful or well formed, but his is.

It's long, thick, and perfectly curved.

Memories of drawing him inside my mouth Friday night tumble through my head.

I wouldn't necessarily mind—

"Looks like you found a perk to this marriage after all."

I shake away the mental fog that has descended. I really need to pull it together. This is becoming embarrassing.

I slant a look upward to meet his eyes. "Maybe a small one."

He snorts. "Small, my ass."

One hand drops to his cock before he wraps it around the length and strokes his palm against it.

My mouth tumbles open as air gets clogged in my lungs and desire pools in my core.

Holy cow.

"Feel free to join me in the shower and I'll demonstrate again just how good my big dick feels inside you."

Before I can jumpstart my brain, he swings away, sauntering into the massive marble bathroom.

And yeah...his ass is just as finely sculpted as the rest of him. It's tempting to sink my teeth into the firm flesh and mark him in some kind of primal manner.

I squeeze my eyes closed.

What the hell is happening to me?

The sound of running water fills the silence of the suite.

Even in my hungover state, I hate to admit how tempting it is to roll from the bed and follow him into the shower.

How hilarious is it that I thought Colby would be lousy or selfish in bed?

Laughter bubbles up in my throat because nothing could be further from the truth.

All I can say is that the man definitely knows how to wield his stick. It doesn't matter if we just started having sex. Somehow, he's managed to find all my buttons.

And he enjoys pressing them until I fall completely apart.

But...

If I allow myself to give in and join him, the only thing I'm doing is complicating matters more than they already are.

I sit up and glance into the bathroom, realizing that he's already stepped inside the marble enclosure.

"Waiting for you, wifey," he calls out, voice raised to be heard over the water.

A shiver slides through me before settling in my core at the name and the growly voice that accompanies it.

No. I can't do this.

I can't get sucked in any deeper.

For both our sakes, I need to pull the plug now.

Decision made, I whip off the covers and stumble to my feet. My hand rises to my forehead as the headache roars back to life with a vengeance.

As tempting as it is to crawl back into bed and sleep it off, I force myself to move. I need to slip away before Colby gets out of the shower. I race to the suitcase, rummaging around until I find clean underwear, a bra, yoga pants, and a sweatshirt. Then I throw my hair up into a ponytail before glancing at the bathroom. He's still in there. And from what I can tell, he's humming the same song I sang to him on the plane.

The guilt that rushes in nearly swallows me whole.

Even though I feel like shit for leaving this way, I need time to clear my head and I can't do that around Colby. He muddles everything.

I rush around and grab everything I packed for the weekend before dragging the small piece of luggage behind me and exiting the suite.

It's only when the door clicks shut that a puff of relief escapes from me.

I step out of the shower and grab a plush towel off the heated rack before drying my face, hair, and chest. For a second or two, I consider wrapping it around my waist and heading back to the bedroom. Instead, I toss it over the glass wall of the enclosure.

Why bother?

Britt melts into a puddle whenever she sees me naked. At the very least, she's rendered speechless at the sight. And right now, that's exactly what's needed to soften her up.

The only thing on my mind is sliding back inside the tight heat of her body.

If I thought one time would be enough to dampen these budding feelings of attraction, I was mistaken.

The more I have, the more insatiable I become.

What's glaringly obvious is that this weekend wasn't enough to quash the growing need I've developed where she's concerned.

So...

All I can say is that what happens in Vegas is definitely *not* staying in Vegas.

After I rock her world, we can discuss this whole marriage situation we've gotten ourselves into. I glance at the thick silver band wrapped around my finger and brace myself for a wave of panic to crash over me for tying myself to another person. One I barely know.

Strangely enough, it never happens.

Even though this was an impulsive decision made while drunk off my ass, I kind of like the idea that Britt belongs to me.

Does that necessarily mean that we'll be sitting in porch rockers while watching our grandchildren play in the yard when we're eighty years old?

Fuck, no.

At some point, we'll have to dissolve the marriage. Hell, I bet this kind of thing happens all the time. This is exactly why party atmospheres and quickie weddings don't mix.

Years down the road, I'm sure it'll be a hilarious story.

One I might even share with my family.

I pause, unable to imagine what my parents will say when they find out about this.

Make that *if* they find out about this.

Thoughts of the fam are enough to wilt my boner. And since that's not the vibe I'm going for, I shove them from my head before sauntering into the sprawling bedroom without a stitch of clothing. Luckily, the idea of sliding deep inside Britt's welcoming heat is enough to stiffen me right up again.

My gaze falls on the rumpled bed, only to find it empty. With a frown, I swing in a semi-circle but don't find any sign of Britt. It takes a handful of seconds to realize that not only has she pulled a vanishing act, but so has her clothing.

Along with her suitcase and purse.

What the fuck?

Did she seriously take off and leave me here?

The moment hurt wells up inside me, I stomp it out.

Screw that.

I stalk over to my duffle and rifle around in it. A second later, my fingers lock on a pair of boxers. After the cotton material has been hauled up my thighs and the waistband snapped into place, I scoop up my phone and hit her number.

It goes straight to voicemail.

With narrowed eyes, I stare out the wall of windows that overlooks the Strip. It doesn't look nearly as magical in the harsh light of dawn as it did when I'd pressed Britt against the thick glass and fucked her senseless.

Well...this isn't how I saw my morning playing out.

I drag a hand over my face and attempt to convince myself that what happened this weekend doesn't mean a damn thing.

It's not like we were going to stay married.

So...does it really matter if the hottest sex of my life just bailed on me without a fucking word?

Do I care?

Nope. Not one damn bit.

What I need is to shake it off and keep it moving.

Just like she did.

Two hours later, I'm still in a foul mood as I throw my duffle over my shoulder and head down to the lobby to meet up with everyone. I glance at the time on my phone. The shuttle should arrive in ten minutes to take us to the airport.

Certainly can't say that Vegas wasn't interesting.

That's for damn sure.

As soon as the elevator opens on the first floor, I step out and make my way through the lobby. Wolf, Fallyn, Carina, Ford, Stella, Riggs, Viola, and Madden are already there and waiting with their luggage.

"Hey." Wolf smirks as he scans my face. "You look like hell, dude."

With a snort, I flip him the bird.

"And your disposition matches your appearance," he snickers.

It's tempting to give him the finger for a second time in as many minutes.

"Where'd you and Britt disappear to last night? One minute, we're all doing shots and the next, you guys are gone."

Yeah...there's no way I'm announcing that he's not the only married man in the group.

Can you even imagine what their reactions would be?

Wolf glances around the bustling space. "Where's Britt? I figured she'd be with you."

Just as I'm about to admit that I have no idea where that girl is,

Stella says, "Something came up and she had to catch an earlier flight back to Western."

Ha!

Likely story.

I'll be interested to discover why she felt the need to run from me when I finally catch up with her ass on campus.

Because if that girl thinks she can ditch me after we tied the knot, she's dead wrong.

IN THE DARKEST NIGHTS, I STUMBLED, COULDN'T SEE THE LIGHT.
LOST IN A MAZE, COULDN'T FIND WHAT'S RIGHT.
BUT DEEP INSIDE, A FIRE BURNED,
REFUSING TO FADE AWAY.
A VOICE INSIDE ME WHISPERED, 'YOU'LL FIND YOUR WAY.'

I'M RISING UP, STRONGER NOW THAN I'VE EVER BEEN.
EVERY SCAR'S A STORY, AIN'T LETTING THEM WIN.
THROUGH THE UPS AND DOWNS, I'LL FIND MY TRUTH.
IN THE CHAOS OF IT ALL, I'LL FIND MY YOUTH.

THROUGH EVERY FALL AND EVERY DOUBT, I'LL STAND TALL.
GONNA SHAKE OFF THE PAST, GONNA GIVE IT MY ALL.
WITH EACH NEW DAY, LEAVING OLD FEARS BEHIND.
EMBRACING EVERY CHALLENGE, GONNA FREE MY MIND.

BRITT

16

I stare at the book sprawled out on the table where I'm working at The Roasted Bean, a coffee house on campus that caters to the student population. I love popping in, grabbing a cappuccino and studying. It's cozy and I'm usually able to get a lot done.

That, unfortunately, isn't the case this afternoon. I've been here for more than an hour and have barely plowed my way through one assignment.

Focus is definitely not my friend at the moment.

It's been that way since I returned from Vegas a few days ago. Even worse than that, I've taken to skulking around campus, so I don't run into the hot hockey player.

It's a pain in the ass.

My brain keeps tumbling back to the weekend.

I *still* can't believe I married Colby McNichols.

Colby!

McNichols!

Mr. Manwhore Extraordinaire.

The baby-faced assassin.

How could I have allowed this to happen?

I've racked my brain, trying to dredge up as much as I can about that night, but the memories remain frustratingly murky.

There were shots—of course.

A ton of laughter.

And then sex.

A lot of really good sex.

I'll say one thing about the guy—he knows exactly what he's doing in that department. A shiver dances down the length of my spine at the memories that bloom to life before settling in my core.

And the first night...

When he'd pressed me against the glass and had his wicked way?

Yeah...that experience is singed into my brain for all eternity.

At some point, we'll have to sit down and discuss the situation and how we go about dissolving our sham of a marriage.

I just need to work up the courage to face him. It's not like Colby wants to be married to me any more than I want to be tied to him. The guy is probably freaking the fuck out right now.

Hell, maybe he's already set the wheels in motion.

Although, he hadn't lost his shit when he'd realized what we'd done.

Nope. He'd been cool, calm, and collected.

I'm the one who'd freaked out.

I pinch the bridge of my nose and release a steady puff of air from my lips. In the past, if there were situations I wasn't able to tackle on my own, I'd enlist the assistance of my family. Mom would swoop in and take over. It's what Sharon does best. Within a matter of days, the circumstance would be resolved.

Given the status of our relationship, that doesn't feel like an option. If I reach out for help, she'll descend, and I'll be forced to return to LA. I'm nowhere near ready to do that.

Uncle Sully pops into my head. I chew my lower lip and contemplate turning to him for help. Over the previous months, we've grown even closer than before.

It's been really nice.

The last thing I want to do is cause problems between him and my mother. He's already keeping it a secret that I'm here, living in the same city.

So, he's not an option.

Which means I need to figure this out on my own.

I'd like to think it'll prove to my family I'm a mature adult who's more than capable of handling her own life, but it's doubtful anyone who marries a stranger in Vegas while drunk can use this scenario as proof of adulting.

It takes effort to shove those thoughts from my head and refocus my attention on my textbook. I have a test coming up in a few days and if I don't wrap my brain around the terminology and concepts, I'll end up failing.

Just as I congratulate myself for reaching the end of one page and flipping to the next, someone drops down across from me. The tiny hairs at the nape of my neck prickle with awareness. I don't have to glance up to know who I'll find.

Even though a few feet separate us, the woodsy scent of his cologne slips around me, cocooning me in familiarity. Arousal explodes in the pit of my belly as my mind tumbles back to what it felt like to wake up beside him, our bare legs tangled together.

With a shaky exhale, I steel everything inside me before forcing my gaze to his.

Staring at his male beauty is like having the air knocked from my lungs.

It's not like I didn't realize that he was handsome, but after days of absence, the memories have dulled. Maybe it was even purposeful on my part. A self-protective mechanism. With him seated across from me, looking all broody and irritated, I don't have any other choice but to acknowledge it.

When I remain silent, unsure how to open the dialogue, his scowl deepens as he crosses his brawny arms over his chest. As unaffected as I want to remain, that's impossible under the intensity of his scrutiny.

This isn't how I imagined our reunion playing out.

"Well, hello...*wifey*."

His deep voice crashes over me like a tidal wave before threatening to drag me out to sea.

My tongue darts out to moisten parched lips.

I have no idea how to respond. My brain misfires, drawing blanks.

All the times I've caught sight of Colby on campus or even at Slap Shotz, he's been surrounded by groupies, his expression a perpetual smirk as if he doesn't have a care in the world.

His appearance is a direct contrast to that.

"I have to admit that you've been rather difficult to track down." He cocks his head. "Almost as if you've been hiding from me. Your husband. Can you imagine that?"

I throw a quick glance around the café, hoping no one is paying attention to our conversation. The last thing I want is for this to get out. All it would take is one spark to ignite and suddenly, the entire joint is burning to the ground.

He might not understand that, but I do.

From a few tables away, a handful of girls stare at him with hungry eyes.

It's tempting to roll mine.

The guy certainly draws attention like flies to shit.

It's just another reason I need to nip this...whatever the hell this is in the bud and end things before it spirals any further out of control.

Although granted, it seems a little late for that.

The last thing I want to do is jeopardize the life I've created for myself at Western.

Catching sight of Axel in Vegas was a close call.

Way too close.

It only drove home the realization of what I have to lose. For the first time in years, I have a group of girlfriends. I'm living an ordinary life and attending classes. All the things I missed out on as a teenager. And my creativity is finally flowing.

I refuse to give it up.

Maybe hiding out isn't a long-term solution, but for now, I want to hold onto it for as long as possible.

"Keep your voice down," I mutter, still trying to get all my out-of-control emotions back under submission. "I am *not* your wife."

He raises a brow. It's thick and sculpted, fitting his profile perfectly. Although, it would be a challenge to find any imperfections in Colby's appearance. He's too damn handsome for his own good.

And mine.

"Well, that's interesting, because I have paperwork that claims otherwise."

My eyes widen at that bit of news. "You do?"

"Yup. Found it in my pants pocket the morning you took off." His eyes resemble chips of blue ice. "I have to say," he muses, "girls usually run toward my dick. Not away from it."

Heat scalds my cheeks. "Sorry," I mumble. "Something came up and I had to leave."

Even though he nods as if accepting the lie, the curl of his upper lip says otherwise. "Right."

I straighten on the couch and attempt to work up some indignation. "What? It's true." Not wanting to argue, I shift and change the subject. "So...about this, um, you know..."

"Marriage? Is that the word you're searching for?"

"Yeah." I don't understand why he's making this convo awkward. We should be on the same page.

When his lips quirk, my gaze dips to them, and a burst of heat explodes in my core as memories of what they felt like coasting over my body crash over me. It's enough to leave me shifting on the couch.

When he tugs his bottom lip between sharp white teeth, a groan nearly escapes.

Ugh...how embarrassing would that be?

I force my gaze to his, only to find that an answering heat has sparked to life within his blue depths.

Muscles coiled tight, he leans forward, closing some of the distance between us. "Is there a particular memory from the weekend that you'd care to share? Because I have several."

"No," I squeak, mortified that he can read me with so much ease.

Or reduce me to a puddle of goo.

It's demoralizing.

All right...so maybe I do understand. They don't call him the baby-faced assassin for nothing.

Clearly, the nickname has been well earned.

Heat suffuses my cheeks. "Shouldn't you be looking for a way out of this?" There's a beat of silence before I add, "From what I've heard, you don't even date. Or probably sleep with a girl more than once."

Humor ignites in his eyes as he sits back again, lounging as if he's a king on his throne. "So, you've been asking around about your new husband? Guess you're not nearly as indifferent as you'd like me to believe."

I roll my eyes. "Don't flatter yourself."

"You know what?"

I press my lips together. The question seems more rhetorical in nature than anything else.

"I kind of like being an old married man."

My face scrunches. "Now that's highly doubtful. Wouldn't it crimp your overactive social life?"

He flashes a knowing grin before lifting his arms and stacking his hands behind his head. The movement makes his biceps pop beneath the sweatshirt he's wearing. "Interested in that too, are we?"

This man's cockiness knows no bounds.

If it weren't aggravating, it would almost be impressive.

"No, I'm not." I shift and force out the rest, wanting the comment to come across as nonchalant. "I'm just saying that married men don't sleep with groupies."

"Some do."

My mouth tumbles open.

Before I can blast him into next week, he tacks on, "But you don't have anything to worry about." He gives me a wink. "I'm all yours."

I release the air trapped in my lungs, unsure why we're having this pointless conversation.

Although, that doesn't stop me from firing back a few questions of my own. "Really? The guy who can't keep his dick in his pants isn't going to roam? Is that really what you're telling me?"

His eyes glitter as he cocks his head. "Now why would I do that when I have a beautiful wife waiting for me at home?"

The heated expression sets off a chain reaction deep in my belly until it feels like I'm on the verge of incineration.

"We don't live together."

"*Yet.*"

The way he drops that little word feels more like a bomb that rocks my world to the very core.

"You can't be serious," I whisper, sounding as if I'm being choked from the inside out.

His arms drop to his sides as he scoots to the edge of his chair and leans forward, hinging at the waist as if seconds away from pouncing. "Does it really look like I'm joking?"

That's the scary part.

The one that doesn't make any sense.

The man looks dead serious.

It's enough to have my mouth turning parched.

It takes effort to shake myself out of the spell he's woven around me in the ten minutes we've been conversing. All I can say is that Colby McNichols is more dangerous to my well-being and sanity than I gave him credit for.

I hold up a hand, surprised to find it trembling. "I've done a little research about what we need to do to dissolve this marriage. It's not difficult—"

"I did the same, and an annulment is out of the question."

"Why?"

He raises a brow as a slow smile spreads across his face. I'm pretty sure the girl seated at the table behind us just gasped. "Maybe you don't remember consummating our marriage the night of, but we certainly did the morning after." There's a beat of silence before he adds, "Right before you skipped town."

"Stop saying that. We're not married," I growl, ignoring the dig.

"The great state of Nevada would claim differently."

"Well, it doesn't have to stay that way."

"Unless we want it to."

His words rob the air from my lungs as we stare at each other for a strained beat of silence. "What?"

It's carefully that he repeats, "We can stay married if we want to."

"I don't understand." I shake my head in confusion. "Is that what you want?"

He settles back on the chair again before shrugging.

The gesture might seem casual.

The look on his face is anything but.

F uck.

Britt is staring at me like I'm the very devil come to drag her to hell.

What's become clear is that I'm going about this all wrong.

It's tempting to drag a hand down my face, but I force myself to remain still. The girl is like a startled animal. Any sudden movements on my part and she'll bolt from the coffee shop. It took days to track her ass down so we could have this convo. I'd checked with her friends, scoured campus, and stalked her apartment building like a creeper.

It's like she's purposefully avoiding me.

It was a stroke of luck when I walked past The Roasted Bean and spotted her in the window. Even though I don't like blowing off class, this situation needs to get hashed out before either of us can move on.

Separately.

Or together.

When I'd shoved through the glass door of the shop fifteen minutes ago, there'd been an entire spiel on the tip of my tongue about contacting our family lawyer to dissolve the marriage.

I mean, come on...we're college students.

Maybe Fallyn and Wolf wanted to tie themselves down this early in life, but that's not what I imagined for myself.

And contrary to everything spewing out of my mouth, it's not what I want now.

It's just...

This chick can't get away from me fast enough, and I'd be lying through my teeth if I didn't admit that it chafes my ass. For the first time since meeting at Slap Shotz, it finally feels like I've wrestled the upper hand away from her.

And I'm nowhere near ready to relinquish it.

Any other girl on this campus would be jumping at the chance to be married to me. They would have blasted the news all over social media by now, announcing it to the world at large.

Britt hasn't done that.

In fact, she doesn't want our nuptials getting out.

Although...it could be because she doesn't have any social media to speak of. Which is weird as hell for a girl her age. What does she do with all the selfies she takes if not post them to her socials?

My brows beetle at that thought.

Have I ever caught her taking a selfie?

I dredge my memories.

Nope. Not even one.

When the girls took photos in Vegas, she'd scooted out of most of them. If I hadn't been watching so closely, I wouldn't have noticed.

I blink back to the conversation when she mumbles, "I don't know. I just assumed we'd be on the same page with this."

"Well, you know what they say about assuming." There's a beat of awkward silence before I blurt, "You make an ass out of both you and me."

Her brows furrow as she stares as if I'm a bug smeared across her windshield. Or some strange species she's never encountered before.

It's not good.

This convo is circling the drain as we speak.

Under normal circumstances, I'm smooth with both the lines and the ladies.

Unless her name happens to be Britt.

Then, I'm a total shitshow.

Needing to move on, I clear my throat as she picks up her drink and takes a sip. "Have you mentioned your newly minted relationship status to your family?"

Her eyes widen as she coughs and sputters before wiping her mouth. "Are you kidding me? Hell no."

"Why not?"

She presses her lips into a tight line, refusing to respond.

When I raise a brow, she finally huffs out a breath. "They would be less than thrilled about the circumstances."

"Do they live around here?" I shift. "We could road trip it and tell them together. I'd like to meet my new in-laws. Don't worry. I'm great with parents. They love me."

The color filling her cheeks gets leeched away. "As fun as that adventure sounds, it's not possible. They're in California."

When she doesn't offer up any more details, I prompt, "Is that where you grew up?"

"No." Just when I think it'll become necessary to interrogate her for a few more stingy pieces of intel, she mutters, "We moved there almost a decade ago."

"Huh. I wasn't aware of that little factoid."

"There's a reason for that. It's because we don't know one another. And that's probably the way it should stay."

I stroke my chin, digesting the tidbits I've been able to squeeze out of her. The more I learn, the more I want to unravel this girl and figure out what makes her tick.

"I don't know, firecracker. Consider my curiosity piqued."

Fear flickers across her pretty features. The emotion is there and gone before I can fully register it, leaving me to wonder if it was just a figment of my imagination. What I don't miss is the way her hand shakes as she wraps her fingers around the cappuccino for a second time and lifts it to her lips.

Even though it's the last thing that should be on my brain, my attention zeroes in on her mouth and the way it puckers when she takes a drink. Just remembering what it felt like wrapped around my dick is enough to have it stirring in my joggers.

It's only when she sets the cup down again that she says, "I think it would be for the best if we rectify this mistake ASAP. Quietly."

Should her comment piss me off?

Probably not.

Under normal circumstances, I'm the one who pulls away and pumps the brakes, holding girls at a distance.

Never wanting them to get too close.

When the hell did our roles become reversed?

Now Britt's the one doing all those things to me.

To me.

I don't like it one damn bit.

And it's totally throwing off my mojo.

I need to regain a little bit of control here.

"I have an idea."

"If I recall correctly, that's how we got into this mess in the first place."

A smile ghosts across my lips as I brush aside the comment. "How about you come to my game tomorrow, and we'll discuss our options afterward."

"Options? What options?" She drops her voice as her brow furrows. "Neither of us wants to be married."

I rise to my feet so that it becomes necessary for her to crane her neck to hold my gaze. "Unlike you, I haven't made that determination yet."

"Colby..." Her eyes widen as her voice dips. "We don't have anything in common. Staying married would be foolish."

"That's not true."

One swift step brings me around the coffee table until I'm standing directly in front of her. Unable to resist the urge, I lean down and cage her in with my bigger body. She flattens against the couch cushions, attempting to put more distance between us, but I'll be damned if I allow that to happen.

My gaze stays locked on hers, sifting through the golden depths in silence. When she swallows, the delicate muscles of her throat constrict.

"You certainly seem to enjoy kissing me." I press closer until the warmth of her breath can feather across my lips. It's nothing short of intoxicating. "Among other things."

Her eyes flare.

Before she can deny it, I add, "And I liked it too." I brush my mouth across hers. "See? That's something we have in common. I'm willing to bet there's more. Maybe we need to take the time and explore it."

Even though it's tempting to crush my lips against hers, I force myself to back away. It might just be one of the hardest things I've ever had to do.

But the hazy look that now fills her eyes?

Totally worth it.

I swing away and head for the exit. "I'll see you tomorrow."

IN THE DARKEST NIGHTS, I STUMBLED, COULDN'T SEE THE LIGHT.
LOST IN A MAZE, COULDN'T FIND WHAT'S RIGHT.
BUT DEEP INSIDE, A FIRE BURNED,
REFUSING TO FADE AWAY.
A VOICE INSIDE ME WHISPERED, 'YOU'LL FIND YOUR WAY.'

I'M RISING UP, STRONGER NOW THAN I'VE EVER BEEN.
EVERY SCAR'S A STORY, AIN'T LETTING THEM WIN.
THROUGH THE UPS AND DOWNS, I'LL FIND MY TRUTH.
IN THE CHAOS OF IT ALL, I'LL FIND MY YOUTH.

THROUGH EVERY FALL AND EVERY DOUBT, I'LL STAND TALL.
GONNA SHAKE OFF THE PAST, GONNA GIVE IT MY ALL.
WITH EACH NEW DAY, LEAVING OLD FEARS BEHIND.
EMBRACING EVERY CHALLENGE, GONNA FREE MY MIND.

BRITT

I bundle my jacket around me and slip from the car before staring up at the arena.

How did I allow Colby to talk me into this?

Oh, that's right...he agreed to sit down and discuss the state of our marriage after the game. I almost wince at that internal thought. What I meant to say is that he agreed to discuss how we'll move forward with our divorce.

Argh.

That doesn't sound any better.

The lesson I've learned from this debacle is that there'll be no more drinking in Vegas.

Maybe they'll just be no more Vegas.

End of story.

It's only since meeting Stella, Juliette, Carina, Viola, and Fallyn that I've attended a few hockey games. They had to drag me kicking and screaming to the first one. I expected to be bored off my ass. Color me surprised when I wasn't. It's fast-paced action from the moment the puck gets dropped at center ice until the buzzer rings at the end.

I stare around the well-lit parking lot as boisterous fans swarm the arena.

What I've learned over the past months is that hockey is a popular sport.

Just as much as football.

Even though I'm not going to see Colby for a couple of hours, my belly is already a tangle of knots. I press a palm to my lower abdomen, hoping to settle the butterflies that are attempting to wing their way to life.

As I hustle up the wide stone steps that lead to the entrance of the building, my phone buzzes with an incoming message. I fish it out of my pocket before glancing at the screen.

> Better not be a no-show. I'd hate to hunt your ass down afterward. Because when I get my hands on you...

A shiver trips down my spine.

It's a peculiar mixture of excitement and anxiety.

Before I can fire off a response, I collide with a small, compact body and bounce back a step. I glance up, an apology poised on the tip of my tongue. I should have been paying better attention to where I was going instead of staring at my phone.

"Hey, Britt."

"Ava!" A genuine smile curves my lips. "How are you?"

"Good. I was going to text and see if you wanted to get together sometime this week. Maybe grab something to eat."

I loop my arm through hers and steer us to the side and out of pedestrian traffic. It's like a swiftly moving current, and it's only a matter of time before we get swept away by the crowd.

"Are you here for the game?"

Her face scrunches as she gives her blonde head a shake. "Nope, just finished up on the ice. I was hoping to get out before the horde descended."

I glance around. "Looks like you're too late for that."

"It would seem so."

With a shift, I throw out the offer. "Any chance I can convince you to stay and watch the game?"

She glances at the building and nibbles her lower lip. "I don't know..."

"I bet your dad would appreciate your show of support," I cajole.

A reluctant smile hovers around the edges of her lips as she shakes her head. "Damn. You fight dirty. Know that?"

A chuckle escapes from me as I grin. "Always."

"Fine. You talked me into it. I'll watch the game with you."

"Yay! Now you can meet the friends I've been telling you about."

"Let me throw my bag in my car and then we can head inside."

Ten minutes later, we navigate our way through the thick crowd inside the chilly arena. I stop and look around for the girls. It takes a few minutes to spot them. As soon as I do, Juliette pops to her feet and waves.

I give Ava a little squeeze. "You'll like them. They're really nice."

Sometimes I get the feeling that Ava isn't necessarily comfortable around people our own age. Like me, she was homeschooled so she could focus on training. She knows that I had private teachers as well, but she doesn't know the reason for it.

"We'll see," she mumbles, sounding none too sure.

I get her skepticism. Girls can be catty and mean. From what I've gleaned from our conversations, it's even more so in the ice-skating world. Everyone's in competition with each other. They might smile and be nice to your face, but they'll stab you in the back the moment it's turned. Even though I don't know Ava well, there's something delicate about her that brings out my protective instincts.

As soon as we reach our seats, I make introductions. Just like I knew they would, everyone welcomes Ava with open arms. Especially when I tell them that she's Coach Philips' daughter. There's a ton of questions and friendly banter. It doesn't take long for Ava's muscles to loosen as she jokes around with them.

"So, Britt," Fallyn says, mischief sparkling in her blue eyes. "Is there a reason we didn't have to twist your arm to meet us here tonight?" Instead of waiting for a response, she taps her chin with her finger and pretends to ponder the question. "Hmmm. I wonder what that could be..."

Carina snorts. "Let me guess—what happened in Vegas didn't stay in Vegas?"

My eyes widen and my mouth tumbles open. There's no way she could have found out that we tied the knot.

I haven't told a soul.

And it's doubtful Colby did either.

No matter what he said at the coffee shop, we're not staying married.

"Excuse me?" I squeak as my heart constricts. "What do you mean?"

All the girls turn their attention my way.

Fallyn gives me an odd look before saying with a laugh, "Just that you two shared a room for the weekend."

Oh, right...we shared a room.

Air escapes my lungs as I force a smile. "Sorry, forgot all about it."

Lie.

It'll be a long time before I forget about that weekend. Or can look at a floor-to-ceiling window in a suite without remembering what it felt like to be pressed against it and thoroughly—

Yeah.

Carina leans around Juliette, who's seated beside me. "Then you two didn't sleep together? Because from everything I've heard, forgettable is the last thing Colby is in bed."

Warmth rushes through my veins before pooling in my core until I'm squirming.

She's not wrong.

"I wouldn't know," I lie. "We're just friends."

Kind of.

Maybe.

Stella waggles her brows. "Are we talking strictly friends or friends with benefits?"

"Strictly friends."

"Interesting. I didn't realize that Colby McNichols had friends who also happened to be girls," Viola chimes in. "Someone needs to write this down."

Ugh.

The last thing I want to do is lie to my new friends, but there's no way I can tell them the truth.

My attention gets snagged by Colby as he rounds the corner and heads our way with his stick slung over his shoulder blades. He's a big guy. Tall and broad with muscles for miles. In skates and padding, he looks larger than life.

Our eyes catch and hold as he glides past.

Even after the connection is severed, my focus stays fastened to him.

"Friends, my ass," Ava whispers with a nudge.

That comment is enough to rip me out of the Colby-induced trance that's fallen over me. When she raises her brows in silent inquiry, a smile simmering across her lips, my shoulders slump.

It's almost a relief when the whistle is blown and the players file off the ice. The lights are dimmed, and the music is cranked up. A spotlight falls on the ice as the visiting team is announced and then the Western Wildcats. Fans jump to their feet, cheering and clapping as the players from the home team are called. There's even more whistling and air horns when Colby takes to the ice.

Without a doubt, he's a fan favorite.

Once the arena is illuminated, the first line takes their positions as the rest of the team heads back to the bench to wait for their shifts. The puck gets dropped and everyone explodes into action. Hayes fights for possession before passing it off to Colby, who races across the ice, blades digging into it. After he crosses the blue line, he flicks the black disc to Ford Hamilton, who drives it toward the net. A defenseman for the other team slams Ford into the boards. The sound of the hit echoes throughout the arena.

Carina winces as Viola chuckles. "Wanna bet that someone's going to be administering a little TLC tonight?"

"He's the biggest baby," Carina says with a laugh. "He'll milk it for days."

Ryder McAdams intercepts the play before sending it back to Hayes, who in turn passes it to Colby. He flies by the net and shoots.

Air gets trapped in my lungs as the puck slips past the goalie and the long blast of a horn blares throughout the arena.

As Colby circles around the back of the net, his gaze locks on mine, holding it captive as he skates back to his side of the ice. A jolt of electricity sizzles through me until my fingertips and toes buzz with it.

Ava clears her throat. "Oh, girl...you've been holding out on me."

I open my mouth to deny the accusation but can't seem to push out the words. Instead, I snap it shut and press my lips together.

I am in so much trouble.

Even though the girls talk and gossip throughout the game, my attention stays pinned to Colby. I don't know much about hockey other than what I've picked up over the past few months, but even I realize that he's talented. As much as it pains me to admit it, I understand what all the fuss is about where he's concerned. Not only is this guy hot and muscular, but he's a gifted athlete.

And, from what I've been able to surmise—smart and funny.

Not to mention good in bed.

Who wouldn't want to get their hands on him, even if it's just for a night or two.

The final buzzer rings and the Wildcats bring home another win. It's tradition for everyone to head over to Slap Shotz to celebrate.

Although, that's not in the cards for us tonight. The only reason I showed up to this game was to hash out this farce of a marriage.

Fallyn rises to her feet and the rest of our group follows suit.

"Let's wait for the guys in the lobby," she calls over her shoulder, all the while maneuvering through the thick crowd. Everyone agrees as we make our way toward the hallway where the player locker room is located.

"And that would be my cue to take off," Ava says.

"You're welcome to join us," Juliette offers.

Her expression softens at the invitation. "Thanks. I appreciate it, but I've never been one to hang around with my father's players. It's always been a big no-no in my house."

"That makes sense," Viola muses. "I'm sure your dad doesn't want you getting involved with any of them.

Ava suppresses a smile. "Nope."

"It was really nice meeting you," Viola says.

"You too." Her gaze encompasses the girls. "All of you. This was fun."

"We'll have to plan a night out at Blue Vibe to do a little dancing," Carina suggests.

"Count me in," Stella says.

Ava throws her arms around me and whispers, "Thanks again for the invite. And you're right—your friends are great."

"Told you so."

"Text me," she says with a wave before taking off.

"I will."

And then she's gone, disappearing through the throng of spectators.

"I like her," Carina says with a nod, blonde ponytail bobbing with the movement.

"Me, too." I smile, glad everyone got along. They really are a great bunch of girls. I'd love for Ava to get to know them better.

I glance around, noticing that there's a ton of people surrounding a handsome, older man. When he turns and smiles at a guy who looks to be similar in age before reaching out and clasping his hand, I can't shake the feeling that there's something familiar about him.

"Who is that?" I ask Viola, gesturing toward the growing group. It's like he's a celebrity in his own right.

Maybe both men are.

"Oh, that's Gray McNichols."

McNichols?

Before I can connect the dots, she adds, "Colby's father. He played in the NHL for a while before becoming a sportscaster on ESPN."

Except for the fact that Colby is blond, and his father is the opposite with darker hair, the resemblance between the two men is uncanny.

"And the guy he's talking to is Brody McKinnon," Juliette cuts in with a grin. "My father."

My brows shoot up. "Wow. He's—"

"Don't say hot," Juliette mutters, expression turning sour.

Carina flashes a grin as her shoulders shake with silent mirth. "She hates it when we talk about how dreamy her dad is."

Juliette glares at her roommate.

"He kind of is," I whisper to Carina.

"Oh, trust me...I know it," she says with a chuckle.

"Hey, you're dishing about my older brother," Stella adds. "And that's just gross. Keep your pervy daddy issues to yourself."

"Now where would the fun in that be?" Carina shoots back with a smile.

My gaze slices to Gray McNichols as he wraps his arm around a slender woman before dropping a kiss against the top of her dark head. I'm guessing that's Colby's mother. Even though Colby resembles his father, he and his mom also have features that are similar.

If his parents are waiting around, they'll probably want to get together once he's released from the locker room, which means we won't get a chance to talk.

Damn.

Now that I'm no longer in avoidance mode, I just want to set the wheels in motion for this divorce.

Or annulment.

Or uncoupling.

Or whatever the hell you want to call it.

But I can't do that until we're both on the same page.

19

I slick on some pit sauce and slam my locker door shut before shoving my feet into my shoes. Then I plow my hands through my damp strands, pushing them away from my face.

"Why the hell are you in such a rush, McNichols? You gotta couple of bunnies who are gonna help you celebrate our W tonight?"

My gaze flickers to Hayes as I avoid answering the question. "I'm in no more of a hurry than usual."

The way his eyes narrow tells me that he's not buying what I'm attempting to sell.

He whips off the towel from around his waist and uses it to dry his face and then chest. The guy is buck-ass naked and couldn't care less.

I tap my foot, anxious to get the hell out of here and find—

"Would this have anything to do with the hot little honey you shared a room with last weekend?"

Sometimes I forget just how perceptive Hayes can be. He gives off this casual, I-don't-give-a-crap vibe, but I've discovered that there's more to him buried beneath the surface.

It's like calm waters and all that shit.

"What makes you say that?"

"The fact that you're answering a question with a question."

I roll my eyes. "Fine. It might have something to do with her."

A smug grin slides across his lips. "I suspected as much." He grabs his boxers and hauls them up his thighs before snapping the waistband against his abdomen. "You're fucking interested."

It's on the tip of my tongue to deny the accusation.

Because that's exactly what it is.

Instead, I drop my voice and do the unthinkable. "What if I am?"

He glances around the rowdy locker room with an expression of wonderment. "What world am I living in where Colby McNichols is actually interested in a chick?"

Ford swings around and stares at Hayes. "I'm sorry, what did you just say?"

Our center grins gleefully. "Turns out the baby-faced assassin over here has a little crushy-crushy on a girl."

Ford's wide eyes slice to mine before he shakes his head. "No way. I don't believe it. Not even for a second."

"Well, believe it because it's true," Hayes continues.

Heat slams into my cheeks as more people turn and stare like I'm a circus oddity.

Christ.

I knew this was a bad idea. I should have denied everything.

Hayes better watch it at our next practice because I'm going to lay him out flat.

Maybe a few times.

I groan when Wolf chimes in.

"I thought as much after the weekend." He jerks a thumb in my direction. "You should have seen how butthurt he was after she took off Sunday morning. Reminded me of a kicked puppy. Then he pouted the entire flight and made me switch seats and hold his hand."

"You offered," I ground out.

"My guess is that she got a good look at the size of his pecker and decided it wasn't worth her time," Bridger adds with a grin like the asshole he is.

Screw this.

With a wave of my hand, I stalk toward the heavy metal door. "All right, I'm out. See you dickheads later."

They all laugh and boo that I'm not sticking around to take their abuse. Just as I escape into the hallway, a wad of white tape almost nails me in the head.

Fuckers.

I give them the finger.

With friends like these, who needs enemies?

Even though there's no way I'd admit it after that, most of these guys are like brothers to me. Sure, maybe we like to harass each other but you don't bother doing that unless your friendship runs deep.

As I swing into the lobby where everyone has congregated, I search the crowd for Britt. It was a relief to catch sight of her in the stands during warmups. I might have strongarmed her into getting together later with the promise of discussing our marriage, but I wasn't certain she'd show.

My steps falter.

It's going to take some time to wrap my brain around the fact that I'm actually married.

Married.

By the time I do, we'll be on our way to a divorce. Sadness and disappointment crash over me at that thought.

My brows pinch together and my heart hitches when I don't find her. As my gaze scans the group for a second time, I catch sight of my parents. I had no idea they'd be here tonight. Most of the time, they'll call or shoot me a text and give me a heads up. As soon as our gazes collide, Mom grins and Dad waves as they make their way over.

Under normal circumstances, I'm always happy to have them in the stands.

At the moment, though?

Not so much.

All I want to do is find Britt.

So I can get my hands on her.

It's been way too long.

The kiss we shared at The Roasted Bean has in no way quenched the hunger running rampant through my body. If anything, it only whetted my appetite for more. That's all it takes for memories of what it felt like to sink deep inside the welcoming heat of her body to bombard me.

My cock stirs with interest.

Down, boy.

This is definitely *not* the time for that.

Mom is the first one to pull me in for an embrace.

Then Dad gives me a hearty hug with a clap on the back. "You played a solid game!"

"Thanks."

His praise has always meant the most to me. How could it not when I feel the need to live up to his level of talent on the ice? It's no easy feat when your father played in the NHL for a decade and helped bring home two Stanley Cups. Most kids worship athletes that they've never met in real life or know on a personal level.

The same can't be said for me.

Dad has always been my hero. As a kid, I spent hours studying his game film, wanting to play just like him.

"We thought if you weren't busy, we could grab something to eat," Mom says.

Fuck.

Again...under normal circumstances, I'd be more than happy to skip the bar and chill with my parents, but not when I've been anticipating spending a little alone time with Britt.

That's the moment I spot her standing off to the side and everything inside me settles. Now that I know she stuck around and didn't take off, I can finally breathe again.

Although, by her pantomiming efforts, she's gonna give it her best shot.

Like hell will I allow that to happen.

"Colby?"

Mom's voice breaks through the chaotic whirl of my thoughts.

I rip my gaze away from Britt long enough to say, "Umm...give me a moment. Okay?"

I'm on the move before either of them can ask any questions.

Once Britt realizes that I'm headed in her direction, she gives her head a little shake as her eyes widen.

As if that's going to deter me.

Ha!

When her mouth pops open, I slip my arm around her waist and steer her toward my parents.

"What the hell are you doing?" she whispers between clenched teeth.

"Introducing you to your new in-laws. What'd you think was happening?"

With a sputter, her body stiffens. It wouldn't surprise me if she dug her heels into the floor in an attempt to halt our progress.

Britt isn't the only one with wide, disbelieving eyes.

My parents look stunned by the sudden turn of events.

I certainly can't blame them for that. It's been over four years since I've mentioned any interest in a girl.

"Mom and Dad, this is Britt. Would you mind if she joined us for dinner?" I keep my arm wrapped around her so she can't make a run for it.

"Of course not," Mom says, still looking surprised. "We'd love that."

"Thanks." I shoot her a smile, appreciative that she's always so friendly and welcoming.

Dad reaches out to shake Britt's hand. "It's nice to meet you."

I might not know Britt well, but I recognize a forced smile when I see it.

"It's great to meet both of you as well." There's an awkward pause before she clears her throat. "I totally understand if you two would prefer to spend some time alone with—"

"Nonsense," Mom says with a wave of her hand as she glances at my father. "Gray and I would enjoy the opportunity to get to know you. If you're important to Colby, then you're important to us. And please, call me Whitney."

Have I mentioned how much I love my mom?

She's seriously the best.

Enough tension drains from Britt's body for her to unbend just a little bit. "Thank you."

"Should we get moving?" Dad asks, shoving his hands into his pants pockets and rocking back on his heels.

"Yup." I give Britt a bit of side eye to gauge her reaction. "Want to meet at the bar and grill downtown?"

They nod before we all head toward the exit.

I keep my arm locked around Britt, steering her toward the double set of glass doors.

She leans close enough for her warm breath to ghost across my ear. "Just so you know, if I weren't already divorcing you, this would definitely do the trick."

IN THE DARKEST NIGHTS, I STUMBLED, COULDN'T SEE THE LIGHT.
LOST IN A MAZE, COULDN'T FIND WHAT'S RIGHT.
BUT DEEP INSIDE, A FIRE BURNED,
REFUSING TO FADE AWAY.
A VOICE INSIDE ME WHISPERED, 'YOU'LL FIND YOUR WAY.'

I'M RISING UP, STRONGER NOW THAN I'VE EVER BEEN.
EVERY SCAR'S A STORY, AIN'T LETTING THEM WIN.
THROUGH THE UPS AND DOWNS, I'LL FIND MY TRUTH.
IN THE CHAOS OF IT ALL, I'LL FIND MY YOUTH.

THROUGH EVERY FALL AND EVERY DOUBT, I'LL STAND TALL.
GONNA SHAKE OFF THE PAST, GONNA GIVE IT MY ALL.
WITH EACH NEW DAY, LEAVING OLD FEARS BEHIND.
EMBRACING EVERY CHALLENGE, GONNA FREE MY MIND.

BRITT

W
ell, hell.

This is *not* how I saw this night unfolding.

Now that I'm in his truck, I realize what a bad idea it was to leave my silver Audi in the arena parking lot and take one car. I'm trapped with these people until Colby decides to drop me off.

Ugh.

Someone needs to explain why I make the worst decisions when I'm around this guy.

I peek at him from beneath the fringe of my lashes.

Even though I'm reluctant to admit it, the answer is obvious.

The guy is stupid hot.

But still...

It's not like I haven't been around good-looking men before. I live in LA. It's hot people central there. Everyone is either an actor, model, or singer trying to make it in Hollywood. And for the most part, they're ridiculously health conscious and looking for ways to turn back the hands of time. Whether that's with wheatgrass shots, plastic surgery, goat Pilates, or the newest weight loss drugs that have flooded the market.

After nearly a decade of living and working there, I should be immune to his physical attributes.

Sadly, nothing could be further from the truth.

He flicks a glance in my direction and catches me staring. "What?"

A sizzle of electricity zips across my skin.

That right there is *exactly* what the problem is.

This kind of all-encompassing attraction isn't something I've experienced before.

Not even with Axel.

I keep telling myself that if I give it enough time, it'll eventually dissipate.

I mean...it has to, right?

That, unfortunately, has not turned out to be the case. If anything, these feelings have only intensified since our first run-in at Slap Shotz.

"This was a terrible idea," I blurt, unwilling to share my innermost thoughts with him. "There's no reason for me to meet your parents. You and I aren't actually together."

"Did you forget that we're married?"

I've been so intent on him that it's almost a surprise when he slides his truck into a parking spot outside the restaurant.

"How could I when you're constantly reminding me?"

It's a legit question.

For a guy who's been portrayed as being anti-monogamous, he's warmed to the idea of marriage with a ridiculous amount of ease.

It doesn't make the least bit of sense.

He flashes a slow smile. The one that makes his dimples pop and wink.

As if on cue, my panties flood with heat.

I narrow my eyes. "Stop that right now."

The grin intensifies as he fights back his laughter and feigns innocence. "What? What did I do?"

I stab a finger in his direction. "You know exactly what you're doing."

This man is completely dangerous.

Not to mention, shameless.

He lays a hand over his heart as his expression turns sincere. "Can you really blame me for attempting to seduce my wife?"

"Please." With a snort, I pop the handle and exit the vehicle.

What I need is some fresh air to clear my head.

I don't get more than three steps before Colby pulls up alongside me. He throws his arm around my shoulders and hauls me close enough to feel the sculpted muscles that shift and bunch beneath his sweatshirt as the woodsy scent of his cologne slyly inundates my senses, making it impossible to think straight.

Is it bad that all I want to do is inhale a big breath of him?

And then hold it captive in my lungs?

Those thoughts come to a screeching halt when I glance at the scene unfolding in front of me and stumble. There are a handful of photographers snapping pics of Colby's parents.

The sight is all it takes for icy cold tendrils of panic to wrap around my heart and squeeze until it becomes impossible to breathe. Even when we were in Vegas for the weekend, I didn't feel this kind of panic and fear. Maybe that's because Sin City is brimming with celebrities and famous people. You can't swing a stick without hitting one.

It was easier to blend in with the raucous crowds.

Kind of like hiding in plain sight.

But here?

With the McNichols family?

Anyone with Colby will garner interest. It wouldn't take that much digging to figure out who I really am.

His arm tightens around my shoulders as he shoots me a concerned look. "Is there a problem?"

It never occurred to me that paparazzi would be here snapping pictures. Maybe it should have. I don't follow sports, but from everything I've heard, Gray McNichols is a big deal.

"Britt?"

I blink out of those thoughts and force my attention from his parents. It's tempting to take a step in retreat. And then another. Along with a third until I've distanced myself from them.

"Yeah?"

He repositions me until we're facing each other on the sidewalk before resting his hands on my shoulders. The weight of them does the impossible and soothes the worst of the panic trying to eat me alive.

His serious gaze searches mine as if it's possible to read my thoughts without me explaining a word. "What's going on?"

I break eye contact long enough to throw a cautious glance at the small group.

Another photographer joins the fray.

"I didn't realize there'd be paparazzi." My voice comes out sounding as if I'm being strangled.

Colby flicks a look at the commotion on the sidewalk before shrugging. "Yeah, sometimes they find out where he'll be and want pictures or sound bites. It's annoying but not a big deal. Dad is usually good about giving them what they want so they'll leave us alone."

I'm not unfamiliar with the practice. It's something we do as well.

I gulp down my nerves. Any minute they're going to explode from me. "Right. I just...don't want my picture taken. Okay?"

His thick brows pinch together as he studies me as if I'm a strange specimen he's stumbled across. "Yeah, sure. Why don't you head inside and wait for us while I join my folks and snap a few photos."

The relief that crashes over me is almost enough to weaken my knees. "Really?"

He strokes his fingers along the curve of my jaw as his voice dips. "Of course. The last thing I want to do is make you uncomfortable."

When we're about twelve feet away, Colby's father waves us over. As soon as the photographers realize that his son has made an appearance, they lift their cameras and snap a bunch of shots. The flash goes off as I duck my head, allowing my hair to fall in front of my face, and slip from his embrace before speedwalking inside the restaurant.

It's only when the glass door closes behind me that I realize I'm trembling. I release an unsteady breath and watch from a safe distance as the three of them are photographed together. After about five minutes, Gray raises a hand, putting a stop to the impromptu photo shoot.

"You know, I never considered myself a woman who'd go all why choose, but damn, those two are *fine* with a capital F."

It takes effort to rip my gaze away from Colby and stare at the older woman who's sidled up beside me while I wasn't paying attention. She's probably somewhere in her mid to late forties and wearing a gaudy faux fur jacket.

At least, let's hope the fur is faux.

Because...eww.

Instead of waiting for a response—as if I have one—she glances at the trio again.

It's tempting to tell her that she's got a little something-something on her chin. But I suspect she wouldn't give a damn.

"Are you with that handsome specimen of a man?" she asks.

Before I can respond, the three of them saunter through the front entrance, commanding everyone's attention. Colby's gaze slices to mine as he beelines in my direction and slips an arm around my waist, steering me toward his parents.

"Guess that answers the question," the woman says with a laugh.

Colby frowns, throwing a glance over his shoulder. "Do you know her?"

"Nope." The hostess leads his parents to a table in the main dining area. "Although, she was just commenting how much she'd enjoy being in the middle of a McNichols sandwich."

His wide eyes cut to mine before his head whips in her direction for a second time. "I'm sorry, she said what now?" Disbelief laces his voice.

It's kind of adorable.

A smile trembles around the corners of my lips. "Oh, I think you heard me the first time."

"Guess I was really hoping that I didn't." Before I can tease him any more, he says in a hushed tone, "And for the love of all that's holy, don't mention a word of it to my mother. She's reached her limit with women objectifying my father."

I can only imagine what Whitney McNichols has put up with being married to the handsome NHL player turned national sportscaster.

Once we reach the table, Colby pulls out my chair. He smirks when I raise my brows.

After I settle on the seat, he pushes it in before leaning close. "Just so you know, I wasn't raised by wolves. Manners were instilled within me. And just in case you're curious—I'm house trained as well. I won't even leave the toilet seat up."

My gaze gets snagged by his parents, who are grinning at us. Heat slams into my cheeks as I pick up my glass of water and take a sip. I'm hoping it'll douse the flames that have been ignited deep inside.

Within seconds of Colby dropping down beside me, a waitress arrives to take our drink order and rattle off the house specials. I'm barely paying attention. As nice as these people seem, I just want to get this over with and get out of here.

"So, Britt. Tell us about yourself," his mom encourages before glancing at her son. Speculation dances in her eyes as if she's excited by the prospect of him settling down. "Colby hasn't been very forthcoming regarding the details of your relationship."

I flick a beseeching look at him, hoping he'll jump in and rescue me.

I have no idea what to tell her.

It certainly won't be the truth.

As I mentally fumble for an answer, a middle-aged couple stops by the table. The man's gaze encompasses all four of us before settling on Gray.

"Hello, Mr. McNichols. I apologize for interrupting your dinner, but I was wondering if we could get an autograph and quick photo. I'm a huge fan. Way back to when you played for Hillsdale University."

By the expression on Gray's face, he'd prefer to decline the request. It's almost a surprise when he rises to his feet with a nod.

"Sure. No problem." He glances at his wife and his expression softens. "Hillsdale University...that was a long time ago. Wasn't it, Whit?"

Her lips bow up in response. "Almost another lifetime."

That interaction lasts for about five minutes as the man launches into a story about his son playing high school hockey. Just as Gray wraps up the conversation, saying goodnight to the man and his wife, someone else wanders over.

And then a few kids who are excited to meet an NHL legend.

I have to hand it to Gray McNichols. He's patient and kind when talking with fans. I know exactly what it's like to want to say no.

To enjoy a rare bit of privacy.

Normalcy.

But you can't do that.

Because then you're a stuck-up bitch who doesn't care about her fans or remember where she came from.

Before you know it, someone looking for their fifteen minutes in the spotlight comes out of the woodwork to tell an obscure story that proves exactly what a conceited C U Next Tuesday you are. Most of the time, they're flat-out lies or some twisted version that no longer resembles the truth.

A few years ago, my childhood neighbors wrote a tell-all book about what it was like to watch me grow up. Not only was it creepy, but a total invasion of privacy. It hurt even more because we'd been close to them.

"Would you mind if I took a group shot?"

Dread coils tight in the pit of my belly as a fresh wave of nerves crashes over me. My chair scrapes against the wood as I shove it away from the table and jerk to my feet. "I'll be right back. I'm, ah, going to the restroom."

I walk away before the guy can pull his phone out and snap away. When you're in the public eye, suddenly there are no boundaries. Even if I said no, he might have taken one anyway.

The backdoor of the restaurant catches my eye on the way to the bathroom. For a second or two, I consider sneaking out and taking off. I'm sure Fallyn or Ava would come to my rescue if I needed them.

Hell, I'll ride share home, if that's what it takes.

I shove through the door, grateful to find the small room empty. My hands bite into the smooth porcelain of the sink as I stare back at my reflection. Beneath the bright lights, my skin has been leached of all color.

Even though I tell myself that I'm panicking for no reason, it does nothing to alleviate my concerns.

Deep breath in and then slowly out.

Repeat.

Repeat.

Repeat.

I study my face in the mirror, looking for similarities.

There are none.

None that are a dead giveaway.

I don't resemble my alter ego in the slightest.

My hair, makeup, and clothing are different.

Everything has been transformed.

And yet...I'm still living in fear.

It only takes one person to make a comment.

Even as a joke.

When my phone chimes with an incoming message, I slip it from my pocket and glance at the screen.

You okay?

As much as I want to hide out indefinitely, that's not possible.

I need to get back.

If fans are still snapping pics, I'll sneak out the back door. Then I'll shoot Colby a text and tell him that I didn't feel well.

It's not a total lie.

It's just not the truth.

Decision made, I slip from the bathroom only to find the guy who has been a constant on my mind leaning against the wall with his arms crossed over his chest.

A squeak escapes from me as my heart riots against my ribcage. "What are you doing here?"

"Making sure you didn't ditch me."

I snort, unable to believe that he can read me with such ease. It's disconcerting. "Please. Like I'd do something like that."

He hikes a brow. "You took off in Vegas."

Well...there's not much I can say to that, is there?

Before I can respond, he reaches out and snags my fingers, drawing me close enough to wrap up in his arms. I hate just how comforting I find the gesture.

"Does it really bother you that much to have your photo taken?"

I chew my lower lip, unsure how to respond.

The truth isn't an option.

Even though it's tempting to blurt it out and clear my conscience. I hate all this lying. When I made the decision to step away from my old life, it never occurred to me that I'd make such good friends and it would become necessary to hide the truth. Or that I'd constantly need my guard up in order not to make a misstep and reveal too much.

But can I trust Colby to keep my secret?

We might be married, but we barely know each other.

In the end, I shake my head. "I'm just not very photogenic."

"I don't believe that for a second. You're gorgeous." His eyes narrow. "I get the feeling there's more to it than that."

"Nope. Looks like your Spidey senses are on the fritz."

"Well, you don't have to worry. My father told everyone that he's done and asked for some privacy."

I'm curious if his fans will abide by the request.

Unfortunately, it looks like I'm about to find out.

Colby slips his arm around my waist and steers me back to the table.

His mother's sparkling gaze bounces from him to me and then back again. "All right, I want all the details. How long have you two been going out? You're so comfortable with each other. It's really lovely to see."

Oh crap.

It probably would have been helpful if we'd concocted a story, since we're not about to reveal the truth.

A nervous laugh escapes from me. "Oh, no. We just—"

"Got married," he says.

My jaw turns slack as I stare at Colby with wide eyes.

One glance around the table tells me that I'm not the only one stunned by his response.

W ell, fuck.

That's not how I planned to share the news of my nuptials.

Needing to occupy my hands, I pick up my glass and drain the water. From over the rim, I stare at my parents and mentally prepare myself for their reaction.

There's only one other time that they've been rendered speechless.

That was more than four years ago.

And Britt?

Her eyes look like they might fall out of her head and roll around on the table.

If I were smart, I'd have kept my big trap shut.

I have the feeling that if we were to do a deep dive into my psyche, we'd find that what I'm really trying to do is bind Britt even tighter to me so she can't escape.

At every turn, that's what it seems like she's trying to do.

And I can't fucking stand it.

This is the first girl I've met who isn't impressed by my family or that I'm headed to the NHL after my senior season. She doesn't melt into a puddle when I flash my dimples.

I have the sneaking suspicion she wouldn't look twice in my direction if I didn't chase her ass down on the daily.

Like seriously...who is this chick?

And why does she act like I have a highly infectious disease she's deathly afraid of catching?

It's a conundrum that needs to be solved.

Mom is the first one to regain her power of speech as she waggles her finger between the two of us. "I'm sorry...did you just say you're married?" There's a pause. "As in—*married*?"

"To each other?" Dad tacks on, as if trying to play mental catchup.

I glance at Britt. Her lips are smashed so tightly together there's a good chance they'll disappear.

"Yup."

Mom clears her throat. "Okay. Um...when did this happen?"

I have to hand it to the woman. She's cool, calm, and collected.

Just like always.

There's not much that rattles her.

Luckily for me, we've always been tight. I couldn't have asked for a better mother. No matter what happens in my life, I can always turn to her for advice. Or at least with help breaking something to my father.

"Last weekend."

Dad scrubs a hand over his face and mutters, "In Vegas, I presume."

"Which means that congratulations are in order." Mom glances around for our waitress who hustles over as soon as they make eye contact. "Could we get a bottle of your best champagne, please?"

"Of course." The woman vanishes as swiftly as she appeared.

Within five minutes, our crystal flutes are filled with golden bubbly liquid. I've never been one for champagne. If I'm going to drink, it's beer. But I'm thankful that Mom is attempting to smooth over the situation since Dad hasn't said much.

I'm sure I'll get an earful later.

When she raises her glass, the three of us do the same. "Gray and I want to welcome you to our family, Britt. We look forward to spending more time together and getting to know you on a deeper level." Love shines brightly from her eyes as she turns her attention to me. "Colby is an exceptional man, and if you married him, then you recognize it as well and that's all I've ever wanted. That also tells me you're special because our son doesn't open his heart to just anyone." Her gaze settles on my father. "I wish you two just as much happiness as we've found."

Dad's expression softens as a smile tips the corners of his lips. "To Colby and Britt."

We clink our glasses before sipping the sparkly liquid.

I peek at Britt. The stiffness of her posture has disappeared, and her expression has relaxed, making her look even more beautiful.

That's all it takes for air to get trapped in my lungs.

Maybe this relationship started off as an impulsive decision fueled by too much liquor, but who's to say it can't be more?

Who's to say it already isn't?

IN THE DARKEST NIGHTS, I STUMBLED, COULDN'T SEE THE LIGHT.
LOST IN A MAZE, COULDN'T FIND WHAT'S RIGHT.
BUT DEEP INSIDE, A FIRE BURNED,
REFUSING TO FADE AWAY.
A VOICE INSIDE ME WHISPERED, 'YOU'LL FIND YOUR WAY.'

I'M RISING UP, STRONGER NOW THAN I'VE EVER BEEN.
EVERY SCAR'S A STORY, AIN'T LETTING THEM WIN.
THROUGH THE UPS AND DOWNS, I'LL FIND MY TRUTH.
IN THE CHAOS OF IT ALL, I'LL FIND MY YOUTH.

THROUGH EVERY FALL AND EVERY DOUBT, I'LL STAND TALL.
GONNA SHAKE OFF THE PAST, GONNA GIVE IT MY ALL.
WITH EACH NEW DAY, LEAVING OLD FEARS BEHIND.
EMBRACING EVERY CHALLENGE, GONNA FREE MY MIND.

BRITT

I give one final wave to Colby's parents as they disappear around the corner. Only then do I spin and whack him on the chest. "I can't believe you told them we're married!"

"Ow." He lifts a hand to rub the injured area. "Why not? It's the truth. We *are* married."

"Not for long," I say with a grunt, stalking to his truck parked down the street.

"TBD," he says, trailing after me.

My clenched fists land on my hips as I swing around and glare. I'm seriously going to throttle him.

The grin he flashes does nothing to soften my stance.

Well...almost nothing.

Damn him.

He clicks the locks on his truck before opening the passenger side door in one smooth movement. "Your chariot awaits, madam."

I flatten my lips, refusing to allow them to tremble. I get the feeling that if I give Colby an inch, he'll take a mile.

After pulling into traffic, he throws a glance my way. "Should we talk at your place? I'm sure it'll be a lot quieter than mine."

I jerk my head into a tight nod.

Tonight I'm pulling the plug and ending this sham of a marriage.

Ten minutes later, I shove the key into the lock and push open the door to my apartment before flicking on the lights. As he strolls into the entryway and then the dining/living room combination, his gaze bounces around the space as if trying to absorb everything at once. It makes me wish that I'd taken the time to hide some of the more personal objects that had been left lying around. I'd assumed we would talk at a restaurant.

After a long stretch of silence, his gaze settles on me. "You live here alone?"

"Yup. When I applied to Western in the summer, I didn't know anyone."

He nods, gravitating to a credenza before picking up a silver-framed photo. My palms dampen as he studies it.

His gaze flickers to mine. "Is this your family?"

"Um, yeah."

"How old were you when this was taken?" With a tilt of his head, he scrutinizes it. "About eight or nine?"

"Probably around there." I force my feet into motion, closing the distance between us before plucking the frame from his hands. Relief rushes through me when he doesn't ask any more questions.

As I set it back on the table, he beelines toward the couch and picks up the guitar.

Damn it.

Why didn't I put the instrument away instead of leaving it out?

He strums a few cords. "You play?"

I jerk my shoulders, trying to shake off the growing tension that fills every muscle. This guy is making me twitchy. "A little."

"Wanna play something for me? We can open this conversation with a song."

It's not a question I have to think about. "Nope."

"You sang to me on the airplane," he reminds, voice turning cajoling.

"Only because you were in distress."

The slow smile that spreads across his lips sends a punch of arousal straight to my core. "Would you believe I'm in distress at the moment?"

It takes effort to swallow past the thick lump wedged in my throat. "Not a chance."

Having Colby here is like being responsible for an overactive child in an art gallery. I need to keep a close eye on him, or he'll rip the place apart and be into everything.

I've invited a few friends over since moving in, but I try to keep entertaining to a minimum. I'm also careful to hide anything that could potentially tie me to my old life.

It's taking every ounce of self-control not to leap at him and rip the instrument from his hands.

I've never allowed anyone to touch or play with it.

Not even my siblings.

Instead of acting on the rush of emotion coursing through me, I settle on the couch in the hopes he'll do the same.

I just want to get this over with.

Anxiety leaks from my muscles when he follows my lead and drops down beside me.

My fingers tap an insistent beat on my jean-clad thigh as I force myself to remain calm. "We need to end this now."

There.

I said it.

Even though he appears outwardly calm and collected, the unnerving way he stares tells me he's anything but. It's enough to have another round of nerves detonating at the bottom of my belly.

"What's the hurry? Why are you so opposed to the idea of spending a little time together to see if this could work?"

I wait for him to flash a charming smile or chuckle. Something that will show me that he's joking around.

It never happens.

Instead, his gaze stays pinned to mine.

A beat of silence passes.

Then another.

Oh shit.

That's when I realize he's serious.

My mouth dries as my brain cartwheels.

I shake my head, not understanding why he'd want to bother.

There's no way that Colby McNichols is interested in being tied down.

To me. A girl he barely knows.

Unable to stand the intensity of his gaze for another second, I rip mine away. "Why delay the inevitable? It won't work between us."

"Why not?"

I open my mouth, grappling for a response.

There are a million reasons.

The biggest one being that I'm not who he thinks I am.

I swallow down my anxiety and attempt to remain calm. "Because we're two different people moving in opposite directions."

He scoots closer before reaching out and placing his larger hand over mine. My pulse skitters when he toys with my fingers. "How can you be so sure? We've barely gotten the chance to know one another."

My attention falls to the place we're now connected, and my heart skips a painful beat before thudding into overdrive. "Colby..."

"What?" His voice deepens as he slants a look my way.

The fire that flickers in his ocean-blue depths is almost enough to have me going up in flames. My brain tumbles back to Vegas and the night he pressed me against the glass before sliding deep inside my body. The glittering lights of the city stretched out below us had only heightened the intensity of my orgasm.

"We shouldn't," I whisper in a voice that barely sounds like my own.

He inches closer before cocking his head. "Shouldn't what?"

"Sleep together." There's a pause before I tack on, "Again."

One brow slinks upward as if the thought had never crossed his mind. "Oh?"

"It'll only confuse matters."

He has to understand that, right?

"Actually, I think it'll help clarify them for both of us."

Before I can collect my thoughts and come up with another reason why us having sex is a disastrous idea, his hand slips around the nape of my neck before tugging me forward. His grasp isn't so tight that I couldn't pull away or put a stop to what's unfolding, but there's a part of me that doesn't want to.

The sex we had in Vegas was amazing, and I'm dying to confirm that I overembellished it in my memories.

It'll make walking away that much easier.

When I don't protest, a smile curves his lips seconds before they crash into mine. I open, allowing him entrance before he can sweep his tongue across the seam.

That simple caress is all it takes for me to go from zero to a hundred.

One hand stays wrapped around the back of my neck as the other slips beneath my sweater and drifts upward until he can cup my breast. A groan rumbles up from deep within him. The guttural sound makes everything inside me clamor for more.

He pulls away just long enough to mutter, "I've been thinking about these all damn week."

With that, he yanks the soft pink cashmere up my body and over my head before tossing it to the floor. It's my favorite sweater, but at this moment, I don't give a damn what happens to it. All I can think about is the way he's touching and kissing me. His hands are strong and possessive, and he knows exactly what to do with them.

As loathe I am to admit it, I haven't been able to stop thinking about him either. A couple of days ago, I was jolted out of a sexy dream and ended up rubbing one out because I was so damn achy. There was no way I was going to fall back to sleep without finding a little relief. It only slams home the realization that Axel never turned me on to this degree.

He pulls back as his gaze rakes over my chest. "Fuck, baby. You're so gorgeous. As sexy as this bra is, it needs to go."

His hands slip around my back to unfasten the hooks. It takes him less than fifteen seconds before the band around my ribcage loosens and the silky straps slide down my arms. The cups shielding my nipples from view fall away. The tiny buds tighten as the cool air of the room wafts across my skin.

His gaze stays pinned to my chest as he reaches out to palm my naked breasts. "They're just as perfect as I remember."

When he tweaks one stiff peak, a gasp works its way up my throat before slipping free.

His attention flickers to my face. "Do you like that?"

"Yes." There's no point in lying when the truth is obvious.

There've been a few men in my past, but not as many as people assume. My mother was always at my side, chasing off the ones who came sniffing around. She made sure that my focus was on the empire we were attempting to build.

He pinches the other one and elicits the same response.

With a growl, his mouth collides with mine as he presses me against the cushions and settles on top of me. His thick erection nestles against the vee between my legs. The way he grinds against my clit, bumping it at the perfect angle, is dizzying. I can't stop myself from shifting, silently begging for more of the addictive sensations that reverberate throughout my body.

He pulls away long enough to growl, "You drive me fucking crazy, you know that?"

It's precisely what he does to me.

His gaze stays fastened to mine as he nips my lower lip, tugging it before setting it free. And then he's delving in for more. There's the scrape of teeth and the slide of tongues. Just when I think I'll come from this alone, his mouth drifts to the point of my chin before grazing my jawline.

It's not a conscious decision to bare the column of my throat. More like instinct. The need to feel his touch everywhere. Another round of arousal detonates in my core as he sucks at the delicate flesh. Impatience spirals through me as my nipples brush the cotton of his sweatshirt. I want to feel his chiseled muscles pressing against my softness. My fingers drift to the hem before giving it a tug. That movement is all it takes to capture his attention.

"You want it off, sweet girl?"

"Please."

Another rumble escapes from deep within his chest as his eyes darken. "Fuck but I love the sound of that word on your lips."

He rises just enough to tug the thick material over his head before tossing it aside. My gaze dips to the tantalizing sight of sun-kissed abdominals.

The T-shirt is the next to get shed until he's just as bare chested as I am.

There's no doubt about it. His body really is perfection.

As stunning as a statue you'd admire in a museum.

There's a whirl of golden blond hair on his chest that arrows down his eight pack before disappearing beneath the waistband of his jeans. It's tempting to flick open the button and shove them down his lean hips and thighs.

I'm dying to get another glimpse of his cock.

It can't possibly be as thick and beautiful as I remember.

"Are you done checking me out yet?"

I slant a glance upward. Both heat and humor simmer in his ocean-colored depths.

"For now."

With a smirk, he lowers himself until he's fully stretched out on top of my body. His naked skin feels so good against mine. The kiss that unfolds between us is surprisingly less frenzied than the one that came before it. It's like he was afraid I might say no and now understands there's no need to rush. We can take our time and enjoy the moment.

Deep down, I realize this is a bad idea, but there's no stopping it. I'll deal with the ramifications tomorrow.

Tonight, I want to feel him buried deep within me until I have no other choice but to shudder around him.

Just like in Vegas.

His tongue slides inside my mouth to mingle with my own. It's the slow brush of velvet with the light scrape of teeth.

My arms tangle around his neck to draw him closer.

"So damn greedy," he whispers before licking at my lips.

And then he's dipping lower to my chest. His hands drift to the outer sides of my breasts before pressing them closer. He licks one pert tip before sucking it into the warmth of his mouth.

Pleasure blooms inside me as I arch, only wanting to get closer.

He's right about being greedy.

When I'm with Colby, my brain clicks off and I stop thinking about what my future will look like and the tough decisions I'll be forced to make. I'm only able to focus on the delicious sensation that careens through my veins.

For better or worse, everything else gets blotted out.

He releases my nipple before zeroing in on the other, giving it the same ardent attention. He sinks lower until he's eye level with the waistband of my jeans. His gaze flicks to mine as the fingers hover over the metal button.

I jerk my head into a tight nod before the question can leave his lips.

"Thank fuck," he mutters, attacking both the button and zipper.

He makes quick work of the thick denim, tugging it down my hips and thighs. The jeans meet the same fate as the sweater until I'm left in a thong. He sits back and allows his hungry gaze to rove over my nearly naked length. Everywhere it touches, heat ignites as if it's a physical caress.

"Have I mentioned that you're gorgeous?"

My lips bow at the compliment. I've been given thousands of them over the years, but for some reason, it means more coming from Colby.

"Pretty sure that you did."

"Well, I'm saying it again, because it's one hundred percent the truth. I could stare at you for hours."

His words arrow to the very heart of me before exploding on impact. It takes effort to stomp out the riotous emotion attempting to break loose inside me. "I think you're just horny."

"Oh, I'm horny all right," he agrees. "For my wife."

A bolt of electricity sizzles through me at the reminder, leaving me breathless.

His fingers slip beneath the band of my underwear before he

slides it down my legs. A tortured groan escapes for him as he removes the tiny scrap of silky material from my body.

His hands drift up and down my calves, almost as if strumming the flesh. "Now, be a good girl and open your legs wide. I've missed seeing my wife's pretty little pussy."

My heart skips a painful beat as I do as he asks.

His gaze drops to the vee between my thighs, and he stares until I'm squirming beneath the intensity of it. Until heat floods my core and I know I'm slick with arousal from the possessive way he watches me.

"So fucking gorgeous."

The first brush of his fingertips across my delicate flesh has a moan breaking free. Even though I got myself off a few days ago, it wasn't nearly this delicious. He caresses me a few more times before shouldering his way between my thighs until the warmth of his breath ghosts over me. Anticipation rushes through my veins as air stalls in my lungs.

I don't have to wait long.

The first touch is almost enough to have me coming off the couch. My fingers tunnel through his thick hair to hold him in place. Or maybe it's to keep me tethered to the earth so I don't float off into the atmosphere.

Just like our previous kiss, there's nothing frenzied about his movements. Instead, each one seems calculated to elicit the most pleasure. His tongue strokes across my center before circling my clit. When he spreads my lips wide, my eyes almost roll to the back of my head.

I can't help but squirm, trying to get closer.

When a whimper breaks free from me, his gaze locks on mine. "So damn greedy," he repeats.

It won't take much more of this exquisite torture before I'm an incoherent mess.

If I'm not already.

His tongue dances around the little bundle of nerves until it throbs with a life all its own. Only then does he thrust his tongue deep inside my pussy.

"Are you ready to come for me?"

So ready...

When I shift, only wanting to feel him deep inside my body, he taps my clit with the tips of his fingers. I gasp as the area is flooded with a potent concoction of pleasure wrapped in pain.

"Answer the question."

"Yes," I groan. "I want you to make me come."

A smug smile flashes across his face. "I know you do. You're practically crying for it—*for me*."

Oh god...

It's true.

The only other time I've been this turned on was—

Another garbled sound escapes from me as he buries his face against my softness. His tongue strokes across my skin before he nibbles at my clit.

"So, so sweet."

This time, he attacks me. One scrape of teeth against my sensitive flesh and I lose all control. A moan falls from my lips as my back bows off the cushions. Every muscle turns whipcord tight.

It's only after the last tremor racks my body that I force my eyelids open and find him watching me. I don't think I've ever seen anything sexier in my life than Colby's blond head between my spread thighs, his sharp blue eyes searing mine.

A shiver skitters down my spine.

Unsure what to say or how to break the intensity of the moment we now find ourselves in, I whisper, "Thank you."

The smirk returns full force. "Oh, don't thank me just yet, sweet girl. I'm nowhere near done with you."

With that, he scoops me up into his arms.

I hold Britt close as I stalk to her room. The warm weight of her feels so damn good in my arms. Every time I think I can't be more into this girl, I somehow up the ante.

Once I set her down in the middle of the queen-sized mattress, I take a step back and allow my gaze to roam over her naked form.

Fuck but she's beautiful spread out before me like a damn feast. Her caramel-colored hair is fanned out around the lavender bedding. I'm pretty sure I've never wanted anyone as much as I want this girl.

One weekend spent together wasn't nearly enough. After she skipped town, I'd assumed dismissing her from my mind wouldn't be an issue.

Turns out that nothing could be further from the truth.

Even though she just orgasmed, a heated look fills her golden eyes.

When she spreads her legs wide, giving me a tantalizing view of heaven, every thought spinning through my brain leaks out of my ears.

Fuck.

Fuck.

Fuck.

My tongue darts out to lick my lower lip before sucking the firm flesh into my mouth. Her honeyed taste explodes on my tongue. It makes me want to dive back in and eat her pussy all over again.

And I will...

After.

"What are you waiting for, Colby? Don't you want to come?"

Oh, this girl...

Did she really just throw my own words back at me?

She can't possibly understand what she's getting herself into.

And perhaps that's for the best.

If she knew, it would scare the shit out of her.

The force of these feelings scares the fuck out of me.

"Just admiring the sight of you." I flick open the button on my jeans before lowering the zipper and pulling out my cock. "But now that you've mentioned it, I'm horny as hell and ready to come."

One squeeze of the bulbous head and I'm precariously close to blowing my load.

How fucking embarrassing would that be?

To come and not even be inside this girl?

There's no way I can allow that to happen.

When her hands rise to toy with her nipples, my dick swells even more than before. I grit my teeth to keep everything locked up tight where it belongs.

She tweaks the hard little buds before squeezing the softness. "I'm waiting."

I hiss out a harsh breath.

It's tempting to strip off the denim, but there's no way I'll last that long. Not with her touching herself in front of me.

I slip my fingers inside the back pocket of my jeans and take out the condom, ripping open the package with my teeth and suiting up. It's only when I slide the latex over my shaft that I realize my hands are shaking.

Fuck.

The need I feel for this girl—*my wife*—is almost too much to wrap my head around.

It takes a few jerky steps before I'm able to settle between her spread thighs. Our gazes stay locked as I push inside her soft heat. As much as I want to close my eyes and revel in the sensation, that's not possible.

I'm unable to look away from the sight of her beneath me.

I'm desperate to see every flicker of emotion as it crosses her face.

Already my balls are tightening, drawing up against my body.

Ten damn strokes.

That's all it takes for me to lose it.

Thank fuck her pussy contracts around me as she follows me over the precipice and into oblivion.

Jeez.

Maybe I didn't last long, but my orgasm seems to go on forever.

Best.

Damn.

Feeling.

In.

The.

World.

By the time my muscles loosen and I collapse against her, my heart feels as if it'll pound right out of my chest. I just want to bury my face in her floral-scented hair and drag a big breath into my lungs and keep it captive forever.

Those thoughts alone should rattle me enough to run.

I'm not sure what it is about Britt, but I'm totally tangled up in her.

Here's an even more terrifying thought—I don't want to get free.

Not ever.

Unwilling to relinquish the closeness we've managed to find, I roll to the side and take her with me until her lithe body is sprawled against my chest. Only then does contentment steal over me as her fingers trace light patterns across my flesh.

Even though a satisfied sigh escapes from her, I sense the words poised on the tip of her tongue before they're able to burst free. There's a shift in the atmosphere. I've never felt this attuned to another human being before. And that includes the guys I've played hockey with for years. The ones that are more like my brothers.

"Don't say it."

She twists until her chin can rest against her stacked hands. "This was a mistake. We both know that sex won't solve anything between us."

"Um, excuse me...it was damn good sex," I correct. "Don't under-rate it."

The corners of her lips tremble. "Funny...out of all the things I've heard about you, two pump chump wasn't one of them."

I narrow my eyes and give her a mock glare. "It was a solid ten strokes. Maybe even eleven."

"It might have been eight. I was afraid you were going to come before you were even inside me."

Me, too.

It's seriously messed up how little control I have around this girl.

I snort. "Please."

Her brows rise. "Please what? Make you come?"

"Methinks someone is looking to get fucked again." I reach down and stroke my cock, attempting to rally. "Give me ten minutes, maybe a power nap along with a Gatorade, and I'll be raring to go."

Her naked shoulders shake. "Thanks for the offer, but it's totally unnecessary. The point I was trying to make is that it's a complicated situation and what just happened won't help matters."

"I'm of the point of view that it doesn't hurt." Before she can fire off another response, I add, "Plus, you're my wife. If there's anyone I should be fucking, it's you."

She groans. "Colby...we're not *really* married."

"Actually—"

"You know what I mean."

Unable to help myself, my arms tighten, unwilling to let her slip away. Because that's exactly what it feels like she's attempting to do. I won't have her pulling another disappearing act. "I think we need to spend some real time together to see if what we have is more than just physical."

She mulls over the suggestion. "You want to spend time together?"

"Yup. Quality time."

Panic floods her eyes before it's quickly shuttered away. "I'm not sure that's a good idea."

It's the same expression that flickered across her face when she spotted the photographers outside the restaurant earlier this evening. Which doesn't make the least bit of sense.

"How else can we figure out if we're compatible?" Before she can shoot down the idea, I blurt, "I should move in with you. If it doesn't work out, we file for divorce and part ways amicably. I mean, we already told my parents the happy news."

"You're the one who told them."

I shrug. "Does it really matter?"

"Yes."

Brushing her response aside, I ask, "What do you say, Britt? Are you willing to give married life a whirl?"

"I think you might be crazy," she whispers.

"So...is that a yes?"

Air stalls in my lungs as I wait for an answer.

The only thought pumping through me is the one that demands I lock this girl down tight and make her mine.

My gaze falls to her lower lip as she nibbles it.

"I can see you need more convincing."

I wrap my hands around her ribcage and drag her up my body until my cock is nestled against the vee between her legs. That's all it takes for me to turn to stone.

And it was more like five minutes, not ten.

No Gatorade necessary.

IN THE DARKEST NIGHTS, I STUMBLED, COULDN'T SEE THE LIGHT.
LOST IN A MAZE, COULDN'T FIND WHAT'S RIGHT.
BUT DEEP INSIDE, A FIRE BURNED,
REFUSING TO FADE AWAY.
A VOICE INSIDE ME WHISPERED, 'YOU'LL FIND YOUR WAY.'

I'M RISING UP, STRONGER NOW THAN I'VE EVER BEEN.
EVERY SCAR'S A STORY, AIN'T LETTING THEM WIN.
THROUGH THE UPS AND DOWNS, I'LL FIND MY TRUTH.
IN THE CHAOS OF IT ALL, I'LL FIND MY YOUTH.

THROUGH EVERY FALL AND EVERY DOUBT, I'LL STAND TALL.
GONNA SHAKE OFF THE PAST, GONNA GIVE IT MY ALL.
WITH EACH NEW DAY, LEAVING OLD FEARS BEHIND.
EMBRACING EVERY CHALLENGE, GONNA FREE MY MIND.

BRITT

A frown mars my expression as I hold the door open for Colby. His muscles bulge as he slides past with boxes stacked in his arms.

How exactly did I get myself into this?

One minute, the guy is sinking inside my body and the next, I'm agreeing to the suggestion that he move in.

Temporarily.

I glance around my apartment, no longer able to recognize the space.

Was it really less than an hour ago that it was neat and tidy? Everything in its place?

It now looks like a bomb exploded.

Guy stuff is strewn across every surface. We're talking hockey gear, clothing, an X-box, books, and hair products...

Seriously?

It's like he's moving in forever.

Not just a few short weeks.

I rack my brain.

Did we set a firm timeline for this trial run?

If we did, it's eluding me.

Panic floods my system.

I need to get ahold of myself.

I'm sure it'll only take a week or two for both of us to realize that we have nothing in common.

Except good sex.

As far as I'm concerned, that doesn't count.

He shifts the boxes before pausing. "Should I set this in the bedroom to unpack for later?"

Good lord...he really is taking over. It's like the floodgates have opened and there's no way to close them again.

"Yeah, I guess."

He disappears inside the room before returning a few minutes later. My gaze tracks his movements as he beelines to the counter that separates the kitchen and living area and picks up a bottle of water before lifting it to his lips and chugging. My mouth turns cottony as he tips his head back until the corded muscles of his throat stand out in sharp relief.

Oh my.

My lady parts twitch in pure male appreciation before I stomp it out.

It takes effort to rip my attention away from the sight of him. I'm embarrassed to admit just how difficult it is to think straight when he's in the vicinity.

All I can say is that the man dulls my senses.

Which makes me no better than all the puck bunnies who stalk him around campus.

A groan tries to work its way free from my throat.

He cocks his head. "I'm sorry? I didn't quite catch that. What did you say?"

Shit.

"Was it really necessary for you to move in?"

He leans against the counter and jerks a brow. "When else are we going to spend time together? Between hockey and classes, I don't have a ton of it."

True.

But still...

"Just seems a bit drastic..." I mutter, unsure what else to say.

"Maybe. But we're married. And from what I've seen, married people cohabit."

"So you keep telling me."

His lips quirk and the delicate skin around his eyes crinkle.

How is it possible that the expression only makes him sexier?

I blink away those pesky thoughts.

They certainly aren't helping matters.

He glances at his cell. "I have practice in a few hours. Want me to throw something together for dinner before I leave?"

I'm sorry...did I hear that correctly?

"Are you trying to tell me that you actually...*cook*?"

When he smirks, something pings at the bottom of my belly. "You don't have to look so shocked. Haven't you figured out yet that I'm a man of many talents?"

He's not kidding.

"You're a real renaissance man, Colby McNichols." My attempt at sarcasm comes out sounding embarrassingly breathy.

"Mom taught me when I was a kid. It's a good stress reliever." He throws a wink in for good measure. "Although, not as relaxing as certain other recreational activities..."

I can't help the way my lips twitch in amusement. It's impossible not to smile and laugh in his presence. He has a real knack for lightening the atmosphere.

Guess that would be another one of his many talents.

But I'll keep that observation to myself.

Otherwise, the guy will get a big head.

All right...a bigger head. It swells up any more and he won't fit through the door.

A strange warmth spreads through my veins at the idea of Colby preparing dinner with me in mind.

"What are you best known for?"

He purses his lips as a thoughtful expression fills his eyes.

I hate to admit how adorable it makes him look.

Ugh.

This is bad.

"If I was forced to pick just one thing, I'd say that my lasagna is pretty amazing."

My brows rise. "Really?" I've watched chefs make the dish on cooking shows. That particular entree seems both time consuming and labor intensive.

"If it's easier, you could just whip up something like grilled cheese and tomato soup or spaghetti." Even Mom was capable of boiling noodles and emptying a jar of sauce into a pan.

He frowns. "You're not a fan of lasagna?"

"No, I love it. I'm just saying that if it's..." My voice trails off as I shrug.

His eyes widen as he straightens to his full height. "Wait a minute...you don't think I have the skills? Is that what you're insinuating?"

The shock that reverberates in his voice is enough to make me laugh. "I didn't say that!"

He crosses his arms against his chest and glares. "You didn't have to. It was implied. Which essentially boils down to a challenge. So, grab your purse and let's pick up the ingredients I need from the store." He throws a glance at my fridge. "And we're going to have to fix that sad state of affairs while we're at it."

"Excuse me?"

"You heard me. You have a few yogurts, diet soda, and a block of cheese. That won't do. We need healthy options."

I grumble before snagging my purse off the breakfast bar as we head to the door.

Forty minutes later, we're back with four bags overflowing with groceries. Only one is for the dinner Colby is dead set on making. The rest is a mix of protein bars, healthy baked chips, unsalted nuts, low carb granola, cartons of eggs, turkey sausage, quinoa, tons of ground turkey, along with fruits and veggies.

I didn't realize he was such a clean eater.

The things you learn about someone when you live together.

I almost wince at that thought.

He unpacks all the ingredients, spreading them out on the counter.

"Do you need any help?" Not that I would know where to begin.

He shakes his head. "Nope. Why don't you sit down and keep me company while I throw everything together."

I settle on the chair as he moves around the kitchen with ease. He might not be familiar with mine in particular and where everything is stored, but that doesn't seem to matter. He places a large pan on the stove and ignites the burner. When it's hot, he adds the chicken sausage and breaks it up into smaller pieces with a wooden spoon. Then he fills an oversized pot with water and adds a few shakes of salt to it before setting it to boil.

There's something soothing about watching Colby cook. Now that he's preoccupied, I'm able to stare at him to my heart's content. My gaze drops to his hands as he chops a few bulbs of garlic before adding it to the meat and stirring. Once the chicken sausage has browned, he adds a large can of organic tomato sauce to the pan and sets it to simmer before cracking two eggs in a bowl and then adding them to a ricotta mixture.

The guy is definitely skilled with his hands.

As that thought tumbles through my head, I gulp and force my attention away. It wouldn't take much to get used to him in my space.

And that's the last thing I want.

We weren't meant for the long haul.

Sadness flares to life inside me before I snuff it out.

I'm pulled from the tangle of my thoughts when he says, "You mentioned that your family is now in California. Where'd you live before that?"

I blink and refocus my attention. Even though I don't like talking about my past, it's better than dwelling on the lifespan of this marriage.

"Actually, it wasn't that far from here."

He glances at me in surprise. "Really?"

"Yup."

"Do you have family in the area? Is that why you decided to attend Western?"

I clear my throat and admit something I probably should've earlier. "I do." There's a pause before I confess, "Sully."

This time, he stops and swings toward me in surprise. "Sully? The owner of Slap Shotz?"

A smile quirks the corners of my lips. "The one and only."

"I didn't know that. Is he your uncle?"

When he continues to stare, I pop to my feet and beeline to the cabinet for a glass before filling it with cold water from the fridge. "Yeah. Guess I forgot to mention it earlier."

My mind unconsciously tumbles back to all the times I was desperate for a break and showed up unannounced on his doorstep.

"Are you two close?"

I nod. "We are. He and Aunt Mary are great. They never had children, so they kind of treat me like one." No matter how much time slips by, when we're together, it's comfortable and easy. I trust them implicitly.

It took years to realize just how precious those kinds of relationships are. When you have fame, people behave differently toward you. They stop treating you like a person.

And you become more of an object.

Something to be coveted.

To my knowledge, Uncle Sully has never told a soul that Bebe is his niece or that he's even acquainted with her.

"How come you didn't stay with them for at least the first semester? Maybe then you would have met someone to live with."

I shrug. "They offered, but I wanted my own space. And I didn't want to cramp their style. They're used to being on their own." And so am I.

A comfortable silence falls over the two of us as he stirs the sauce and adds the noodles to the boiling pot. For the first time since moving into the apartment, the place is filled with delicious scents. My belly growls in response.

"Everyone on the team loves Sully," Colby adds. "He's the best."

My lips lift into a genuine smile as everything inside me loosens. From the few times I've hung out with the girls at the bar, that much is obvious. He has a lot of love for the team, and they return it tenfold.

"He's easy to get along with."

There's a pause as he changes the subject. "So, tell me what kind of meals your parents made growing up."

It's tempting to bark out a laugh.

As a kid, we didn't get a lot of homecooked dinners. Mom is a lot of things, but a Michelin-star chef is not one of them. As soon as we could afford it, she hired a private chef. I was usually working or traveling, so I missed out. Uncle Sully and Aunt Mary are amazing and sometimes send over leftovers, but that doesn't happen nearly often enough.

"Um, I guess the normal kind of stuff like spaghetti—"

He glances at me while stirring the sauce. "From a jar?"

My lips tremble at the disgust woven through his voice. "Of course."

He shakes his head. "That's practically child abuse."

"Um, I don't think so. And tacos."

"Can I assume there were a lot of taco Tuesdays in your past?"

"And sometimes Thursdays and Sundays."

"So, you like Mexican?"

"Even though we ate a ton of it as a kid, I do. It's definitely a comfort food."

His expression turns thoughtful. "Noted. The way to your heart is through tacos."

I snort, wanting to disabuse him of the notion.

Except...he's probably not wrong.

"Have you been to Taco Loco?" he asks.

I rack my memory. "No, I don't think so."

"We'll have to go sometime. You know, when we have date night. They have the best Tacos in town. Maybe even in the state."

"That's a pretty big claim."

"It's one I stand firmly behind." He drains the noodles in a strainer set in the sink. "What else?"

"Macaroni and hot dogs. Chicken nuggets. Sometimes grilled cheese and tomato soup."

"My stomach hurts just thinking about eating all that."

"Yeah. Not exactly the dinners of champions, is it?"

"Nope. What about when you were older?"

I take another drink of water before setting the glass down on the table. "Once we could afford it, Mom hired a private chef to cook for us or we ate out."

"You've mentioned your mom a couple times. What about your dad?" His gaze flickers to me as he layers the noodles, ricotta mixture, and meat sauce. "Are you close to him?"

Nerves skitter across my flesh, leaving behind a trail of goosebumps in their wake.

It's important to tread carefully while talking about my parents.

"Yeah, I am." I pause for a moment to collect my thoughts. "My father is a good man. More of the strong silent type. Lowkey. He's happy to allow my mom to make all the decisions and then go along with whatever she says. She has a strong personality, and he doesn't really challenge her."

The few times he tried, she steamrolled right over him.

"Interesting."

His brows draw together as he concentrates on layering the lasagna before sprinkling the top with mozzarella and sliding it into the oven. Then he sets the timer on his phone.

"Now we wait an hour and fifteen minutes."

I glance at the clock on my phone. "Will you have enough time to eat before practice?"

"Probably not. I'll have some when I get back. After two hours on the ice, I'll be starving."

He slides onto a chair before peppering me with questions about my childhood. When they turn to the not-so-distant past, I decide to ask a few of my own.

"Tell me more about your family. Your parents seem great. Really accepting of the decisions you make. Even when you shock the hell out of them." That's what impressed me most.

His expression softens. "They're amazing. When I was younger, my dad was on the road a lot and my mom always held down the fort, making sure that we had a stable home. Her kids always came first."

My heart clenches with envy.

"When Dad was gone, she's the one who schlepped me to the rink five days a week with all my siblings in tow." He smirks. "It was pretty much their second home."

"Are you all still close?"

He nods. "Yup. I'm sure my brothers will follow in my footsteps and play here at Western."

"And your sister?"

"She's an equestrian."

"Sounds like your upbringing was pretty idyllic."

I'm even more envious than before.

He shrugs as a flash of darkness enters his eyes. "It was. But having a father who played in the NHL and then worked in broadcasting isn't all it's cracked up to be."

"Oh?"

For the first time, he's the one who breaks eye contact. A heavy silence falls over us as he gets tangled in his thoughts.

I reach out and lay my hand over his. "You don't have to tell me anything you don't want. Whatever happened in the past isn't any of my business."

He draws a deep breath into his lungs before forcing it out again. "That's where you're wrong. You're my wife, and I want you to have a better understanding of me." He jerks his shoulders. "Maybe this'll help."

Instead of asking questions, I squeeze his hand, just wanting him to know that he's not alone.

"When you're famous or related to someone who's a professional athlete, people try to get close to you or want things from you. It's something that was really driven home to me in high school. Although looking back, I think I was always cognizant of it."

I clear my throat. He has no idea how close to home this hits. "I can imagine."

"You have to be careful and constantly question people's motives. Even when you've known someone for years." His brows pinch together. "Guess I kind of forgot that. When I was a senior in high school, I started dating this girl."

His lips quirk at the corners and it's so tempting to tease him because I'm shocked that he's gone out with anyone. But there's something about his tone that keeps me silent.

"We attended the same school and had the same circle of friends. We hung out a few times by ourselves and she'd show up to all my games. After about a month or so, I asked her to be my girlfriend, and for a while, everything was cool. Even though I liked her, I knew that we wouldn't attend the same college. We both agreed that it didn't make sense to stay together after senior year." His tongue darts out to moisten his lips. "It was important that we were both on the same page. I didn't want to go away as a freshman and have a long-distance relationship. Not with the pressure of hockey looming over me."

He pauses.

The question shoots out of my mouth before I can stop it. "What happened?"

A mix of emotions crosses his face. Anger. Sadness. Embarrassment. "A few months before graduation, she told me that she was pregnant."

My eyes widen and I bite my lower lip to keep all the questions trapped inside as I wait for him to continue.

"I was upset about the situation but mostly, I felt bad that I was careless and allowed this to happen. I knew my parents would be disappointed. That conversation was probably the most difficult one I've ever had with them."

I squeeze his hand, wanting to bring him back to the present. I can tell that he's getting lost in the memories.

"I bet."

"My mom called Anna's parents right away, wanting them to know that they would pay for whatever was needed for her and the baby. It was important to them to be involved." His lips quirk. "Mom was great. She told me that we'd figure out everything together and that I wasn't in this alone."

"Your mom sounds pretty amazing." Not all parents would react that way. It's doubtful my own would.

His lips quirk slightly. "She is."

If Colby ever mentioned having a child, I'm pretty sure I'd remember it.

And he hasn't.

So that can only mean...

"Over the course of two or three months, my parents shelled out somewhere around a hundred thousand dollars because her family didn't have insurance. Her dad kept pressuring me to set a date and marry Anna, even though we were seniors in high school. He said that they didn't care about a big, fancy wedding." He drags a hand through his hair. "A baby was one thing. Getting married after just turning eighteen was another."

"That's a difficult situation to be in when you're just a kid yourself."

"Yeah. They really applied a lot of pressure. They threatened to go to the news outlets if we didn't give them more money and set a date. Anna missed a lot of school, and I didn't see much of her. I figured it was because she didn't feel good. Morning sickness and stuff like that. So, one night, I decided to stop by her house. Her parents weren't home, and she didn't really want to let me inside. But I said that we had to talk. I needed to see her and get everything hashed out. I was tired of her parents calling all the shots and making unrealistic demands. Even though she was scared, she agreed. She looked terrible. Pale and thinner than I remembered. After I told her that I'd marry her if that's what she really wanted, she broke down and said that she wasn't pregnant. That she'd *never* been pregnant."

My eyes widen as my hand flies to my mouth. "No!"

Air leaks from his lungs until he looks deflated. "Yeah. Her parents put her up to it. They saw it as an easy way to make some cash and set their family up for life."

"Oh god, Colby. That's so terrible. I can't believe something like that happened to you."

"It was a really fucked-up situation. After that, I pulled back and evaluated everyone in my life and whether they could be trusted. It was a tough lesson to learn."

It's so tempting to come clean and admit that I understand exactly what he's talking about. People have tried to use me, and it always hurts because, in the end, it only reinforces that your worth is tied to what you're able to do for someone. How much you're willing to give them. It's disheartening.

Instead, I slip around the table and pull him into my arms. "I'm so sorry that happened to you."

"Thanks. I spent some time after that working with a therapist because I was really pissed off and depressed. It just felt like my trust had been broken and I wasn't sure there was a way to repair the damage."

Guilt mushrooms up inside me.

"It's understandable that you would feel that way. It's so important to talk about what's going on deep inside instead of pretending it doesn't exist."

"Yup, that's what I learned." There's a moment of silence as he pulls away enough to search my eyes. "This isn't a subject I've ever discussed with anyone else besides my family and therapist. But I wanted you to know. It just felt...important."

His brutal honesty is like a gut punch.

I need to tell him the truth.

My tongue darts out to moisten my lips. Before I can work up the nerve, the timer beeps, interrupting our conversation.

I take a step in retreat as he rises to his feet before snagging two mitts from the counter and pulling the pan from the oven. The cheese is perfectly browned as he sets it on the stove to cool.

As delicious as the aroma is, my appetite has vanished. I don't think I could eat a single bite. "It smells really good."

"I promise that it'll taste even better," he says, the heaviness of our previous conversation fading.

I slip back onto my chair before squeezing my eyelids tightly shut. It's only when I sense his presence that I force them open and find him hunkered down in front of me. He reaches out and cups my cheek with one large palm. Solemnity fills his blue depths.

"I'm going to take such good care of you that you'll never want to get loose."

After what he just divulged, it's shocking that he's not the one searching for a way out.

Even though he hasn't admitted it, my guess is that he's still affected by what happened in high school.

In only makes me feel worse than I already do.

When I remain silent, he searches my eyes. "Nothing to say?"

I shake my head. A thick lump gets lodged in my throat, making it impossible to breathe.

He presses close enough to ghost his lips over mine. Neither of us close our eyes. Instead, they stay locked on each other.

"You have no idea how much I'm looking forward to coming home tonight." His voice drops. "To my wife."

Warmth blooms in my chest before spreading outward. There's no way to stop it from seeping into every cell of my being.

"I better get moving. If I'm late, Coach will have us skating suicides." He grimaces before pressing his mouth against mine. "After I get back, I'm going to enjoy that lasagna. I'll also enjoy hearing you tell me how damn good it was." His lips hover over mine again. "And then I'm going to enjoy eating your pussy before sliding deep inside it until you shudder around my cock, milking it until there's nothing left to give."

I drag a shaky breath into my lungs.

He pulls back enough to search my expression before his lips lift into a smirk. "You gonna come nice for me, sweet girl?"

Oh god.

I melt into a puddle every time he calls me that.

I clear my throat and attempt to fight my way out of the Colby-induced haze that has descended.

It's not easy. Especially after what he confided. It would be impossible not to have a better understanding of who the man I married is.

"Maybe. Guess you'll just have to wait and see."

A chuckle slides from his lips. "You're adorable when you're trying to appear unruffled." The fingers of his other hand settle on the vee between my legs before applying enough pressure to get my attention.

I gulp.

"How much do you want to bet that little pussy is already soaked?"

It's not a wager I'd be willing to take.

From the smirk on his handsome face, he knows it.

Is all but reveling in it.

Heat flares in his eyes as he strokes my slit through my jeans. I don't realize that I've widened my legs until he cups my heat. I should be embarrassed by how easily he's able to turn me on, but I'm way too aroused to care.

"Colby." His name comes out sounding more like a whimper.

"What, sweet girl? What do you need?"

Everything.

Everything he's willing to give.

"Bet you'd like to come, wouldn't you?"

My teeth scrape across my lower lip. "Yes," I admit.

His fingers continue to circle, stroking over my clit with every pass. My muscles coil tight with anticipation.

He leans forward, nipping my lower lip with sharp teeth before sucking the plump flesh into his mouth and then releasing it with a soft pop. "Unfortunately, I gotta go."

When his hands fall away and he straightens to his full height, I gasp. "You're just going to leave me?"

A mixture of heat and humor simmers in his eyes as he jerks his thumb toward the door. "Yeah. Gotta get to practice. But don't worry, I'll be back to take care of what I started in a couple of hours."

"Are you being serious?"

"Yup. I already told you that I can't be late."

With that, he swings away, sauntering out of the kitchen and picking up his duffle. As he walks past the doorway again, he flashes a shit-eating grin as if proud of his handiwork.

My jaw is still on the floor.

I can't believe that he fired me all up and then...

And then...

Just walked away!

It's tempting to throw something at his head.

"Oh, and wifey?" There's a beat of silence. "Don't you dare touch that sweet little pussy before I get back. You might not have realized it, but all your orgasms belong to me now," he calls out before closing the door behind him, leaving me alone.

As the silence settles around me, I realize just how turned on I am and how quiet it is in the apartment without him breathing life into the place.

Argh!

I drag a hand through my hair and force out an unsteady breath. It's the delicious scent of cheese, noodles, and sauce that penetrates the thick haze that has fallen over me. Instead of sitting here and stewing, I force myself to pull out a dish and cut a small section from the pan.

Steam rises from the square as I slide it onto my plate and resettle at the table. With the side of my fork, I cut through the layers before raising my utensil to blow on it. When it's cooled, I slide the piece into my mouth.

That one taste is all it takes for my eyelids to feather close as I savor the medley of flavors.

Oh.

My.

God.

He's right.

This is delicious.

Damn him.

He really is a man of many talents.

I tap my foot as the elevator rises to the third floor. Had I been smart, I would have taken the stairs. Then I'd already be inside the apartment with my hands on Britt.

Not to mention my mouth.

As that thought flickers through my brain, I realize just how impatient I am to see her again. The three hours I spent at the arena felt more like an eternity.

During practice, my attention kept wandering to the clock on the scoreboard.

It's the first time I've been distracted at practice.

By a female.

Sharing what happened with her earlier felt right. And I'm not sorry I did it. I want Britt to have a better understanding of who I am. Why I've spent the past four years screwing around and not allowing anyone to get too close.

She's the first person that I want to take a chance on.

Hopefully, now that I've opened up, she'll realize how serious I am and do the same.

The more time we spend together, the more fascinated I find myself. I want to peel back all those layers one by one and figure out who she is beneath it all.

Once the metal doors slide open, I step into the hallway. As sore and tired as I am, I hustle toward her apartment. Anticipation thrums through me until it's all I can think about.

I've never come home from practice to someone waiting for me.

I like it.

More than that, I like *her*.

My heart skips a beat as that thought ricochets throughout my brain.

I pause in front of the door before fishing the key she gave me out of my pocket and shoving it in the lock. Just as I'm about to twist the handle, the sound of a guitar drifts from within the apartment.

I pause and press my ear to the door, straining to hear the notes.

After a handful of seconds, her voice accompanies the instrument. A shiver scampers down my spine as I flatten even more against the wood. I'm catapulted back to the Vegas flight.

My eyelids feather shut as both the guitar and her husky voice wash over me.

And here she tried to tell me that she barely played.

Little liar.

It's obvious from the minute or so I've been standing here that she has natural ability.

So why downplay it?

Why not own it?

Britt has never struck me as insecure or a shrinking violet.

I almost snort.

Quite the opposite.

She has confidence in spades, and it's sexy as hell.

It takes a few moments to realize that she's singing the same song as before. Now that I'm not freaking out, I'm able to focus on the lyrics and melody. It's not something I recognize.

Did Britt write it herself?

The question circles around in my brain. It only adds to the growing list where she's concerned.

I squeeze my eyes closed and refocus on the song. I might not be able to recognize it, but there's something familiar about her voice. Almost as if I've heard her sing something else with a faster beat.

With a frown, I smash myself against the door. Maybe then I'll be able to—

"Hi, Colby!"

Startled from my thoughts, I bang my head against the wood.

Fuck.

My teeth sink into my lower lip to keep the string of curse words trapped inside before straightening to my full height and pretending like I wasn't just standing here, trying to eavesdrop.

Although, it seems much too late for that.

"Hey, Lance. What's up? How's everything going?"

He beams in response, the smile overtaking his expression. "You remembered my name. I wasn't sure if you would."

I shrug. "Of course I remembered. We hung out and had a good time."

He glances at the apartment I'm loitering in front of. "So...are you and Britt dating now?"

Dating my wife?

Guess I am.

"Um, yeah. Something like that."

Here's hoping he doesn't ask her the same question, because it's doubtful our answers would match up.

"That's cool." His brows slide together as his nose twitches. "You know...Britt is a good friend of mine."

I tilt my head, wondering where this conversation is going. "Uh huh."

His tongue darts out to lick his lips. "And I don't want to see her get hurt."

I force a smile. "I have no intention of hurting her."

He mulls over my answer for a second or two. "But it could happen anyway."

"You're right," I admit. "It could. But I'll do my best not to cause her any pain. Promise."

"You're the first guy I've seen her spend time with since she moved in."

"Oh?" I can't help but like that.

Even if I'm forcing her to do it.

With a nod, he steps closer and drops his voice. "I was hoping that

maybe something would happen between us, but it never did."
There's a pause. "I think we're probably better off as friends. You
know?"

"Sorry it didn't work out. She's lucky to have you in her life,
watching out for her."

His chest puffs up at the compliment. "Nah, I'm the lucky one.
There are a lot of girls around here who won't even give me the time
of day, but Britt isn't like that. She's cool and down to earth."

"Yeah," I agree. "She is."

His eyes turn serious as they bore into mine. "Which is why you'll
answer to me if you hurt her." He cracks the knuckles of both hands.
"I hope you understand."

My brows skyrocket. It's tempting to ask if he's playing around,
but I can see by his stony expression that he's as serious as a heart
attack.

"You have my word," I say solemnly.

He nods before clapping me on the arm as his face transforms
back into a smile. "Good. I'm glad we could have this little chat."

Ahhh...

"Yeah, me too."

Just as I'm about to turn the key, he nods toward the apartment.
"She's pretty talented, isn't she?"

"She really is." The question shoots out of my mouth before I can
stop it. "You've heard her play before?"

"A couple times after we finish studying. She's been working on a
new song. I told her that after she finishes it, we should video it so
people can take a listen. Who knows, maybe she'd get famous." He
shrugs. "Or, at the very least, find a few followers."

Curiosity eats at me. "What was her response?"

"That she wasn't interested in finding followers. She just wanted
to focus on creating music."

Huh.

Interesting.

Most people would do just about anything to find a little fame.
Especially if they have a talent that can be exploited on social media.

It's just another example of how different this girl is. Sometimes it feels like the more I learn, the less I understand.

As tempting as it is to pump Lance for more intel, I'm impatient to see Britt.

I jerk my head toward the door. "I should probably get moving, but I'll catch you soon, all right?"

"Yup." He takes a few steps toward his own apartment before swinging around with a cheery smile. "Remember what I said."

He's joking, right?

It's not every day that someone threatens me with bodily harm.

"It would be hard to forget," I mutter, twisting the key and stepping inside the entryway. The fragrant aroma of lasagna still hangs heavy in the air.

If I closed my eyes, it would feel like home.

Mom would be proud.

It's only when I step farther into the beautifully decorated space that I realize Britt is curled up on the couch with a textbook splayed open on her lap. Her guitar is propped against the wall in a corner.

"Hi," she says.

"Hey." I nod toward the well-loved instrument that looks as if it's seen better days. "Were you just playing?"

Her gaze flickers away for a second or two as she shakes her head. "Nope."

Caught off guard by the lie, disappointment flares inside me before I stomp it down.

"Huh. That's weird. Pretty sure I heard music coming from inside."

Instead of responding, she sets the book on the coffee table and jumps to her feet. "Do you want something to eat?"

Before I can respond, she slips past me and swings into the tiny kitchen. Unable to help myself, I drop my bag in the living room and gravitate toward her. It's like there's an invisible string connecting us.

I'm beginning to wonder if there's anywhere she could lead that I won't follow.

She opens a cabinet door and pulls out a plate before beelining to the stove where the pan sits. I peek over her shoulder and notice that one slice is missing.

When she spins around, nearly crashing into my chest, our gazes catch and hold. Every muscle tightens, going on high alert. I'm waiting for the smallest sign that she wants to finish what we started before I took off earlier. It's all I've been able to think about.

Maybe I shouldn't have left her hanging...

Or maybe I just want her to feel even a tenth of the need that courses through me where she's concerned.

One agonizing heartbeat passes and then another before she clears her throat. The growing tension between us dissolves as she thrusts the plate toward my chest.

The smile she flashes looks strained around the edges. "Here you go."

"Thanks." I glance down and realize that she's given me two thick wedges.

"I bet you're hungry," she says by way of explanation.

"Starving." My gaze remains fastened to hers. "But not for this."

Her eyes widen and the delicate lines of her throat constrict as she swallows.

My brain trips back to the weekend in Vegas and the way she looked on her knees, staring up at me as she took my cock.

Said appendage twitches and rises in my sweatpants with growing interest.

She tucks a stray lock of caramel-colored hair behind her ear. "What are you hungry for?"

"You."

I set the plate on the counter before eating up the distance between us. And then my hands are cupping her cheeks, and my mouth is crashing onto hers. That's all it takes for her sweetness to flood my senses until I'm dizzy with it.

How I walked away earlier, I have no idea.

Everything about this girl consumes me.

Our tongues tangle as our teeth scrape. Arousal pumps through every cell of my being.

When we finally come up for air, she gasps, "Colby..."

"Tell me, sweet girl...did you miss me as much as I missed you?"

I nip her lower lip with my teeth before peppering kisses across her face.

"I wish I could say no."

Satisfaction swells inside me like an overinflated balloon. I was half expecting her to tell me the same and that I'd have to fight her to admit the truth.

It's a relief that we've moved past that.

"But you can't."

She shakes her head. "No."

"And you hate it."

"I really do," she admits with a sigh.

A grin spreads across my face. "Good. It would seem like my evil plan is working."

Her lips quirk. "Unfortunately, I think you might be right."

In the darkest nights, I stumbled, couldn't see the light.
Lost in a maze, couldn't find what's right.
But deep inside, a fire burned,
Refusing to fade away.
A voice inside me whispered, 'You'll find your way.'

I'm rising up, stronger now than I've ever been.
Every scar's a story, ain't letting them win.
Through the ups and downs, I'll find my truth.
In the chaos of it all, I'll find my youth.

Through every fall and every doubt, I'll stand tall.
Gonna shake off the past, gonna give it my all.
With each new day, leaving old fears behind.
Embracing every challenge, gonna free my mind.

BRITT

26

I pinch my eyes shut as the muscles in my lower abdomen cramp. It feels like they're being squeezed in a vise.

That's all it takes for a whimper to escape from me.

Most months are like this.

Some are worse than others.

This one is bad.

Really bad.

Bad enough that I didn't even attempt my nine o'clock class this morning. Instead, I shot my instructor an email to let her know that I wasn't feeling well. Colby rolled out of bed as streaks of orange and red painted the horizon with vibrant color. He kissed me and said something about getting to an early morning practice and that he'd be back later.

That was hours ago.

I'd fallen back to sleep for a little bit.

Now I have a headache and lower back pain to go with a side of cramps.

Ugh.

Sometimes being a girl sucks.

This is one of those times.

At some point, I'll have to find the wherewithal to haul myself from bed and go to the store for supplies. I'm down to two regular tampons. I have the sneaking suspicion this one is going to call for super plus absorbent.

Just as I'm dozing off, the apartment door opens and heavy foot-steps fill the silence of the space before stuttering to a stop over the threshold of the room.

"Hey, what are you still doing in bed? I thought you had class this morning."

I crack open my eyes and meet his concerned stare. "I don't feel good."

I refrain from getting into specifics. If he's anything like Axel, he doesn't want to hear about "girl issues."

Colby's brows furrow as he beelines toward the bed and drops down on the edge. His palm settles on my forehead. "Do you have the flu?" His eyes scrutinize my face. "You don't feel warm. Tell me what's going on."

Even through the pain, I can't help the smile that quirks my lips. "Are you a doctor now?"

A matching expression settles on his. "We both know that if you're in need of a thorough examination, I'd be more than happy to provide one free of charge. Although, I'll need to get you naked."

I wince as another cramp racks my belly.

Argh.

It's like my insides are being twisted.

"I don't think that's going to be happening anytime soon."

"You have your period?"

Heat floods my cheeks. It's certainly nothing to be embarrassed about, but still...

"Yup. Seems like you arrived at the correct diagnosis, Dr. McNi-chols. Now, if you'll just leave—"

"You should have told me what was going on. What do you need?"

My brow furrows. "Need? I don't understand."

He reaches out and strokes his fingers through my hair. I can't help but lean into the comforting touch, enjoying how easy he is with his affection.

"All right. Let's go about this a different way. Describe your symptoms."

"I, ah..."

Is he joking?

When he arches a brow, I realize he's one hundred percent serious.

I clear my throat and glance away. "I really appreciate your concern, but this isn't something we need to discuss."

"Why not?" Confusion flickers across his handsome features. "How else am I going to make it better if I don't know what your symptoms are?"

My gaze slices back to his in surprise. "Make it better?" I echo, unsure I heard him correctly.

"Yeah. Depending on what they are, I'll either give you ibuprofen, acetaminophen, or one of those combo meds that has caffeine in it."

When I continue to stare in silence, he rolls his eyes as if I'm too dense for words. "Please don't tell me that you're embarrassed. I have a sister and a mom. It's a monthly occurrence. No way to avoid it."

My brow furrows, unable to believe we're delving headfirst into this topic. "So...you'd get them stuff?"

He pops a shoulder and continues stroking my hair. "Why wouldn't I? It wasn't out of the ordinary for my sister to get really bad cramps. Sometimes she'd have to get picked up from school because they were so painful. If she needed something and my parents weren't around, I'd run to the store and grab it." He searches my eyes as his voice softens. "It wasn't a big deal."

I shake my head. "It's times like these when I realize that I don't know who the hell you are."

He snorts.

"Or maybe you're just really different from the guy I assumed you were."

"Maybe your takeaway should be that we need to actually get to know one another before making snap judgments," he murmurs.

"You could be right."

He cups my cheek. "Did you take pain meds yet?"

I nod. "A couple hours ago."

"Are you still having bad cramps?"

"They're like knives slicing through my belly."

"Ouch. All right, I'm going to run to the store and pick up a few things." His thumb sweeps over my lower lip before he rises to his feet. "Is there anything else you need while I'm out?"

I glance away, watching him from the corner of my eye.

God, but I hate to ask...

He cocks his head and continues to watch me.

This is so embarrassing.

"Pads or tampons?"

Air rushes from my lungs. It's like a balloon deflating. "Tampons."

"What size?"

"The biggest ones you can find."

"No problem." He reaches down and strokes his fingers through my hair one more time before pressing a kiss against my lips. "I'll be right back. If there's anything that comes to mind while I'm out, text me. Okay?"

I nod, grateful he's here.

And isn't making a big deal out of this.

Thirty minutes later, Colby returns with a couple of grocery bags in tow. He sets the first one down on the bed as I drag myself to a seated position, curious about what he picked up. What he thinks a girl with her period needs.

This should be interesting.

As long as he bought tampons, it's all good.

Nothing else matters.

He settles on the edge of the mattress before delving one hand into the plastic and pulling out the first item.

It's a small box of pills.

"Those combo meds I was talking about. Not only do they help with headaches and cramps but bloating, fatigue, and muscle aches as well."

My brows rise. "I've always just taken acetaminophen."

He turns the box over. "This one has that but other things as well."

He passes the container to me so I can read the list of active ingredients for myself.

"I wasn't sure how much the cramps were bothering you, so I bought some hot and cold patches."

When my face scrunches, he says, "You peel and stick them on your lower abdomen. They're mentholated and will help with the cramps. My sister swears by them."

Huh. I've never used anything like that.

He reaches into the bag again before pulling out an oversized package of pads.

"It's the multi-pack." He taps the colorful wrapper. "This has everything from light to heavy."

Then he adds a couple of blue boxes with a sporty looking woman on them. "I know you said heavy duty, but there was a sale. Buy two and get a third for free. There's a variety. I figured you'd use them at some point."

The tampons run the gamut from tiny and light to oversized and super-duper absorbent.

"I wasn't sure if you had a gelled eye mask for headaches, so I grabbed one of those as well."

I shake my head and fight back the tears that are threatening to fill my eyes. Stupid hormones. "I can't believe you bought all this. I really appreciate it."

"I'm your husband. That's what we do." He flashes a lopsided grin. "Plus, there's more."

"More? How's that possible?"

What more could there be to buy?

He reaches into the bag again and pulls out an oversized chocolate bar.

"Did you know that dark chocolate is rich in magnesium? Apparently, that helps relax uterine contractions."

Laughter gurgles up in my throat. "Are you being serious?"

"One hundred percent. Plus, it just tastes good. I'd challenge anyone to eat chocolate and not feel better."

Well, the man makes a valid point.

"And lastly, I noticed that you have a Kindle. So, I picked up a gift card. That way you can buy a few books and get your mind off everything. I've never been much of a reader, but isn't that what books do? Transport you to another place?"

"Colby..." My voice trails off as thick emotion fills it. "Thank you."

I really didn't expect any of this from him.

More than that, I can't remember the last time someone took care of me in this kind of manner. As if I were important.

"You have sisters," he says, interrupting the whirl of my thoughts. "I'm surprised your family didn't do the same."

This time, I do bark out a laugh. "No. My mom was a nurse and would give us painkillers, but she always acted like that time of the month wasn't a big deal and you didn't whine about it. Instead, you powered through and kept working."

Colby frowns. "Well, that sucks. If you're in pain or have symptoms, they need to be treated."

How is this man for real?

"You're being too good to me," I force myself to whisper when I've got my emotions under control.

"You're my wife," he says simply. "All I want to do is be good to you."

He rises to his feet and heads for my bathroom. "I'm going to run you a hot shower. After that, we'll apply a patch to your belly, and I bought some soup for lunch. Then you can download a new book or take a nap. Up to you."

I can only stare as he saunters out of the room. After a few heartbeats, my gaze falls on everything he bought that's still spread out on the bed.

Even though I've never been much of a crier, I burst into tears.

IN THE DARKEST NIGHTS, I STUMBLED, COULDN'T SEE THE LIGHT.
LOST IN A MAZE, COULDN'T FIND WHAT'S RIGHT.
BUT DEEP INSIDE, A FIRE BURNED,
REFUSING TO FADE AWAY.
A VOICE INSIDE ME WHISPERED, 'YOU'LL FIND YOUR WAY.'

I'M RISING UP, STRONGER NOW THAN I'VE EVER BEEN.
EVERY SCAR'S A STORY, AIN'T LETTING THEM WIN.
THROUGH THE UPS AND DOWNS, I'LL FIND MY TRUTH.
IN THE CHAOS OF IT ALL, I'LL FIND MY YOUTH.

THROUGH EVERY FALL AND EVERY DOUBT, I'LL STAND TALL.
GONNA SHAKE OFF THE PAST, GONNA GIVE IT MY ALL.
WITH EACH NEW DAY, LEAVING OLD FEARS BEHIND.
EMBRACING EVERY CHALLENGE, GONNA FREE MY MIND.

BRITT

I t's been a week since my period, and weird as it sounds, that's when everything shifted between us. It's like tumbling down a hill.

I couldn't stop it from happening even if I wanted to.

There's a part of me that wonders if I still want to untangle myself from this man.

The biggest shocker in all this is that I actually like Colby McNichols.

No one's more surprised by this turn of events than me.

There were times last semester when I'd catch sight of him strutting around campus with his posse of puck bunnies and would roll my eyes. He came across as a player who was more than happy to take advantage of the groupie situation.

And maybe that was true. But what I've learned over the previous few weeks is that there's more to him than meets the eye.

Here's a bit of irony that hasn't escaped me—I hate being judged and dismissed because of what people think they know. And that's exactly what I did with him. I slapped a few labels on the guy and deemed him not worthy of my time.

Trust me, that epiphany hurt.

The other night when I couldn't get comfortable, he reached over and started stroking my pussy. When I told him that I wasn't interested in having sex because the bed would end up looking like a crime scene investigation, he smiled and said that he didn't care.

Even though it was tempting, I declined the offer.

Axel was always so weird about doing it when I had my period.

Instead of pulling away, he continued to caress me, telling me that an orgasm would help with the menstrual cramping. So, while I was wearing a tampon, he stroked my clit until I came with an explosive rush.

And I'll be damned if he wasn't right.

It did ease the cramping.

Someone needs to explain to me who the hell I married because I really don't know.

It's given me serious pause.

I've started to wonder if this is a relationship worth pursuing.

If that turns out to be the case…then I'll have to come clean and tell Colby the truth. We can't build a foundation on top of lies.

If that's what we're actually doing…

It feels crazy that I'm considering making this situation permanent.

"Ready for bed?"

My heart leaps into my throat as I blink back to the present and find Colby standing in the room, wearing nothing more than a pair of form-fitting boxers that leave very little to the imagination.

He's like the sun. Staring directly at him for prolonged periods of time will end up burning my retinas.

He's just so beautiful.

Chiseled perfection.

"Um, yeah."

A slow smile lifts the corners of his lips as the intensity of his gaze sharpens. "Feeling better?"

I nod as everything inside me softens.

A lot of that is thanks to him. He really stepped up and offered support when I needed it. Even if it was just for my period, his thoughtfulness meant the world to me. It's impossible to sweep that aside and pretend it never happened.

"Good. I'm glad."

Unsure what to say, I blurt, "You'd make an excellent boyfriend."

He gives me a funny look. "Or husband."

Heat scalds my cheeks. "Right. Sorry. Guess I forgot."

"Then I must be doing something wrong." He pads to the bed before slipping beneath the covers and patting the place next to him. "Come here. Let's see if I can rectify that situation."

As soon as I settle on the mattress, he wraps his hands around my waist and hoists me onto his lap until I'm straddling his thighs. My legs end up on either side of his torso so that we're facing one another.

My tongue darts out to moisten my lips. "What are you doing?"

"I haven't laid my hands on you for a couple of days, and I miss it."

"You gave me an orgasm the other morning," I remind.

He smirks. "So I did. But my cock misses being inside my wife's perfect little pussy."

Liquid heat pools in my core at his dirty words.

Truth be told, I've missed it as well. All the orgasms he's given me this week have been amazing, but I miss his thick length filling me until I can't take another inch.

A shiver slides through me as that image somersaults through my brain and my hips unconsciously rotate until I'm squirming against his hard thighs and groin. That's all it takes for him to stiffen up.

His eyes lower to half-mast. "Mmm. That's exactly what I've been missing, sweet girl."

My palms settle on the warm skin of his chest. I can't help but stroke them across all those sinewy muscles.

His fingers flex, biting into my flesh. He studies me, his gaze sifting through mine as if he's able to glimpse my innermost thoughts. I've always been so good at keeping them buried deep down.

Whether it's a conscious decision on his part or not, Colby makes me feel seen.

Which doesn't make sense. It's not like we've known each other very long and yet...

His eyes hold mine ensnared. "Tell me what's going through your head."

I blurt out the truth before I can overthink it. "There aren't many people who see me. *The real me.* And I think you just might."

The corners of his lips tip upward as if he's pleased by the admittance. "You're right. I do. And when we're together, you're all I see. When we're apart, you dominate every fucking waking thought. For the first time in my life, I want something more than hockey." There's a beat of silence. "I want you."

The soft words are so unexpected that hearing them is like getting the air knocked from my lungs and leaves me feeling stunned.

When I remain silent, at a loss, one hand snakes around the nape of my neck before pulling me forward until his lips crash onto mine. As soon as we collide, I open. Impatience simmers through my veins. His tongue slips inside my mouth to tangle with my own. It's as if he's intent on devouring me. There's so much possessiveness in his touch and I love it.

Love how much he wants me.

Wants this.

His hold tightens as his hungry mouth roves over mine. Everything inside me melts as his other hand drops to his boxers and he shoves the cottony material down until his thick erection can spring free. He hooks the fabric of my panties with one finger before yanking it to the side.

He breaks free long enough to growl, "I need to feel your pussy wrapped around my dick, choking the life out of it."

Those words have my inner muscles contracting around nothingness. Like him, I need him inside my body, filling me to the brim. I shift, squirming as hot licks of need rush through me.

In this moment, everything around us falls away.

There's only him.

And me.

It wasn't so long ago when I felt that nothing was better than lyrics melding together perfectly with the notes of my guitar to create a song.

I was wrong.

This is a thousand times better.

His hands wrap around my hips, lifting and shifting until he's able to slide deep inside my pussy. Until he's buried to the hilt and soft sighs of contentment escape from both of us.

"Fuck, baby. You feel so damn amazing."

He keeps me locked in place as if he doesn't want me to move a single muscle.

Not even a twitch.

Our eyes stay fastened.

There's nothing more intimate than holding someone's gaze while they're buried deep inside the heat of your body.

It goes without saying that Colby McNichols is gorgeous.

But the expression on his face?

The unspoken emotion that fills it during such intimacy?

Even more so.

"There's no way I could ever grow tired of this," he says with a groan.

I can't imagine that happening either.

"I'm going to fuck you nice and slow, sweet girl. I'm going to show you exactly how much I want this. I want *you*." He finally shifts, pulling out just a bit before sliding back in. "And when I'm done, you won't question any of it. You'll just know. Like I do."

Tears prick the backs of my eyes.

It takes effort to blink them away and not allow them to fall.

What is this guy doing to me?

He rolls his hips again. On the upward stroke, he growls, "You're my wife. You belong to me. Do you understand?"

I bite my lip as he does it again, picking up tempo.

Every time he drives inside me, he repeats the words like a mantra.

His hands loosen from around my hips before drifting upward until his fingers can play with my nipples. It doesn't take long before they're hard little points that beg for his attention.

"You're my wife," he says more forcefully as he tweaks both sensitive buds in tandem, making me cry out with pain wrapped up in pleasure.

When I bite my lower lip, his palms settle on my cheeks as he continues to flex, hitting a spot deep within. I'm so close to splintering apart. It won't take much before I'm teetering on the precipice. And then, like Humpty Dumpty, no one will ever be able to put me back together again.

In this position, I feel everything. It ricochets throughout my being before echoing in my fingertips and toes. When it all becomes too much, my eyelids drift shut, needing to savor every delicious sensation.

"Open your eyes, sweet girl. I want you to see exactly who's fucking you."

I follow the directive and meet the steeliness that shines in his blue depths. Only then does he withdraw before surging forward until he's buried deep.

"Tell me who you belong to."

When he repeats the movement, his thick length filling me to the very brim, a whimper escapes from me.

His hands tighten around the sides of my head as he drags me closer. "Tell me," he growls. "Tell me that you're my wife. That my cock is the only one this pussy will ever need."

His dirty words only push me closer to the edge.

He grinds against me.

With each new thrust, he repeats the command.

As turned on as he is, he pulls almost all the way out and holds perfectly still. His jaw is tightly clenched as his eyes glitter.

"Tell me right now whose wife you are, or you won't get fucked."

I gasp.

My inner muscles twitch, clenching with the need to lock around his erection. It's the only thought that pounds through my head. He's done the unthinkable and reduced me to a quivering mass of hormones. Nothing else matters at this moment but the insatiable need I have for him to drive inside me, fucking me into oblivion.

"Please, Colby," I sob, wriggling around on his lap, trying to draw him deeper inside my pussy.

But he holds himself back, making it impossible.

Every cell feels as if it's been charged with electricity. As if it's traveling through my body, searching for an escape.

The feel of it is agonizing.

"Say it. Tell me who you belong to."

The head of his erection stays poised against my opening.

I try in vain to clench around him.

How can he stand this torture?

How can he hold himself back?

While he's made me orgasm every day this week, sometimes multiple times, he hasn't come at all.

The muscle in his jaw ticks a mad rhythm.

It's the only telltale sign that he's fighting himself just as much as he's fighting me.

It's become a battle of wills.

A standoff.

One I won't win.

One, I realize, I don't want to win.

He drags my face even closer until his mouth can collide with mine. His tongue licks at the seam of my lips before shoving inside. There's the scrape of teeth as the kiss turns frenzied. My hips buck against his, searching for relief.

He pulls away just enough to stare into my eyes. "Don't you want me, sweet girl?"

"You know I do."

Doubt flickers in his expression.

It's enough to kill me.

"Then say it. Give yourself over to me."

"I want you, Colby."

His palms tighten around my cheeks to hold me in place. "Tell me that you're my wife."

Even though I should keep some distance between us until he

knows the truth, I can't help but blurt, "I'm your wife. I belong to you."

With those seven little words, he surges deep inside me until we're fused together.

It's like a detonation within my core, and an orgasm explodes throughout my being. The force of it nearly robs my lungs of oxygen. As soon as I cry out, he tumbles over the edge. His hands stay locked around my head as our gazes remain fastened the entire time.

"My wife," he chants over and over until I have no choice but to believe that this will end up being our reality.

That it can't turn out any other way.

No matter the obstacles that seem insurmountable.

No matter what secrets I have yet to share.

The arena buzzes with anticipation as I jump onto the ice for warmups. The puck drops in thirty minutes and already the stands are packed. It's a sea of orange and black. Heavy rock pumps through the loudspeakers in an attempt to hype the crowd. When the fans are amped, the energy in the arena turns electric, making us feel invincible on the ice.

There's nothing unusual about the adrenaline humming through my veins.

But tonight, it's more than just pregame jitters.

As I circle our half of the ice with my stick lying against my shoulders, taking long strides to stretch my muscles, my gaze combs over the spectators, looking for one person in particular.

It's been a long time since I've invited someone to watch me play.

For the past four years, I've closed myself off emotionally, not wanting to get hurt again.

But Britt is worth taking a chance on.

Not because I drunkenly tied myself to her in a spur-of-the-moment decision.

But because I actually like her and want this to work.

The longer I go without spotting her in the stands, the more it messes with my head until she's all I can think about.

Focus on.

I've never experienced anything like this before.

Not even with Anna.

She never felt like the beginning and end of my world.

Britt is different.

I realized it the first time I laid eyes on her.

All it took was one conversation to confirm it.

Maybe I was able to force her into admitting that she belongs to me and is my wife the other night in bed, but it's not enough. I want her to say it because that's how she truly feels.

Not because I'm holding her orgasm hostage.

Sometimes, it feels like I'm walking a tightrope. I'm trying to show her how amazing we could be so she'll give us an honest shot. But I'm also trying to give her the time and space to wrap her head around what I've already accepted.

That we belong together.

It's not like I was looking for a relationship senior year of college, months from when everything in my world will change, but that's exactly what happened. And I'll do everything in my power to make it work.

As I loop around for a second time, I'm slammed with the realization that Britt might not show up. Sure, I'd thrown out the invitation and she'd agreed, but that doesn't necessarily mean she'll do it.

Maybe she forgot.

Or is busy doing something else.

Like scouring the internet for divorce attorneys.

Even the thought terrifies me.

There's only so many times I can force her to say that she's my wife and I'm her husband while we're having sex.

Fun fact—it gets me off every fucking time.

Who would have thought?

It's only when Hayes pulls up alongside me that I force my attention to him.

His gaze searches mine from behind his visor. "You good?"

I jerk my head into a tight nod. "Of course. Why wouldn't I be?"

"I don't know." He shrugs his padded shoulders. "You seem distracted."

Fuck.

He's right.

I didn't think it was noticeable.

"Nope. Not at all."

I hold my breath, hoping he'll do me a solid and drop the topic.

Should have known better.

"Does this have anything to do with the chick you're shacked up with?"

"Her name is Britt," I snap, tension gathering in my muscles and straining against my skin. Any moment, it'll burst free.

She's not just some chick.

Although...Hayes doesn't know that.

Mostly because I haven't said a word about it.

Or her.

Everything with this relationship has been on the downlow because that's what Britt wanted. Only now do I realize how much it bugs me. I don't want to hide this like it's a dirty little secret.

Like *I'm* a dirty little secret.

There's no reason we can't tell our friends that we're dating.

We don't have to necessarily share that we tied the knot in Vegas.

At least, not right away.

Yup, this is definitely a convo we'll be having later.

"Right. Britt. So, it's serious then?"

I stare straight ahead, refusing to respond.

Until everything is hashed out with her, I'm not saying a damn word.

Although, I want to.

When I remain silent, he glances at the stands. "Is that why she's wearing your jersey?"

I swing around so fast that I nearly take myself out. Hayes' laughter rings unwantedly in my ears.

Fucker.

"Tell me you've fallen for a girl without telling me you've fallen for a girl."

I knock into him with my shoulder.

Hard.

"Asshole."

She's not there.

The guy is screwing with me.

"You need to get your head out of your ass and focus on what's important." He stares at me as if I'm pitiful. And at the moment, that's exactly how I feel. It's not good. "You're the last person I expected this from." He glances at our teammates. "Everyone around here seems to be getting wifed up. It's like an epidemic."

Wifed up.

Hayes would shit a brick if I admitted the truth.

Actually, all the guys on the team would.

As tempting as it is to blow his world apart at the seams, I clap him on the back instead. "Thanks for your concern, but there's nothing to worry about. It's all good."

"It better fucking be. We need to bring home a championship this year. Our final season before we graduate."

A prick of sadness fills me. I've been playing hockey since kindergarten. As soon as I could walk, dad laced up my first pair of Bauers. And I've been a part of more house and travel teams than I can remember. But these guys?

They're like brothers to me.

There's nothing I wouldn't do for them.

Someone needs to bury a body?

I'll bring my shovel.

It's like *that.*

I force those thoughts aside before refocusing on Hayes. "It'll happen. Everyone's gelling on the ice and we're only getting better. There's no way we won't take home a Frozen Four championship."

"All right, man." His easy disposition returns as humor flashes in his eyes. "Just so you know, I wasn't kidding before. Your girl really is here."

I snort, unwilling to be suckered for a second time, and look like an even bigger pussy. "Uh huh. Whatever you say."

With a grin, he raises a gloved hand toward the stands and waves. "And she's seriously wearing your jersey."

The guy is a total moron if he thinks I'm going to fall for this again. Maybe I'm turning out to be a simp, but Hayes doesn't need to know it. It takes every ounce of self-control not to turn and scan the bleachers for the umpteenth time.

It's only when I round the corner that I allow my gaze to comb over the crowd with more care. Even though I've spent the past couple weeks doing everything in my power to prove that I can be the husband she needs, I need to accept that Britt's not there yet.

For some reason, she's holding back.

Something is standing between us.

And I'll be damned if I don't figure it out so that it's no longer in my way. I'll tear down her walls brick by brick with my bare hands if that's what it comes to.

As those thoughts settle within me, I catch sight of her sitting with Juliette, Carina, Viola, Stella, and Fallyn. Or the girlfriends, as they'd become known in the locker room.

Looks like Hayes was telling the truth.

Even better than that...she really is wearing my jersey.

The one I was too chickenshit to give her because I was afraid she'd turn me down flat.

Or worse, laugh in my face.

But there she is with the wildcat emblem on the front and my number stamped on the sleeves. Pride swells within me. The sight of her sends a thrill shooting down my spine as a surge of warmth spreads through my body, invading every cell like a virus.

My lips lift into a smile.

She looks fucking gorgeous. Almost as good as she did spread out naked beneath me.

It makes me wish I'd swallowed my pride and given it to her myself.

Our gazes stay fastened as I skate past.

The moment is broken when Hayes claps me on the shoulder. "I hate to break this to you, but you're fucked."

I don't bother to deny it, because deep down I know he's right.

I'm totally fucked.

Seeing her ass in the stands, wearing my jersey, only slams it home with more force until there's not a single doubt in my mind.

The players from both teams vacate the ice as the lights are dimmed and the music gets cranked until it echoes throughout the arena and vibrates in my ears. The visiting team is announced and then it's the Wildcats' turn. The bright glare of the spotlight falls on each player as they skate to center ice to wait for their teammates.

Even though I can't see the stands, I know that the fans are on their feet cheering. The place hums with pent-up energy just waiting for the opportunity to break loose. I might not be able to see Britt, but I know she's there.

The heat of her gaze sears my flesh as if it were a physical caress.

Once the arena is illuminated, the first line takes their places. Wolf does a few final stretches before lowering his center of gravity and waiting for the puck to get dropped. It's easy to see that the guy is in his zone.

A fresh burst of nerves explodes in the pit of my belly as I wait near the red center line. This is the first time since I've been playing hockey that it felt like they might eat me alive.

And it has everything to do with the girl watching me.

The one who's now my wife.

My wife.

It's a dizzying thought.

As soon as the puck gets dropped, Hayes fights for possession before passing it to me. The second the small black disc touches the end of my stick, I take off. My blades dig into the smooth surface as I race to the other side of the ice. When a defenseman swarms, I pass to Ford.

We've watched a shit ton of game film this week and know what a solid team the Eagles have this season and what to expect. It makes me realize that we'll have to dig deep and fight hard if we're going to dominate.

This win won't be handed to us on a silver platter.

It'll have to be wrestled from their hands.

Sweat trickles down the back of my neck during the second

period as I race off the ice for a shift change and guzzle down water. Even though my attention is focused on the game, I'm still aware of Britt. I want her to see that I'm a difference maker when I'm out there.

I want her to wear my jersey with pride.

Toward the end of the third period, the score is tied 2-2. I glance at the clock. There's only a few minutes left before the final buzzer rings.

I can tell from the expressions on my teammates' faces that they're gassed. It's been a rough couple of hours.

But we're all still out there, working our asses off.

We haven't given up.

And we're not about to.

We won't stop until the final buzzer.

I might bitch and complain about how grueling practice can be, but it's times like these that I'm glad Coach skates us until the younger guys are red-faced and puking, barely able to stand upright. There's always a few who don't come back after their freshman season because they weren't prepared for this level of practice and play.

It takes dedication and work.

There are guys who think the new coach is a hardass who wants to make our lives miserable, but that's not the case.

Well, maybe it is.

But there's a method to his madness.

The harder you work during practice, the more conditioned you are for the games, the easier it is to dig deep and find just a little bit more to give. Instead of concentrating on the exhaustion attempting to suck you under, you draw on the mental fortitude and toughness it takes to get through five AM practices and two-a-days in the offseason.

Our old coach was good.

Really good.

But Coach Philips is better.

He's drilled us into the ground and built us back up again.

I glance around.

And it's worked.

As fatigued as these guys are, they have just a little bit more in the tank to give.

Will it be enough?

No idea.

But I wouldn't bet against us.

Ryder slams an Eagles' attackman into the boards and knocks the puck loose. The sound of the hit reverberates throughout the arena. Bridger scoops it up before passing it off to Ford, who drives toward the opponent's net. Defensemen descend, and the puck goes flying. Fans jump to their feet, wanting to get a better view of the action that's unfolding on the ice. The tension and excitement in the arena escalates until it turns suffocating.

From the bench, Coach bellows as Maverick knocks into a player and passes the black disc to me. As soon as it lands on the blade of my stick, my skates dig into the ice. My pulse quickens as my heartbeat pounds in my ears and I focus on the goal. Ford bodies up a player long enough for me to rip off a shot. Air gets clogged in my throat and time slows as I wait to see if it'll go in or not.

The seconds on the clock tick down.

The goalie slides, raising a gloved hand. The puck grazes the tip before sailing past and hitting the net.

Ford claps me on the back. "Fuck yeah, baby. I could kiss you right now!"

Relief crashes over me as I laugh. My gaze slides over the cheering spectators before locking on Britt. With a smile, I point to her and the crowd roars its approval.

With a shake of his head, Hayes singsongs what he'd said earlier. "Tell me you've fallen for a girl without telling me you've fallen for a girl."

I do the only thing I can and flash him a smile because I'm tired of denying it.

I've fallen for a girl.

I've fallen for my wife.

IN THE DARKEST NIGHTS, I STUMBLED, COULDN'T SEE THE LIGHT.
LOST IN A MAZE, COULDN'T FIND WHAT'S RIGHT.
BUT DEEP INSIDE, A FIRE BURNED,
REFUSING TO FADE AWAY.
A VOICE INSIDE ME WHISPERED, 'YOU'LL FIND YOUR WAY.'

I'M RISING UP, STRONGER NOW THAN I'VE EVER BEEN.
EVERY SCAR'S A STORY, AIN'T LETTING THEM WIN.
THROUGH THE UPS AND DOWNS, I'LL FIND MY TRUTH.
IN THE CHAOS OF IT ALL, I'LL FIND MY YOUTH.

THROUGH EVERY FALL AND EVERY DOUBT, I'LL STAND TALL.
GONNA SHAKE OFF THE PAST, GONNA GIVE IT MY ALL.
WITH EACH NEW DAY, LEAVING OLD FEARS BEHIND.
EMBRACING EVERY CHALLENGE, GONNA FREE MY MIND.

BRITT

29

A rousing cheer goes up as the Wildcats hockey team saunters through the door and into Slap Shotz. Hands reach out, stroking over their arms as people attempt to claim their attention.

Their adoration doesn't bother me.

I've grown used to it over the years.

The strange part is that I'm not the one they're clamoring for.

It's Colby.

And his teammates.

My fingers are safely ensconced in Colby's larger hand as we make our way through the bar. It's been that way since he walked out of the locker room after the game and cut a direct path to me where I was waiting with Juliette, Carina, Viola, Stella, and Fallyn. Even Ava showed up to help cheer on the Wildcats.

This relationship is moving faster than the speed of light.

It's both scary and exhilarating at the same time.

Part of me wonders if I'm ready for it.

Then again, I'm not sure how much of a choice I have in the matter.

I keep telling myself that we can take our time and figure it all out.

But Colby needs to hear the truth. I can't keep hiding it from him. That knowledge sits at the bottom of my gut like a heavy stone. One that continues to grow with the passing of each day.

We settle at a couple of tables that have been shoved together in the back. When I drop down next to Colby, he pulls the chair closer until I'm practically seated on his lap.

Since Fallyn isn't working tonight, Erin, the other waitress, takes our order.

Colby turns toward me and whispers, "Guess it's all out in the open now, huh?"

I glance at him and find our mouths scant inches apart. My breath hitches with the need to close the distance between us and taste him. "Seems that way."

It hadn't occurred to me when I showed up at the game earlier this evening that everyone would assume there was something going on between us. People wear his name and number all the time and it doesn't mean a thing. As soon as I took off my jacket and the girls saw it, I was bombarded with questions until I came clean and told them everything.

All right...maybe not *everything*.

Colby searches my eyes. "And you're good with it?"

I allow the question to circle through my brain for a few seconds before nodding. "Yeah, I am."

A slow smile spreads across his lips. "Good. So am I."

He bridges the gap between us until his lips can sweep over mine. "I can't wait to get you home tonight. Are you going to let me fuck you in that jersey and nothing else?"

The idea sends a thrill shooting through me. "Maybe."

Heat blooms in my cheeks. It would be impossible not to think about all the ways he lays his hands on me and just how much I love it.

He nips at my lower lip before growling, "I think we can do better than that, don't you?"

It's only when my uncle climbs onto the makeshift stage on the other side of the bar that we turn our attention toward him.

"Our boys brought home another win tonight!" he booms into the microphone.

A deafening cheer goes up that nearly shakes the walls.

Sully raises his hands to be heard over the roar of the crowd. "And you know what that means!"

"Karaoke," everyone in the joint screams in response.

A smile lights up his face as he nods. "You got it!"

His gaze coasts over the bar before connecting with mine. If he's surprised to see me with Colby, his expression never falters. I probably should have mentioned it to him and Aunt Mary. They've been so good to me since I moved here. Kind of like de facto parents. It's obvious that he loves both the Western Wildcats hockey program and the players. That being said, I'm not sure how he'll feel about his niece not only dating a player but being married to one.

It only drives home the knowledge that I've been lying to the people in my life.

I glance at the man next to me.

Especially him.

A couple of Colby's teammates lumber onto the stage and sing 'You Got It' by New Kids on the Block. It's an oldie but a goodie. Ford jumps up and belts out Justin Timberlake's 'I'm Bringing Sexy Back.' Carina just shakes her head, but it's obvious that she's loving every minute of it since he's pretty much serenading her. Ryder drags Juliette up there and together they belt out Evanescence's 'Bring Me to Life.' They're surprisingly good. It's obvious from the way they stare at each other that they're in love.

It's next-level swoony.

Colby nods toward the stage. "Maybe you should get up there and sing. You've got an amazing voice. More people should hear it."

That's all it takes for my mouth to dry, making it impossible to swallow. "No thanks. It's just a hobby. Something I like to fool around with."

He raises a brow. "I don't know many people who can write music and play the guitar. You must have been in choir or taken vocal lessons when you were younger."

I don't want to lie...

But I'm reluctant to share the truth.

"In middle school, I took choir and then yeah, I had some vocal training."

"I'd love to hear the song you've been working on while you play the guitar. When we get home, will you do that for me, sweet girl?"

I chew my lower lip as the prospect circles around in my brain.

Would he recognize my voice if I did?

It's a scary proposition.

"I'll think about it."

He presses closer until his lips can drift over mine. "Want to get out of here?"

Actually, I do.

I don't care if we've been here for less than an hour.

As I nod, a trio of girls take over the stage. They're giggly and obviously drunk. They crowd together, hovering over the computer before choosing a song.

Colby strokes his fingers along my palm. I hadn't realized until now that he was holding my hand. Even more surprising is how much I enjoy it.

Want more of it.

Want more of him.

Somehow, when I wasn't looking, he forced himself into my life, and now I can't imagine living without him.

How ironic is it that our relationship feels more real than anything else when all I've done is hide the truth and lie?

I blink back to the moment when the girls take their places center stage and wait for the music to start. As soon as I hear the first few chords, my belly crashes to my toes and bile rises in my throat.

Shake Me Like That.

My hit single.

The one that had millions of views in less than twenty-four hours. It's what catapulted me from teen living in obscurity to household name in less than a month.

If I had to pick one defining moment when the course of my life altered drastically, it would be that song.

It'll always be synonymous with my rise to fame.

Before I realize what's happening, the entire bar is belting it out with the girls who are prancing around and putting on a show.

Colby smirks as he watches them.

It's a shock to realize that he's mouthing the lyrics as well.

The pounding against my ribcage turns painful. Any second, my heart will explode from my chest.

Once the last notes fade, the girls take a bow, and the crowd whistles and claps their approval.

"Now that I have a little more time, I've been binging the show, trying to catch up. Is Bebe still MIA? I haven't heard anything new lately," Carina says.

"Yeah, I think so. So weird," Stella adds before taking a sip of her beer.

"I'm dying to know if she'll accept Axel's proposal," Viola says, which is a surprise. I didn't think she was interested.

There must be a confused expression marring my face because she shrugs as color pinkens her cheeks. "I checked it out after you guys were talking about it the other week and fell down the rabbit hole. What about you, Britt? Are you a Bebe fan?"

How am I supposed to answer that?

I pull the collar of Colby's jersey away from my neck. It's as if the material is choking me.

"I've, ah, seen the show a time or two."

That's not a lie.

While the rest of my family enjoys watching themselves on screen, I don't. I obsess about all the little things that bug me about my appearance.

"I wonder if she's in rehab. Didn't her mother say in a recent interview that she's at a retreat for rest and relaxation? I'm pretty sure that's Hollywood speak for when someone's detoxing," Fallyn adds.

The beer I just consumed threatens to make an encore appearance.

I swipe my sweaty palms against the thighs of my jeans. It takes effort to fight down the icy shards of panic that are multiplying in the pit of my belly as I attempt to keep my voice level.

Instead of getting drawn into the convo, I turn to Colby. "Are you ready to go?"

He nods before rising to his feet and pulling me up with him.

"What I'm ready for is to have you all to myself," he whispers before pressing his lips against my cheek.

If he notices that I'm trembling from head to toe, he doesn't mention it.

30

A strange silence falls over us as we leave the bar amid boos from our friends. It's like the mood has shifted, and I'm unsure as to the reason. For the duration of the ride back to the apartment, she stares straight ahead and chews her lower lip as if lost deep in thought.

I ask a few questions, but it becomes obvious after a handful of them that she isn't paying attention. Nerves prickle at the bottom of my belly as I continue to shoot apprehensive looks her way.

Even though she made it sound like she was content with our relationship being out in the open, my biggest fear is that she'll change her mind and tell me this isn't working. That it's been a few weeks and she's ready to cut me loose and move on.

Once we're in the elevator, I reach out and tug her into my arms. She fits perfectly. Almost as if she were made for me.

Or maybe I'm the one who was made for her.

I don't know anymore.

What I do know is that I don't like the feelings of uncertainty bubbling up inside me.

The ones that have me wondering if I'm going to lose what I've only just found.

And it doesn't help that I have no idea what she's thinking.

What I've discovered about Britt is that she's difficult to read. She's a master at keeping everything buried deep down inside where it can't see the light of day.

In silence, she slides the key into the lock before throwing the apartment door wide. As I trail after her, I realize that I need to do everything in my power to convince her that we can make this work.

The only other choice is to let her go, and I'm nowhere near ready to do that.

There's a chance that I'll never be ready to do that.

Instead of heading to the bedroom, she beelines to the couch and sinks to the edge of the cushion. Tension radiates off her in heavy, suffocating waves as her brows pinch together.

It's briefly that her golden gaze touches upon mine before flitting away. "We need to have a conversation before this goes any further."

Fuck.

I knew this was coming.

I drag a hand through my hair before shoving down my panic and nodding toward the guitar. "Will you play that song for me?"

Confusion flickers across her features. "You don't want to talk first?"

Hell, no.

If she's going to give me the boot, I want to hear the song she sang for me on the plane while playing the guitar. I want to close my eyes and pretend for just a moment this isn't the end.

"We'll do it afterward."

Her gaze bores into mine. "Promise?"

Ouch.

She's really impatient to end this.

Hurt floods through me as I jerk my head into a nod.

"Okay." She reaches for her guitar next to the couch. The wood is dinged up and dented. Worn. But from the careful way she handles it, obviously well loved.

Britt drives a brand-new silver Audi and lives in an apartment by herself. My guess is that if she wanted to buy something pricier with more bells and whistles, she could do it.

She must hang onto it for sentimental reasons.

I can understand that.

There are hockey sticks I've outgrown but they felt good in my hands. Made me feel lucky. Invincible. So, I've hung onto them. They're part of my past and bring back memories that are important to me.

With her attention centered on the instrument, I'm able to eat her up with my eyes. I want to burn this moment into my memory for all eternity.

I can't stop trying to figure out where it all went wrong. It's almost hilarious that I thought we were on track when nothing could be further from the truth.

As she strums a few chords, the notes reverberate throughout the stillness of the apartment, and I recognize the melody. It's been playing on repeat in my brain since Vegas.

> *"In the darkest nights, I stumbled, couldn't see the light. Lost in a maze, couldn't find what's right. But deep inside, a fire burned, refusing to fade away. A voice inside me whispered, 'You'll find your way.'"*

The knotted tension filling my muscles drains. There's something soothing about her voice and the way it washes over me.

> *"I'm rising up, stronger now than I've ever been. Every scar's a story, ain't letting them win. Through the ups and downs, I'll find my truth. In the chaos of it all, I'll find my youth."*

Her voice rises, growing stronger, as she sings the chorus. Her eyelids feather closed as if lost in the music.

Both her beauty and talent are like a gut punch and steal my breath away.

> *"Through every fall and every doubt, I'll stand tall. Gonna shake off the past, gonna give it my all. With each new day, leaving old fears behind. Embracing every challenge, gonna free my mind."*

A chill slides through me as she sings the bridge before ending with the chorus. Only then do her voice and the chords fade.

I'm out of the chair before I realize what I'm doing. It's carefully that I wrap my fingers around the guitar and pry it from her grip before setting it on the couch and pulling her up.

She searches my eyes for just a heartbeat. A mixture of fear and sadness swirls through them. It only reinforces my thoughts that I won't like what she has to say.

"Colby..."

I shake my head, cutting her off. "Whatever you need to get off your chest can wait until the morning."

"But it's important," she tries again.

"There's no way it's as important as this."

My mouth crashes onto hers, swallowing up any further protests before I lift her up. Her legs tangle around my waist as her arms twine around my neck. As soon as my tongue sweeps along the seams of her lips, she opens so they can mingle.

Her sweetness floods my senses and rushes through my veins.

Already I know that I'll never find anything like it—*like her*—in this world.

It only takes a dozen long-legged strides to reach the room we've been sharing. I beeline to the queen-sized bed before setting her on the mattress. Even though I'm reluctant to break contact, I pull away long enough to stare down at her.

Just like earlier, I want to singe the sight of her into my brain for eternity.

She's so damn beautiful.

More beautiful than anyone I've ever seen.

Inside and out.

Especially when she's wearing my jersey.

Even though it's tempting to rip her clothing off, the need to take my time and draw out this experience is what tempers the urge. Maybe I'm incapable of saying the words, but I can show her with my actions just how strongly I feel.

For the first time in my life, I want to make love to someone.

My heart hitches at the realization.

Because that's exactly what it'll be.

Love.

With my forehead resting against hers, I squeeze my eyes tight. "I'm not sure what you've done to me, Britt. I didn't think it was possible to feel this way. Especially after what happened. But I do. And that has everything to do with you."

I've never been one to talk about my feelings or bare my soul, but I can't stop the steady stream of words as they slide from my lips. No matter what happens in the future, I want her to know that what I feel is real.

Special.

It's the moment I realize that I'll be nursing a broken heart for the first time ever.

Even after Anna, my heart wasn't crushed. My pride was hurt, and I was pissed off about being used and taken advantage of. I was embarrassed that her parents threatened my father and his livelihood.

But it wasn't love.

This couldn't be more different.

And it's doubtful I'll be able to move on so easily afterward.

In fact, I can't imagine my world being the same after Britt crashed into it.

I'm not sure if I should thank her or curse her for opening my eyes and showing me what's possible.

"Colby..." Her arms tangle around my neck to draw me closer. The grip she has on me is so tight. Almost like she's trying to squeeze the very life from my body.

Maybe it would be better that way.

It's like I blinked, and everything transformed, never to be the same again.

"Maybe we should—"

"No." I pull away enough to meet her gaze, needing to confirm my suspicions. "Whatever you need to say will change everything between us, won't it?"

Her teeth scrape against her lower lip as a sheen of tears fills her eyes. She jerks her head into a nod. "I think so."

"Then we'll sit down and discuss it tomorrow morning. All right?"

When she remains silent, I plead, "Give me this. Give me tonight. Can you do that?"

"Is that really what you want?"

"Yeah, it is."

"Okay. But it's important, and we can't put it off any longer."

Relief pumps through me as my mouth settles over hers. As soon as it does, she opens, and our tongues mingle with deep strokes that leave me wanting more.

Leave me wanting everything.

I nip the plumpness of her lower lip before drawing away. I want every shred of clothing that separates us removed.

My fingers grip the hem of my jersey before dragging it up her torso and over her head. As much as I want to fuck her in it, I need to feel the warmth of her flesh pressed against mine even more. Her bra is the next to get shed. The button of her jeans is flicked open before the zipper is lowered. The thick denim is tugged down her hips and thighs until she's left in a pair of light blue panties with tiny red hearts decorating them. I bury my face against the thin cotton and inhale a deep breath, drawing her scent into my lungs until I'm dizzy with it.

A whimper escapes from her as I drag my teeth against her clit.

My fingers slip beneath the elastic, tugging them down and tossing the tiny scrap of material to the carpet.

I straighten, needing to soak in the sight before me. With her caramel-colored hair spread out on the lavender comforter and the tips of her breasts already hard, she's like a wet dream sprung to life.

"You really are gorgeous," I rasp. "I've enjoyed every fucking moment that we've spent together."

She blinks as more wetness fills her eyes before holding her arms out to me.

I rip the sweatshirt over my head, taking the T-shirt with it. My jeans and boxers are the next to get shoved down my thighs. I kick them away until I'm as naked as she is.

Just the sight of her has my cock throbbing.

Slow.

Slow.

Slow.

I chant the word in my head like a mantra, wanting to draw out this experience for as long as I can. Wanting to make it one she'll never forget.

One that will haunt her for the rest of her life.

The same way it will for me.

I want her to realize that no one else will ever be able to make her feel the way I do.

All this churns inside my head as I crawl up her body and press my mouth against hers. When she opens, I slide downward, peppering her jawline with kisses before doing the same to the delicate column of her throat. A groan breaks free from her as she bares it. Her arms lift until her fingers can tunnel through my hair as if to lock me in place.

It's not necessary.

There's nowhere else I'd rather be than here with her.

I rain kisses along her collarbone before adoring both breasts. By the time my mouth settles over one hard tip, her back is already bowing off the mattress and she's whimpering for more.

"That feels so good."

"I want to make you feel amazing," I whisper against her flesh.

"You do. Every time."

And yet...it wasn't enough, was it?

I release one nipple with a soft pop before drawing the other between my lips and sucking on it until she's shifting beneath me.

Her desire is like a living, breathing entity and all I want to do is stoke it to life until it consumes her soul.

Once I've worshipped her breasts, I work my way down her ribcage to her pubic bone. She widens her thighs without me saying a word. I shoulder my way between them until her pussy is spread before me like a feast.

Tonight, I plan to make a meal out of her.

"So fucking pretty." My eyes flick upward before capturing hers.

With our gazes locked, I lap at her shuddering softness. That's all it takes for her sweetness to explode in my mouth.

I run the flat of my tongue along her slit before dipping inside her core and circling her clit with the tip of my tongue. I keep up the gentle assault until she's shifting, lifting her hips in an attempt to get closer.

"You like that, sweet girl? You like the way I play with your body?"

"God, yes."

When her muscles tighten, I can't resist adding, "I hope you realize that no one else will ever make you feel this way."

My tongue circles the tiny bundle of nerves.

"No one else but you."

Damn straight.

With that, I push her over the edge, licking her the entire time she screams out her orgasm. It's only when she turns boneless that I press one last kiss against her shuddering softness and climb up her body. My lips settle on hers as our gazes stay fastened. My tongue slips inside her mouth to tangle with her own.

"Do you taste yourself on me?"

She nods.

"There's no way I'll ever get enough of you. Not ever."

I line my cock up against her drenched entrance.

She's so damn wet.

And hot.

All I want to do is bury myself deep inside her body.

And then stay there forever.

This girl is where I belong.

I understand that even if she doesn't.

That's what hurts most of all.

I've spent all these years fucking around and holding girls at a distance.

Until her.

And now that I've finally opened up and allowed someone inside, she doesn't want me.

Whoever said karma was a bitch knew what they were talking about.

When she widens her legs, I slide inside her tight heat. It's so damn tempting to fuck her into oblivion but I hold back, needing to control myself.

It's not easy. I clench my jaw until the muscles ache. Until my teeth are on the verge of shattering.

"Your pussy is so damn hot and tight. Fuck but you feel amazing." I have to force myself to pull out and tease her entrance, giving her just the tip.

Her hands splay wide against my back before the sharp nails bite into my skin as she attempts to drag me closer.

"Colby, please..."

"Do you need more, sweet girl? Do you need some dick filling that pretty little pussy?"

"Please...I've never wanted anything more. Give it to me."

I groan. Her begging is my undoing, and I slide inside until I'm buried balls deep. The pleasure is so great that my eyes nearly roll to the back of my head.

Slow.

I need to take this slow and make it last.

With measured movements, I pull out before flexing my hips and gliding back inside her tight body. Every time our pelvises collide, the pleasure increases until it becomes almost too much for the confines of my skin.

It's only when her pussy spasms, squeezing the life out of me, that I come with a vengeance and roar out my orgasm.

It's altogether possible that the tip of my cock just blew off.

A few minutes later, we both float down to earth.

My heart pounds an unsteady staccato against my ribcage, and it takes time for my breathing to even out until I no longer feel like I just ran a marathon.

Or skated suicides during a two-hour practice.

Even though my brain is hazy, discontentment presses in at the edges. I haven't pulled out, and I can't help but dwell on the very real possibility that this will be the last time I'm buried inside her sweet heat.

It's only when I soften that I roll onto my back and take her with me.

A heavy silence, chockful of unspoken words, hangs heavy in the air. It's as if we're both aware of the impending storm that looms on the horizon. There's no way to outrun or hide from it.

All we can do is stand tall and face it down when it finally arrives.

But that doesn't mean we can't put it off until the early morning light streaks across the horizon.

I bury my face in her hair and draw a deep breath of her floral scent into my lungs. If only there were a way to hold it captive for the rest of my life.

Hold *her* captive.

"I hope you realize that I'm nowhere near done with you," I whisper.

She shifts against me until her gaze can fasten onto mine. "Maybe I'm the one who isn't done with you."

My heart clenches, wishing that were the case.

We make love a few more times before finally drifting off to sleep wrapped up in each other's arms.

Even though I try to brace myself for what tomorrow will bring and close myself off from the inevitable pain, I realize there's no way to do that.

No matter what happens, this will hurt.

IN THE DARKEST NIGHTS, I STUMBLED, COULDN'T SEE THE LIGHT.
LOST IN A MAZE, COULDN'T FIND WHAT'S RIGHT.
BUT DEEP INSIDE, A FIRE BURNED,
REFUSING TO FADE AWAY.
A VOICE INSIDE ME WHISPERED, 'YOU'LL FIND YOUR WAY.'

I'M RISING UP, STRONGER NOW THAN I'VE EVER BEEN.
EVERY SCAR'S A STORY, AIN'T LETTING THEM WIN.
THROUGH THE UPS AND DOWNS, I'LL FIND MY TRUTH.
IN THE CHAOS OF IT ALL, I'LL FIND MY YOUTH.

THROUGH EVERY FALL AND EVERY DOUBT, I'LL STAND TALL.
GONNA SHAKE OFF THE PAST, GONNA GIVE IT MY ALL.
WITH EACH NEW DAY, LEAVING OLD FEARS BEHIND.
EMBRACING EVERY CHALLENGE, GONNA FREE MY MIND.

BRITT

31

I t's the bright sunlight filtering through the gauzy curtains of my bedroom that has me surfacing from a deep sleep. I turn my head and take in the man snoring softly beside me.

I lost track of how many times we had sex last night. Enough for me to promptly pass out afterward.

My gaze rakes over him with more care.

His blond hair is tousled, and his eyelids are feathered closed. His lashes are ridiculously thick as they rest against his skin. His nose is long with a little crook as if it had been broken at some point. It's what stops him from being over-the-top beautiful. His cheekbones are sharp and his face angular.

The man is definitely gorgeous and a real pleasure to look at.

And the women of Western do enjoy staring at him.

All I can say is that Colby McNichols hasn't turned out to be the man I assumed he was. There's a surprising amount of depth and layers to him. Even more shocking than that, I've enjoyed our time together.

I release a long slow breath, knowing that I can't delay the inevitable any longer. I need to come clean about my identity. After working up the courage to do it last night, he shut me down.

Throughout our relationship, he's opened up about his past and been honest with me, divulging details he wouldn't normally share.

And I've been resistant to do the same.

I worry my bottom lip.

I have no idea how he'll react to what I have to say.

Instead of cuddling against him the way every impulse clamors for, I slide from the bed and tiptoe around the room, picking up my clothing as I go. Once dressed, I slip into the hallway.

The plan is to run to the coffee shop around the corner and pick up breakfast.

Then we can sit down and finally hash this out.

Every night that Colby has been at my place, he's cooked dinner. It might not be fancy or elaborate, but it's nice to come home to a prepared meal. Even when it's just grilled cheese and tomato soup. There's nothing better than sitting down and talking about our days. I can always count on him to share funny stories about his friends and teammates that make me laugh.

It only makes me realize how much I'll miss the routine we've fallen into if this fledgling marriage doesn't work out.

Most of all, I'll miss Colby.

Instead of grabbing my jacket, I pull on his black Western Wild-cats hockey sweatshirt. I can't help but lift the soft material to my nose and inhale a giant breath. My eyelids feather closed, and my tummy flutters as his woodsy scent cocoons me in comfort and familiarity.

I love the way he smells.

I snag my purse and keys on the way out before leaving the apartment. Instead of waiting for the elevator, I push through the heavy metal door and into the stairwell. The only thing on my mind is picking up breakfast and returning as quickly as possible. It feels imperative that I get everything off my chest and into the open. Only then can we discuss what our future will look like and the possibility of moving forward. The realization that we could have one that's intertwined is as exciting as it is terrifying.

But the idea of a life without him is even scarier.

Especially after last night and the way he made love to me.

It wasn't just sex.

In a way, it felt as if he were trying to convey so much with his body that he wasn't able to put into words.

And I felt the same.

There was so much I wanted to say.

And couldn't.

If he's willing to make a go of it, then everything will have to change. I'll film the upcoming season, but then I'm done. I want off the show. I'll finish college and work on my music.

My life has never felt farther away from LA and my family as it does at this moment.

And it's freeing.

Almost like a thousand-pound weight has been lifted from my chest and I can finally draw fresh air into my lungs.

Just as I step into the lobby, my cell rings, breaking the silence that has settled around me. My father's name flashes across the screen. That's all it takes for a shiver of dread to scamper down my spine. It's almost as if he can sense over the miles that everything is about to change.

It's a little unsettling.

Instead of picking up the call, I send it to voicemail. As tempting as it is to tell him that I'm done, I need to discuss the matter with Colby first.

We can make decisions together.

Like a married couple should.

A flutter of excitement wings its way to life inside my belly.

I return the slim device to the pocket of Colby's hoodie before pushing through the door and into the bright sunshine. The warmth feels good on my face as the cool air slaps at my cheeks. Lost in thought, I end up slamming into a hard body. Hands lock around my upper arms to hold me in place.

"I'm so—"

The apology dies a quick death on my lips as I glance up and find myself staring into a familiar face.

"Hello, Bebe."

With a stretch, I roll onto my side, only to find the bed empty and the sheets cool to my touch.

That's disappointing.

After last night, all I want to do is sink inside Britt's warmth.

I know that we need to talk.

But still...

I was hoping to make love to her one more time before we sit down for a conversation, and she tells me that our relationship is over. It's like I'm trying to gorge myself, but no matter how much I have it'll never be enough.

I'll always be left wanting more.

Even though I'm reluctant to face what today will bring, I roll from the bed and force my feet into movement. Maybe she's in the kitchen, whipping up some grub.

A bon voyage breakfast of sorts.

As disturbing as that image is, it's one that makes me snort. What I've learned about Britt in the short time we've been together is that she knows absolutely nothing about cooking, and she has zero interest in learning.

And you know what?

That's fine with me.

Guess it'll be one of my selling points as to why she should keep my ass around.

I stumble to a halt.

Holy shit. Is that what my life has come to?

I have to convince someone that I'm worth staying married to?

I shake my head before dragging a hand through my mussed hair.

It's like I entered a parallel universe when I wasn't looking. One where nothing makes a damn bit of sense.

Except when Britt and I are together.

Then, it makes perfect sense.

I yank open a drawer and snag a pair of boxers before hauling them up my hips and over my thighs.

When she first made room in her dresser, I'd thought that was a positive sign of things to come.

Now?

Not so much.

I glance around for the sweatshirt from last night but can't find it.

Hmmm.

Weird.

To be fair, clothing was thrown all over the damn place. It could be anywhere.

I gravitate to the closet and pull out a different one and then a pair of gray sweatpants before walking into the short hallway and peeking in the living area, only to find it empty.

Well, damn.

She's not here either.

My brows pinch together.

Where the hell did she go?

I beeline to the window in the living room that overlooks the parking lot to check for her sleek little Audi. She usually parks in the same spot and it's still there.

So...she didn't just take off on me.

That should be comforting, but it's not.

Just as I'm about to swing around for my phone, my attention gets snagged by a couple loitering on the sidewalk.

My eyes narrow.

I'd recognize Britt's caramel-colored hair anywhere.

And some slick-looking dude has his arms wrapped around her.

Are they hugging?

I smash my face against the glass, attempting to get a better look.

Who the hell is that guy?

And why does he have his hands on what belongs to me?

I scour his face. I'm pretty sure I don't recognize the dude from campus, but there's something oddly familiar about him.

That's all it takes for a giant stone to settle in the pit of my belly until it feels like I'm going to be sick.

Especially when he pulls her closer like they're long lost—

I swing away from the window before shoving my feet into slides and racing from the apartment like my ass is on fire. It takes less than sixty seconds to slam through the door and into the chilled morning air.

"Hey!" The word erupts from my mouth before I can stop it. Maybe if we were in a better place, I could control myself, but that's not possible at the moment. All I want to do is tear this guy limb from limb.

It's only after my voice rings out that Britt fights her way free of his hold before whipping around to stare at me with wide eyes. Any color staining her cheeks gets leached away.

"Colby."

The panic woven through her tone doesn't sit well with me. Is this what she's been hiding the entire time?

Another relationship?

It takes effort to rip my gaze away from Britt and glance at the guy. As soon as our gazes collide, he swallows up the distance between them and slips an arm around her waist as if laying claim.

My hands clench as they hang loosely at my sides. I've always been more of a lover than a fighter, but this douchebag is making me want to throw fists.

A smirk lifts the corners of his lips as his disinterested gaze slides down the length of me before flicking upward for a second time.

"Really, B? A steroid-infused meathead? What does he play? Wait...let me guess." There's a pause. "Football?"

I straighten to my full height. "Hockey." Barely am I able to push the response past my clenched teeth.

I refocus my attention on Britt. She has yet to say anything other than my name since I've arrived on the scene. It's taking every ounce of self-control to keep my cool. Maybe I need to take this down a notch.

It's always possible this guy is a relative.

Maybe her brother?

A cousin?

I release the pent-up air from my lungs and try to stay calm when all I want to do is yank her to me.

And beat the piss out of this guy.

I crack the muscles in my neck. Maybe a quick intro will be enough to clear up this mess. "We haven't met. I'm Colby McNichols. Who the fuck—"

"*Oh my god!*" a girl shrieks at the top of her lungs. "*It's Axel and Bebe! Am I dreaming? Are they really here? Oh my god, oh my god, oh my god!*"

It's like a light switch flicks on, and the guy standing entirely too close to Britt flashes an overly white smile at the girls who have ground to a halt and are staring at him with their mouths hanging open.

Well...they're not just staring at him. They're staring at Britt as well.

Axel and Bebe?

Who the hell are Axel and Bebe?

A memory tickles the far recesses of my brain.

Why do those names sound so familiar?

I'm pretty sure I don't know anyone named Axel or Bebe.

I drag a hand through my hair as more people gravitate to the sidewalk and the group swells in size before doubling and then quadrupling.

"I can't believe it's actually them!" another girl cries.

Weirder than that, she's actually sobbing.

Wetness streams down her face.

What the actual fuck is going on around here?

Have people lost their ever-loving minds?

"OMG, I love your hair, Bebe!"

Bebe?

Why are they calling Britt that name?

Why are all these people acting like they know her?

And him?

Like they're celebrities.

My narrowed gaze slices back to Britt. She's gone deathly still. Almost as if she's frozen to the sidewalk. Panic flashes across her face as she glances around the growing crowd as if unable to believe what's happening.

That makes two of us.

The girl next to me whips out her cell to video the spectacle. "Can you believe this? Bebe's been here this entire time!"

Bebe?

No. They've got the wrong girl.

It's a case of mistaken identity.

That's not Bebe.

I blink and then squint.

No fucking way.

There's no way she's the chick everyone has been speculating about.

It's not possible.

For fuck's sake, we're married.

That's something I would definitely know.

"Are you two now engaged?" a voice shouts from the crowd.

Axel flashes a well-practiced smile. This guy couldn't be more fake. He's like a shiny piece of plastic.

"You'll have to tune in and find out."

That's when I'm hit with the realization that knocks the air from my lungs, making it impossible to breathe.

Bebe is...*Britt*.

Or maybe it's the other way around.

I have no idea.

I'm at a total loss.

Laughter gurgles up in my throat.

A piercing scream is what sends me crashing back to earth with a painful thud. The girl next to me is losing her shit.

"She's here! No, I'm serious! Look at the photo I just sent you."

The din of conversation continues to rise as a load of cars pull into the parking lot and screech to a halt.

All the little clues that didn't add up earlier now fall neatly into place, making me wonder why I didn't piece it together sooner.

The guitar.

Her reluctance to talk about her family.

How stingy she was with details of her past.

The familiarity of her voice.

Her unwillingness to take photos at the restaurant with my parents.

Not to mention, lack of social media.

I'm such a fucking idiot.

I've spent the past four years protecting both myself and my heart so that I wouldn't get played again, and that's exactly what happened. Waves of anger crash over me until my vision is obscured by a thick red haze. It's silently that I fume until her gaze collides with mine.

Only then do I raise my voice, making sure that everyone standing within a hundred-foot radius can hear what I'm about to say. "This might be a good time to tell your boyfriend that you already have a husband."

Her mouth tumbles open as her eyes grow wider.

More people whip out their phones to snap pics.

"Colby." My name comes out sounding as if it's being choked from her body.

For the first time since I've found them together, the fucker next to her doesn't look so damn smug.

Mission accomplished.

Her tongue darts out to moisten her lips. Instead of waiting for a response, I swing around and stalk inside the building, away from the growing circus.

Even though I still want to punch that guy in the face for daring to lay his hands on what's mine, I restrain myself.

Only now do I realize that Britt doesn't belong to me.

She never did.

IN THE DARKEST NIGHTS, I STUMBLED, COULDN'T SEE THE LIGHT.
LOST IN A MAZE, COULDN'T FIND WHAT'S RIGHT.
BUT DEEP INSIDE, A FIRE BURNED,
REFUSING TO FADE AWAY.
A VOICE INSIDE ME WHISPERED, 'YOU'LL FIND YOUR WAY.'

I'M RISING UP, STRONGER NOW THAN I'VE EVER BEEN.
EVERY SCAR'S A STORY, AIN'T LETTING THEM WIN.
THROUGH THE UPS AND DOWNS, I'LL FIND MY TRUTH.
IN THE CHAOS OF IT ALL, I'LL FIND MY YOUTH.

THROUGH EVERY FALL AND EVERY DOUBT, I'LL STAND TALL.
GONNA SHAKE OFF THE PAST, GONNA GIVE IT MY ALL.
WITH EACH NEW DAY, LEAVING OLD FEARS BEHIND.
EMBRACING EVERY CHALLENGE, GONNA FREE MY MIND.

BRITT

"**B**ebe! Are you really married to Colby McNichols?" a girl shouts.

More questions are yelled from the swelling crowd.

"What about Axel? Did you cheat on him?"

"Who are you in love with? Axel or Colby?"

"What about the show?"

"How was rehab?"

"When are you leaving for LA?"

The drone of voices buzzes in my ears until it's tempting to slap my hands over them and squeeze my eyes tightly shut to blot everything out. Instead, I crane my neck and search the sea of onlookers for Colby. My heart twists beneath my breast when I don't find him.

The hurt and confusion written across his face had been palpable.

I hate myself for causing him even a moment of heartache.

It was never my intention to hurt him, but that's exactly what happened.

A pit settles at the bottom of my belly. I need to find him and explain why I kept my identity a secret. I should have tried harder last night to have a conversation. Maybe then everything wouldn't be playing out the way it is.

My biggest fear is that he won't listen to what I have to say.

Ignoring the questions hurled at me, I turn to Axel. "I can't do this with you now. We'll talk later."

Before I can slip away, his grip tightens around my waist to keep me locked in place. "If you hadn't run away and ignored my calls, none of this would be happening," he mutters through gritted teeth just loud enough for me to hear. "Now smile for the cameras. It's about time we were in front of them again."

"Let me go," I growl, shoving at his chest and pushing him back a few steps.

I don't give a damn about the hundred cell phones that are poised to record every move we make. When his grip loosens, I bolt, cutting a path through the thick mob. People reach out, attempting to grab hold of me as they continue shouting questions at my retreating form. It's enough to make me hyperventilate.

It's only after being away from the frenzied crowds for more than six months that it's slammed home just how much I hate them. And how claustrophobic they make me feel.

With a shaking hand, I key in the code before slipping inside the lobby. The door slams closed behind me as people press against the glass, trying to fight their way in. It won't be long before another resident grants them access, but it should buy me enough time to reach the apartment. Instead of waiting for the elevator, I race to the metal door and take the concrete stairs to the third floor. Once I arrive at the landing, I burst into the hallway and find several people milling around, talking to one another.

It's only when my hand rises that I realize I'm not wearing a ball cap. After Vegas, I became more complacent and felt more comfortable on campus without it.

"Something's happening in the parking lot."

"My friend just said that Bebe and Axel are outside," a girl yells. "Let's go!"

I duck my head and stare at the thin carpet as people race past, chattering excitedly.

This is a nightmare.

I pick up my pace, only wanting to reach the safety of my apartment before all hell breaks loose.

It's a relief when I reach the door and slide the key in the lock before bursting inside. With a slam, I collapse against the thick wood. My knees feel more like jelly. It takes effort to keep myself upright. Ever since starting school in the fall, this was my biggest fear.

And now it's come to fruition.

I've been outed.

Everyone knows I'm here.

"Colby!"

I wait for a beat or two, but there isn't an answer.

If I didn't know better, I'd assume I was alone. Except for the suffocating tension that hangs heavy in the air that tells me differently.

He's here.

In the utter quietness, I feel the vibration of his hurt and anger.

I shove away from the door and beeline for the bedroom before skidding to a halt at the scene that unfolds in front of me. His duffle is open on the floor as he yanks the drawer open and scoops out his socks and underwear before dumping them in the bag.

"When were you going to tell me who you were, *Bebe*?"

The way he bites out my name sounds more like an accusation.

And I can't blame him for it.

I went to great lengths to hide the truth from him.

From everyone.

I force myself to the bed before settling on the mattress. My tongue darts out to moisten parched lips as I wring my hands in front of me.

Now that we're alone, I have no idea what to say.

Or how to make the situation better.

But I have to come up with something. Otherwise, he'll walk out of my life and never look back.

"I'm so sorry," I whisper, heart thumping painfully in my chest. "None of this was supposed to happen. I needed a break. Time to figure everything out."

His expression remains inscrutable as he glances toward the window. "From the looks of it, your break is over. Your adoring public is waiting."

I squeeze my eyes tightly closed before forcing them open again. Maybe I was able to blot out my life in LA, but I can't do that here with Colby.

In a matter of a few short weeks, he's become important to me.

"Can we please talk about this?"

A humorless chuckle slides from his lips. "It seems a little late for that, don't you think? Your boyfriend is here. The one who proposed on national TV. The one you failed to mention."

"He's not my boyfriend," I murmur, trying to keep the panic from invading my voice.

When he raises a brow, his stare boring into mine, heat suffuses my cheeks.

"Not really," I mutter. "It was all for the show."

His lips flatten into a tight line as he jerks his head into a nod. "Well, that's just perfect."

"No, it's not. Nothing about my life is perfect." My heart thunders painfully against my ribcage. "The only time I truly feel like myself is when I'm with you."

He cocks his head. The iciness filling his blue depths is enough to freeze the blood rushing through my veins.

"And who exactly would that be? Bebe, the reality star? Or Britt, the college student I married in Vegas? The one who secretly sings? The one who refuses to share any pieces of herself with me? Because I have to be honest, I have no idea who the hell you are."

Tears spring to my eyes. His words slice through my heart, leaving me to feel as if I've been gutted.

"I tried to tell you last night."

"You should have tried harder," he fires back. "Or maybe you should have mentioned that you were living a lie weeks ago."

"You're right." I rise to my feet before inching closer. "I was scared. Scared of how you would react and what would happen if people discovered I was here."

Emotion flickers in his eyes, and the harsh lines bracketing his lips soften.

A kernel of hope blooms inside me that I've finally said something that resonates.

Instead, he zips up the bag and anchors it to his shoulder. "I shared things with you that I've never told anyone before because I trusted you. It would have been nice if you'd given me the same benefit of the doubt."

As I open my mouth to tell him that I wanted to, he stalks past me on the way to the door. He stutters to a stop when he reaches the threshold but doesn't turn back to meet my gaze.

His shoulders sag. "This isn't goodbye."

Thick emotion floods my voice. "Are you sure about that?"

"I need time to figure out if it's possible for us to move forward."

"Take as much as you want. When you're ready, I'll be here waiting. For what it's worth, I really am sorry."

He drops the bag on the floor before swinging around and eating up the distance between us. As soon as I'm within striking distance, he yanks me into his arms. His lips crash onto mine and I open so that our tongues can meld into one. If only it were as easy for us to do the same.

Just as I sink into the embrace, he sets me free and takes a quick step in retreat. Even though he's no more than a foot away, he's never felt more out of reach.

In trying to protect myself and my identity, I hurt the one person I've come to care about. I'd do anything for the chance to rewind time and make different decisions.

Better ones.

"I love you," I whisper, needing him to understand what's in my heart.

Moisture gathers in his bright blue eyes as he jerks his head into a tight nod and swings away. Tears burn the backs of mine as the door to the apartment closes with a soft click.

As the silence settles around me, I realize that even after walking away from my life in LA and leaving behind everything familiar, I've never felt more alone than I do in this moment.

The past twenty-four hours circle around inside my head, and there's nothing that makes it stop.

After leaving Britt's apartment Sunday morning, I headed back to my house. Somehow, I'd managed to convince myself that the spotlight would shine brightly on Britt—*or Bebe*—and I wouldn't have to worry about any spillover.

Ha!

That just proves what an idiot I am.

News spread through campus like wildfire. By the time I pulled up in front of the house, my phone was blowing up with messages.

Are you really hitched to Bebe?

Did you know who she was before marrying her?

Are you moving to LA?

I'm not sure what possessed me to blurt out our relationship status in front of the crowd. Had I been thinking clearly, I would have kept my big trap shut and quietly walked away.

Unfortunately, hindsight is twenty-twenty, and it's too late for that.

The damage is done.

It took less than two hours for my parents to call and ask if I was all right. It sucked to admit that I was just as much in the dark regarding her identity as everyone else.

Dad told me not to worry. He'd already reached out to his lawyer and set the divorce wheels in motion. Even though this situation isn't like the one in high school, all I can think about is how our name will be dragged through the mud. Gossip sites will pick up the story and run with it.

They'll make a mockery out of my marriage.

I fucking hate that it'll be the cause of any embarrassment for my parents.

I've always done my best to keep my nose clean and stay out of trouble.

Now, I look like a flaky athlete who got hitched to a reality star on a drunken weekend in Vegas.

How fucking cliche.

It's only when a sharp whistle fills the air that I'm knocked from the thorny tangle of my thoughts as the players burst into motion.

Everyone but me.

Fuck.

Madden gains possession before passing it up to Ford who takes off, blades digging into the ice.

"Get your ass moving, McNichols," Coach bellows from the benches.

There's a turnover near the crease and Maverick snags the rubber disc, crossing the red center line before flicking it to Hayes. I keep pace with him, waiting for a pass.

Just as I glance away, I get hit from the side and crash into the boards. The air is knocked from my lungs as I struggle to find my balance before dropping to the ice.

For a second or two, I lay there, trying to catch my breath. It feels like my lungs are being squeezed in a vise.

With narrowed eyes, I look up and find Garret Akeman, a second line defenseman, staring down at me with a smirk twisting his lips.

Fucking douchebag.

And if I could wrap my lips around words, that's exactly what I'd say.

"Maybe if you don't make it in the pros, *wifey* will give you a starring role on her garbage reality show."

Rage hits me like a freight train. In all honesty, it's been bubbling up since I discovered the truth. I've been able to keep it locked up tight where it couldn't see the light of day while it simmered.

The last thing I want to do is make an already shitty situation worse.

Except...that hit rips away the thin layer of restraint I've been clinging to.

Even though my body is screaming with pain, I scramble to my skates as Riggs, Hayes, Maverick, and Bridger press closer.

Tension ratchets up in the chilled arena air.

"What did you say, motherfucker?" I wheeze.

Garret sneers. "To paraphrase, I said that you suck at hockey and maybe Bebe will give you a job. You can be her himbo on the show."

A red haze obscures my vision as I skate closer. "You don't know what the fuck you're talking about, and keep Britt's name out of your damn mouth!"

Malice glitters in Garret's eyes as he lifts his chin. "Or what, McNichols? What are you gonna do?"

I don't bother responding to the taunt. Instead, I dive at him. My gloved fist slams into his helmet as we crash into the ice a tangle of limbs. He hits the unforgiving surface with a grunt.

Can't say the sound isn't satisfying.

I've never been one to start shit, but I'll damn well finish it.

He lands a punch that snaps my head back and we roll a few more times before I land on top of him. That's when he throws his gloves to the ice before trying to rip the helmet from my head.

I'm seething inside as hands reach out to drag me away. All I want to do is tear Garret Akeman apart limb by fucking limb. I buck and fight the arms that lock around me, dragging me from my teammate who's still sprawled out on the ice.

"Settle down," Bridger hisses in my ear.

"Damn," Hayes mutters loud enough for me to hear.

"McNichols!" Coach bellows from the benches, his deep voice echoing off the cavernous space. "Get off my ice until you can pull yourself together!"

Other than my own harsh breathing, a blanket of heavy silence falls over the arena.

"Fuck...you really screwed the pooch this time," Bridger mumbles with a shake of his head.

Garret glares as a few teammates assist him to his skates. With a scowl, he wipes away a smear of blood. "You're a talentless hack riding the coattails of your father," he growls.

When I surge forward for a second time, Hayes and Bridger tighten their grip, dragging me away.

"Go cool off in the locker room, McNichols!"

"Why are you listening to one word Akeman has to say?" Hayes grumbles. "He's the talentless hack. Not you."

"Fuck off, Van Doren! You're just a piece of trash here on scholarship!"

Hayes glares, his upper lip curling. "Right back at you, asswipe."

It takes a full sixty seconds before the haze obscuring my vision begins to clear. Only then do I glance around to find everyone staring at me.

Including the coaching staff.

My muscles lose their rigidity as the last of my rage drains away, leaving me to feel worse than before.

"You good?" Bridger asks.

"Yeah," I say with an embarrassed grunt.

He pats my shoulder. "Better move your ass before you get it chewed out again."

Fuck...

I pick up my stick and force myself to skate toward the benches where the coaches are loitering before grinding to a halt in front of Reed Philips. I hate the disappointment that stares back at me.

"Go cool off and get yourself straight."

"Sorry, Coach. It won't happen again."

I don't bother waiting for a response.

What's he going to say?

That it's all good?

We both know it isn't. I shouldn't have acted like some hot-headed punk. It's not who I am. Now that I've had a little time to think, I'm ashamed of my behavior. Garret Akeman runs his mouth all the time and normally, I let it roll off my back without a second thought. Sometimes, I give it right back to him.

What I don't do is lose my shit.

Ever.

It only proves how much the situation with Britt is messing with my head.

I slam into the locker room and drop my stick in the holder before unsnapping my chin strap and yanking off the helmet. Then I drop onto the bench and plow my hands through the sweat-soaked strands.

My heart hammers against my ribcage as adrenalin drains from my body. In the silence of the locker room, I'm all too cognizant of the thoughts that circle through my brain.

I need to get all this shit off. The skates get unlaced before I toss them into my locker. The practice jersey, shoulder and elbow pads come next. Then the socks, shin pads, and pants. Once I'm standing in my cup, I rifle through my locker and find my phone.

I open the home screen and hit Mom's number.

She picks up on the second ring. "Hey, hon. What's up?" There's a pause. "Aren't you supposed to be at practice?"

I sink to the bench as emotion bubbles up inside me. It's been a long time since I felt this overwhelmed. I hate how paralyzing it feels.

"Yeah."

That one-worded response is enough for her to realize there's been a disturbance in the force.

She says something to my brothers before there's a soft click of the door. I can just imagine her shuttering herself away in Dad's study. "Tell me what happened, Colby."

My shoulders wilt as I admit, "I kind of lost it at practice."

"Lost it?"

If I hate to disappoint Coach, it's tenfold with my parents. But there's no way I'm going to lie or withhold the truth. That's not the kind of relationship we have. They've always been my number one supporters. Even when I fuck up. They're there to help pick me up and get me moving again.

"I got into it with Garret Akeman on the ice."

"How come?"

I drag a hand over my face and stare at the orange and black wildcat painted above the lockers.

"Stupid stuff," I mutter.

"Well, it couldn't have been that stupid if you got so upset."

The woman knows me well. It's the reason I called. When there's too much mental crap for me to wade through, she's the first person I reach out to.

She's my phone-a-friend.

My lifeline.

Every.

Single.

Time.

I squeeze my eyelids shut. "It was about Britt."

"Ahhh."

"Everything that's happened has really knocked me off balance."

"That's understandable, Colby. Anyone going through what you are would feel the same way. It's just going to take time."

"I thought I knew her." All right, maybe that's not entirely true. I could sense from the beginning she was holding back. I just never imagined it was something of this magnitude. "This would have been easier to deal with if she'd told me the truth from the beginning."

"Well...I can only imagine that she needed time to build trust before revealing who she really was."

"I guess." That acknowledgment isn't enough to stop the hurt from flooding in.

"Have you figured out where you two go from here?"

I rest my elbows on my outstretched knees before hanging my head. "Nope."

"What you need to decide is if you're ready to walk away and end your relationship."

My heart picks up tempo at the thought. "I've never felt this confused or torn."

"I know, sweetie. Britt's the first girl you've introduced us to since high school. You wouldn't have done that unless you'd developed strong feelings for her."

She's not wrong. But still...

"The trust has been broken, and I'm not sure if it can be repaired."

"Because she didn't tell you who she was right away?"

"Well, yeah," I mumble.

"Kind of seems like she might've had a good reason to be cautious. Look what's happened in just twenty-four hours." When I fail to respond, she continues. "The only advice I can give you is to think long and hard about your future and who you want to share it with."

"Thanks, Mom. You're right."

"Anytime."

"I love you."

"Right back at you, Colby."

After I hang up, the silence of the locker room presses in on me as our conversation circles through my brain.

Mom is right.

It all comes down to what I want my future to look like.

IN THE DARKEST NIGHTS, I STUMBLED, COULDN'T SEE THE LIGHT.
LOST IN A MAZE, COULDN'T FIND WHAT'S RIGHT.
BUT DEEP INSIDE, A FIRE BURNED,
REFUSING TO FADE AWAY.
A VOICE INSIDE ME WHISPERED, 'YOU'LL FIND YOUR WAY.'

I'M RISING UP, STRONGER NOW THAN I'VE EVER BEEN.
EVERY SCAR'S A STORY, AIN'T LETTING THEM WIN.
THROUGH THE UPS AND DOWNS, I'LL FIND MY TRUTH.
IN THE CHAOS OF IT ALL, I'LL FIND MY YOUTH.

THROUGH EVERY FALL AND EVERY DOUBT, I'LL STAND TALL.
GONNA SHAKE OFF THE PAST, GONNA GIVE IT MY ALL.
WITH EACH NEW DAY, LEAVING OLD FEARS BEHIND.
EMBRACING EVERY CHALLENGE, GONNA FREE MY MIND.

BRITT

35

My belly is a tangle of painful knots as I pace the small dining area. Even though I've been expecting the knock, the sound of it is enough to startle me.

I just want to get this over with.

With a swipe of my palms against my jeans, I force myself to answer the door. I swing it open and find Axel waiting on the other side. He's dressed similarly as to when I caught sight of him in Vegas. Like he's ready to hit the club. Lavender dress shirt unbuttoned midway down his chest and black pants. A black leather jacket is draped over his shoulders and his favorite crocodile loafers complete the look. I'm sure his stylist threw this together before he took off.

"Hi. Thanks for coming over."

"Well, it's not like I was going to head back to LA without talking to you. I didn't fly out here to be ignored, B."

Already I can see how this conversation will go.

He brushes past me before I can invite him inside and drops down on the couch as if he owns the place. A bored expression settles on his face as his gaze roves over the interior.

"So...this is where you've been hiding yourself all these months, huh?" His upper lip curls. "I figured you'd be in Costa Rica or Paris. Maybe a spa in the Sonoran Desert." He waves a manicured hand around the space. "Not some shithole college town."

I should thank him for reminding me of who he really is when he's not putting on a show and trying to dazzle the audience. It'll make this convo much easier.

I gravitate to the armchair across from him and attempt to appear just as nonchalant about the situation as he is. "Sorry to disappoint."

He shrugs as if he doesn't care one way or the other. "Look, dude. You can do whatever the hell you want. But I draw the line when it affects me or my career. And right now, your bullshit is spilling over."

I can only blink.

Whatever I was expecting him to say, that wasn't it.

He straightens before leaning forward. His steely gaze stays pinned to mine. "You've spent more than enough months slumming it, trying to find yourself. And we've all been patient. Now it's time to pack up and return to reality." He jerks a brow. "You remember what that is, right? It's the show that pays our bills."

My mouth turns bone dry as I force out the one question that has been gnawing at me for years. "And what if that's no longer what I want?"

For the first time since waltzing into the apartment, genuine humor lights up his handsome face. "Give me a break, B." He throws his arms wide. "Take a good look around. This is what you want? This...*ordinariness*?"

He spits the last word out as if it's a dirty one.

I glance around the apartment. All the little touches I've added over the months have turned it into a home. Maybe it's less than seven hundred square feet in size, but it's become a refuge.

I can pick up my guitar from the corner any time I want and work on a song. I can do it because something I haven't felt in years now hums through my veins.

Creativity.

A genuine need to put pencil to paper and jot down lyrics and musical notes.

What can't be denied is that my tiny apartment is vastly different from the eight thousand square foot luxury rental Mom found in the Hollywood Hills, where we film practically twenty-four seven. I can barely escape to the bathroom without cameras attempting to follow me in.

A shiver of dread snakes down my spine at the thought of returning to that life again.

I don't want to leave the friends I've made. Juliette, Carina, Stella, Viola, and Fallyn have all been so welcoming and friendly. And then there's Ava. She's someone I'm still getting to know. But I think, with enough time, we could be close.

None of these girls are anything like the ones I've met in LA.

They don't smile at my face before stabbing me in the back the second I turn away. They don't talk shit and try to tear me down because their careers haven't taken off the way mine did.

"Yeah, I do."

His pale blue eyes spark with anger as his thinly veiled pretense falls away. "Well, that's too bad. You don't get a choice in the matter. So, do me a favor and go pack your shit." He waves toward the bedroom before glancing at the silver Rolex wrapped around his left wrist. "I want to be on our way to the airport in an hour."

My heart accelerates as I fold my arms over my chest. "No. I'm not leaving."

His expression hardens. "Excuse me?"

"I said that I'm not leaving. I enrolled in classes for the semester, and it's important that I finish them." With a gulp, I attempt to steady my nerves. "If my parents and siblings want to continue the show, they can do it without me. I'm done."

I'm ready for a change.

Even if the people in my life aren't.

"We both know your fucking family can't hold that show together," he says with a snort.

"Cheyenne can sing and act. She could easily slide into my place." And she'd be thrilled to do it. Over the years, my sister has grown resentful that she's always stuck in second place. Relegated to the shadows. It can't be denied that in my absence, she's flourished.

Axel rolls his eyes. "The only thing she's got going for her is a great set of tits."

I spring to my feet and realize that I'm shaking from head to toe. "It's time for you to leave."

He rises before taking a menacing step in my direction. "The only way that's happening is if you're with me."

When he stalks closer, a flurry of nerves explodes at the bottom of my belly.

"Here's the thing, Bebe—I don't care if I have to drag you out by your hair. We're boarding that plane and getting the fuck out of here. You've lost your damn mind if you think I'm going to lose my career because some ungrateful bitch no longer wants the fame and fortune I helped build."

"You didn't build anything." With a shake of my head, I point at my chest. "*I did.*"

Air gets clogged in my lungs when he grits his teeth, the muscle in his jaw ticking as he lunges.

"You touch one goddamn hair on her head, and I'll bury you."

On shaky legs, I swing toward Colby as relief bubbles up inside me.

Axel glares at the muscular hockey player. "I don't know how you got in here, but do us all a favor and show yourself out. This conversation doesn't concern you, asshole."

Colby eats up the distance between us with a handful of long-legged strides before snaking his arm around my waist and hauling me close. The woodsy scent of his cologne does the impossible and calms everything raging inside me.

That's all it takes for my knees to weaken as I lean into his comforting strength.

"Actually, that's where you're wrong. Britt is my wife. Anything that concerns her is my business."

Axel's narrowed gaze slices to me. Only now do I see the hatred burning in his pale blue depths. On some level, I've always sensed his true feelings. Only now does it occur to me that by breaking off our pseudo-relationship, I've dodged a major bullet.

He never gave a damn.

It was always about the show.

"Are you really going to throw away everything we've built over the years for a nobody?"

My gaze locks on Colby's. "This man could never be a nobody. He's my husband." I pause for a heartbeat. "And I love him."

His arm tightens, pressing me closer.

I straighten to my full height. It would be so easy to hide behind Colby and allow him to fight this battle, but this is something I need to take care of myself.

It's important that I end it here and now.

"We don't have anything further to discuss. As far as I'm concerned, there's no reason for us to ever talk again. You need to leave."

He stabs a finger in my direction. "I'll make sure you regret this decision. Do you hear me?" His voice escalates with every word as spittle flies from his mouth. "You'll never work again. Your pathetic excuse for a career is over!"

Fear pools in the pit of my belly before I quash it. As much as Axel wishes he had the power that comes with those kinds of threats, he doesn't.

"Get out."

When he doesn't budge, Colby growls, "You heard my wife. Get the fuck out of our apartment and don't come back."

Color rides high on Axel's sharp cheekbones. Even though it's obvious he wants to argue, he stalks from the living area and into the entryway before slamming the door shut behind him. The thick wood reverberates on its hinges as a deafening silence falls over us.

Colby's hands settle on my shoulders before he turns me until we're facing each other.

"Are you all right?" His brows pinch together as he examines my face. "Did he hurt you?"

"No, he never touched me."

But he would have.

He would have used brute force had it become necessary. I could see it in his eyes and hear the threat of violence filling his voice.

A shiver scampers down my spine as I release a shaky breath.

I've known Axel for years and have seen him lose his shit on producers and other people deemed beneath him, but his ire has never been directed at me because I always played my part and did what I was supposed to.

Until now.

Colby tugs me against his chest until my senses are inundated with his scent. It's enough to calm everything that vibrates within.

Even though it's the last thing I want to do, I pull away enough to meet his steady gaze. "How did you get in here?"

He fishes a small metal object from the pocket of his jeans. "I still have my key."

Emotion swells in my throat. "Did you come back to return it?"

He searches my eyes for a long, painful heartbeat. One that has my nerves stretching so taut that it feels as if they'll snap.

"No, I came back because I wanted to talk. I told you yesterday that I needed some time and space to deal with everything that happened."

I release a steady stream of air from my lungs, relieved that he's willing to hear me out.

Unable to resist touching him, my hand rises to cup his shadowed cheek. "I'm so sorry. I should have been honest about who I was. Maybe it's not something I could have done right away in the beginning, but I should have done it sooner so you could deal with it without the world finding out at the same time."

"I wish it could have happened differently as well. After putting myself in your shoes, I understand why you held back." His voice dips. "And I don't blame you for it."

Shock spirals through me. "You don't?"

"No."

When he doesn't continue, I force myself to ask the one question that has been weighing heaviest on me. It's the answer I'm most afraid of but need to hear.

"What happens now?"

"I guess that depends." He searches my eyes as if it's possible to inspect my innermost thoughts. "Do you want a divorce? I know you never wanted this marriage."

A thick lump settles in my throat, making it impossible to swallow. Out of everything I've done in my life, this by far is the scariest.

My entire future feels as if it's at stake.

"I want to see if we can make this work." I gulp down my nerves and force out the truth. "I want *you*."

Instead of responding, he asks, "Did you really mean it when you said that you loved me?"

I lean onto the tips of my toes and press my lips against his. "I've never meant anything more."

His arms snake around my body as he hauls me closer. "I love you too and can't imagine my life without you filling it."

"Good." I nip his bottom lip, tugging at the plump flesh before releasing it with a soft pop. "I hope that means you'll move back in."

"Baby, wild horses couldn't keep me away."

With that, he sweeps me into his arms and carries me into the bedroom.

COLBY

36

Other than Brit strumming her guitar as she sings the lyrics of her new song on stage, the bar is silent. I'd glance around, but I can't take my eyes off my wife.

And I'm certainly not the only one.

Everyone is captivated by her acoustic performance.

It's standing room only.

Gerry, the bouncer, had to turn people away at the door.

When fans find out that she's going to play a set, they descend on the joint. Sometimes coming from a hundred miles away. Everyone wants to catch a glimpse of Britt McNichols.

She no longer goes by Bebe Benson.

Now that she isn't in hiding, she's blossomed into a different person. I've loved watching her grow and figure out who she is deep down inside. The woman who has been fighting to come out. She's discovering what she likes. And that includes her music.

The songs she's been working on lately are more soulful in nature and less pop.

Like the one she sang to me on the plane.

Stella shakes her head. "I still can't believe that our Britt is actually Bebe. Consider my mind officially blown."

"I'm just glad she's sticking around and not leaving us," Carina adds.

"Me, too," Fallyn says, mouthing the lyrics as Britt croons them on stage.

Wolf squeezes his new wife, burying his face in the strands of her dark hair. "You're so adorable when you try to sing."

Fallyn turns to him with a frown. "What do you mean *try to*?"

He pulls away with a grin. "Babe..."

Her dark brows rise. "Are you saying I'm not good?"

"How about you go back to singing and I'll go back to cuddling you?"

A smile breaks out across her face before she leans forward and kisses him. "Sounds good to me."

Bridger pulls off his ball cap before plowing a hand through his hair. "Well, it's official. Another one bites the dust. I always figured it would be you and me at the end." He nods toward Hayes. "Maybe that guy. Can't see him getting tied down anytime soon."

I rip my attention away from Britt long enough to glance at the golden blond center who's grinning at Larsa Middleton as she trails her hands over his chest. Hayes has always made it perfectly clear that he doesn't have time for a girlfriend. Not with all the family responsibility that rests on his shoulders.

"Sorry, bud. Looks like it's just you, Hayes, and Mav now." My gaze settles on Steele, who's holding court at the end of the table. "And probably your cousin."

"And you're cool if he takes over your room for the rest of the semester?"

I shake my head before lifting the beer to my lips. "It's all his. I won't be moving back anytime soon."

"Cool."

Once the final chords reverberate throughout the bar, thunderous applause breaks out. People leap to their feet, whistling and shouting for an encore. Britt plays one more song before taking a small bow and stepping off the stage. She doesn't get more than a couple of feet before her uncle envelopes her in a warm embrace and kisses her cheek.

Did he just so happen to pull me aside when he found out that I'd married his niece in Vegas?

You bet your damn ass he did.

After we had ourselves a little chat—his term, not mine—he clapped me on the back and told me with a cheery smile that if I caused Britt one moment of heartache, he'd have no problem making me disappear.

Permanently.

I reassured him that there was no way in hell that would happen. I loved her more than anything and my new mission in life was to make her happy. He seemed to accept that response, and we've been having Sunday dinners at his place ever since.

Here's a little something that I refuse to admit to anyone else—my lasagna is better.

But you didn't hear that from me.

My gaze remains fastened onto my wife as she moves through the crowd. People surround her, wanting to talk. She's always gracious about accepting their accolades.

A smile curves her lips as our eyes lock from across the space that separates us. When I grow impatient and rise to my feet, ready to cut a path straight to her and steal her from her fans, she slips away and beelines toward me. The closer she gets, the more my heart picks up tempo.

That's the way it is with this girl.

She's changed everything.

I can barely remember what it was like before she came into my life.

And I wouldn't have it any other way.

As soon as she's close enough, I reach out and nab her fingers before drawing her into my arms. Exactly where she belongs. It's only when she's wrapped up tight that I'm able to breathe again.

"You were amazing up there."

She presses her lips to mine. "Thank you. Did I mention that the song was for you?"

I can't help but grin. "Pretty sure I thanked you last night." There's a pause. "Not to mention the night before that."

Heat fills her golden eyes. "You certainly did."

"Don't worry, sweet girl," I whisper. "I have no problem thanking you all night long."

"Promise?"

"Always."

EPILOGUE

A ir stalls in my lungs when I catch my first glimpse of Britt as she pauses on the beach. Everyone rises to their feet as the music changes.

I don't think I've ever seen her look so damn beautiful.

Her caramel-colored strands have been swept up to the top of her head with a few loose tendrils left to curl around her face. Her gaze locks on mine as she proceeds down the makeshift aisle, each step bringing her closer.

Everyone fades to the background until she's all I'm cognizant of. This girl is my fucking world, and I have no idea how I lived so long without her filling it.

When her lips lift, I return the smile, giving her a wink as she closes the distance between us. As beautiful as she looks in the strapless dress that hugs every delectable curve, I can't wait to strip her out of it.

Hell, maybe we can sneak away during the reception so I can get my hands on her.

If the years we have stretched out before us are anything like our first six months together, then getting hitched in Vegas will have been the best damn decision I ever made.

I can't imagine another woman I'd rather go through life with.

Britt is the one for me.

Just like I'm the one for her.

Which is exactly why we decided to tie the knot all over again. Because that's the kind of thing a couple likes to remember, and the finer details from Vegas are murky at best.

After signing a three-year contract with the Milwaukee Mavericks, we decided on a destination wedding in the Virgin Islands.

Hey, it worked for both my parents and grandparents, so why the hell not?

Everybody's here to help celebrate.

Both her family and mine.

All I can say is that Britt wasn't lying when she said that her family was kind of extra. They're over-the-top cray-cray.

When the producers of her show asked if they could film our wedding as a TV special, Britt told them abso-fucking-lutely not.

All right, those might not have been her exact words, but you get the point.

Her agent even tried brokering a deal for a spin-off show that featured us and the first couple of years of our marriage.

That was also a no-go.

Now that Britt has stepped away from the spotlight, she's more protective of her privacy.

And of us as a couple.

Over the previous months, she's given a few interviews. When asked about our marriage and what I'm like, she responds with a sweet smile and asks for the next question.

I don't think it's possible to love this girl any more than I already do.

Once Britt makes it down the aisle with her father, I reach out and shake his hand before grinning at her like a lunatic. The officiant gives her spiel and before you know it, we're married for a second time. Everyone claps and cheers. All the guys from Western showed up with their significant others.

Even Hayes and Bridger.

With training camp right around the corner, it's impossible not to dwell on how much I'm going to miss playing with the Wildcats. No matter how close I get to my new teammates, there's no way they'll be able to replace them.

When it comes down to it, we all grew up together.

Became men together.

And two of us got hitched together.

Fuck.

Now I'm getting maudlin, and that's definitely not the vibe I'm going for.

Not when I've married the love of my life all over again.

After the ceremony, the party moves to the open-air restaurant on the beach. There's dinner and dancing to cheesy eighties music. Britt sings a few new songs she's been working on and then a throwback. The one that went viral and launched her career to stardom.

All the guests sing along.

I take a moment to glance around the reception. Everyone's laughing, drinking, and having a blast. Which means that it's the perfect time to slip away. Life has been chaotic since we arrived on the island a few days ago. Now that the deed has been done, we can finally chill out and enjoy ourselves.

I nab Britt's fingers and tow her toward the exit. She quickens her steps to keep pace.

"Where are we going?" she asks, her voice sounding light and happy.

"I've missed you, sweet girl. You've been so busy planning all this the past month. I wanted to steal a little time alone with you."

We hit the sand and leave the boardwalk behind. A large silvery moon hangs heavy in the sky, sending cascades of light across the ocean as the rhythmic sound of the waves washing up on the beach fills my ears.

Today couldn't have been more perfect, and I can't imagine sharing it with anyone other than her. When we're a few feet from the water, I drop down and pull Britt onto my lap. My arms slip around her waist to hold her close. A few strands of her hair whip in the wind and slide across my cheek as she snuggles against me.

After I was drafted, Brit decided to transfer to UW-Milwaukee and continue working toward her degree. Then we picked out an apartment with killer views of Lake Michigan.

Life's pretty sweet right now, and there's not a damned thing I'd change about it.

I nuzzle her neck as the warm wind caresses our bare skin. "Are you happy, sweet girl?"

With a smile, she angles her face toward mine. Contentment shines brightly from her eyes. It's an amazing feeling to know that I have everything to do with it.

"Of course I am. Today was perfect, don't you think?"

I nod in agreement. "It was. And you were gorgeous."

"You didn't look so shabby yourself."

"I'll take that as a compliment."

She presses her lips against mine and whispers, "I love you."

"I love you, too." So freaking much that it hurts my heart.

And I can't see that ever changing.

Right now, we're happy to live in our little bubble.

We've had all the big talks, including ones about kiddos.

The plan is to wait a few years, but since we both come from big families, that's what we want for ourselves.

When my hunger gets the best of me, my mouth finds hers. One sweep of my tongue against the seam of her lips and she opens, allowing me entrance just like always. I break away long enough to turn her in my arms so that we're facing one another. She hikes up the flowy material around her thighs until she's able to straddle my legs. I'm already hard as steel.

Her palms settle on my cheeks as our gazes cling. "Do you have any idea how much I love you?"

I didn't think it was possible for anything to deter thoughts of getting my hands on my wife, but the sound of her husky voice and the soft look that fills her expression does the trick.

"I love you too, firecracker. You know that. What I feel for you grows stronger with the passing of each day. You're it for me. You might have needed some convincing in the beginning, but I didn't. One look at Slap Shotz and I was a goner."

"Oh, Colby."

With that, her lips crash onto mine. As soon as I open, her tongue dips inside to tangle with my own. My hands stroke over the long line of her spine before pressing her closer.

When she shifts, I growl. "Baby, you keep that up and we won't make it back to our suite before I have you."

She pulls away long enough to smirk. The silvery moonlight that slants down on us highlights the mischievous glint in her eyes. "Maybe that's exactly what I want."

A tortured groan falls from my lips.

There's no doubt about it—this girl will end up killing me.

But it would be one hell of a way to go.

She peeks over my shoulder to look at the open-air restaurant that glows in the distance. "I think we could probably sneak in a quickie before anyone realizes that we're MIA."

One brow slants upward. "Don't tease me, woman."

In answer, she rises to her knees and shifts her dress around before yanking her thong to the side. My cock stiffens as my gaze settles on the vee between her legs. Need spirals through me as I fumble with my belt, button, and zipper of my slacks until my thick erection is unleashed.

As soon as she slides down my hard length, we both groan and a sense of rightness washes over me.

The best part of it all is that being buried deep inside her body feels like coming home.

Because that's exactly what Britt is for me.

My home.

Where I'll always belong.

In the darkest nights, I stumbled, couldn't see the light.
Lost in a maze, couldn't find what's right.
But deep inside, a fire burned,
refusing to fade away.
A voice inside me whispered, 'You'll find your way.'

I'm rising up, stronger now than I've ever been.
Every scar's a story, ain't letting them win.
Through the ups and downs, I'll find my truth.
In the chaos of it all, I'll find my youth.

Through every fall and every doubt, I'll stand tall.
Gonna shake off the past, gonna give it my all.
With each new day, leaving old fears behind.
Embracing every challenge, gonna free my mind.

BRITT

bonus EPILOGUE

Four years later...

The final buzzer rings throughout the arena as the sea of spectators goes nuts, cheering for their beloved hometown team. The Milwaukee Mavericks have pulled off another win, clinching a spot in the playoffs.

Tonight, there'll be some major celebrations around town.

Hell, probably the state.

Avery's tiny hands settle over her ears as she stares at the crowd with wide eyes filled with awe.

And a little bit of fear.

"It's all right, baby," I tell her. "Everyone is happy. They're celebrating that Daddy and his teammates won the game."

She claps her hands together and gives me a big, toothy grin.

Now that she's walking, Colby insists I bring her to the games so she can watch him in action. Just like he insisted on buying her a pair of little pink skates. If he has his way, she'll follow in his footsteps and play hockey. At two, she's his little mini me and he loves it.

"Should we go see Dada?"

"Dada!" she squeals in excitement.

With that, we pack up all our stuff from the private suite where all the other wives and girlfriends congregate for the games. Avery enjoys it because there are kids to play with, plenty of space to run around, and snacks galore. Even though she's only two, she'll stare out the glass that overlooks the ice and point to her father while chanting his name. When he scores a goal, he looks right at her and makes a heart with his hands.

That always makes the crowd go wild.

Especially the female fans.

It takes a while for us to make our way through the concourse and then past security to where the locker rooms are located. By the time we get there, players are already out of the shower and giving interviews to the press.

A few of Colby's teammates wave as we sneak past. Their gazes soften when they catch sight of Avery in her pink jacket. Colby's number is stitched on the front and back along with his name. There's a Milwaukee Mavericks hat with a little pompom on her head.

Want to see grown men who enjoy beating the hell out of each other on the ice turn to mush?

Show them a two-year-old decked out in team gear.

They melt like butter every single time.

I've never been the jealous type. And I was never concerned about losing Colby to another female. But that's exactly what happened the night Avery was born. She's the spitting image of him with blonde hair, bright blue eyes, and a sunny disposition that charms the pants off everyone she meets.

Not to mention the dimples.

She's the apple of her father's eye and has him wrapped around her little finger.

It's the most adorable thing ever.

Over the years, Colby has matured so much. He's become a man that I trust not only with my life but our daughter's as well.

And if he has his way, there'll be more little McNichols in the future. It's something I want, too. During the season, I work on song writing. From May to September, Colby is home and I'm able to hit the road and play select venues. What I like best is seeing Colby and Avery in the audience.

I wouldn't trade the life we've built for anything.

As I pass Wyatt, one of Colby's teammates, he perks up. "Hey, Britt. How are you doing?" His gaze drops to Avery, who grins at him. There's not a shy bone in this girl's body. "Hey, munchkin." When he holds out his fist for her to bump, she squeals and slaps at it. "One of these days, we're gonna get the hang of it."

I snort. "I wouldn't count on it. This girl marches to the beat of her own drum."

He cups the side of her face in his palm. "She almost makes me want one of my own."

With a laugh, I shake my head. "It might help to settle down with just one girl before you make any life-altering decisions."

Wyatt Hillcrest is known around the league for a lot of things, but monogamy isn't one of them.

And at twenty-six years old, who can blame him?

I nod toward the locker room. "Is it safe for us to go inside?"

The last thing I want to do is mentally scar my daughter.

"Yup. In fact, your hubby is the last dawdler in there."

"Perfect. Thanks."

He takes a few steps away before swinging around. "Tell the old man that he had a good game."

I raise a brow. "You really want me to do that?"

He flashes a shit-eating grin. One capable of dropping panties all over this town. "Absolutely."

"You must enjoy taking your life into your own hands, huh?"

He chuckles as I shake my head and push through the heavy metal door into the spacious locker room.

"Dada!" Avery wiggles out of my arms and takes off, knowing exactly where she'll find her father.

"Sounds like my girls are here!" Colby steps out from a row of lockers wearing gray, low-slung sweatpants and nothing else. My mouth turns cottony at the sight.

If it's possible, he's in even better shape now than when we met in college.

As soon as Avery throws herself at him, he wraps her up tight and lifts her into his arms. My step falters as I watch them. These two are the most important people in my life, and the sight of them together always makes my heart swell until it feels like it's on the verge of bursting.

I can't resist pulling out my phone and snapping a quick pic. If I were a social media kind of girlie, this is one shot that would send Colby's female fanbase into a rabid frenzy. Now that Booktok has taken off, he's a fan favorite.

I mean, come on...just look at him.

Of course he is.

Which is exactly why it'll stay private, for my enjoyment only.

His gaze flicks from our daughter to me before he flashes a sexy grin. "Hey, babe."

"Hey right back at you."

He rearranges Avery in one arm before reaching for me. That's all the incentive I need to swallow up the distance between us. As soon as I'm close enough, he snags my fingers. I stretch onto the tips of my toes to brush my mouth across his.

"You had an amazing game," I whisper. There's nothing more that I love than watching him play. The way he dominates and takes control. It's the same way he is in the bedroom.

He waggles his thick brows. "Does that mean we'll be having our own celebration after this one goes to sleep?"

"That was the plan."

He groans. "Then let's get out of here."

An hour later, Avery is tucked into her crib and snoring softly. I have the feeling that it won't be long before we're moving her into a big girl bed. She's growing up so fast. A little pang of sadness blooms in my chest before I snuff it out and head to our bedroom.

Just like in the locker room, I find Colby bare chested, sitting on the edge of the king-sized bed waiting for me. A pair of flannel pajama pants cover his lower half.

I have no idea why that's so sexy.

By the way his bright blue eyes dance with a mixture of heat and humor, he knows it.

When he holds out his hand, I cut a path straight to him. There's nothing I love more than being held in his strong arms. From day one, they've made me feel safe and protected. He slips them around my body before towing me close enough to rest my head against his broad shoulder.

"What's wrong, sweet girl?"

"Nothing."

He pries me loose until he's able to search my eyes. "Tell me. You know I don't like seeing my girl sad."

"I'm not sad."

He raises a thick brow. "But?"

With a shrug, I force a smile. "Avery's growing up so fast. Pretty soon she'll be out of her crib and into a real bed."

"Well, it was bound to happen," he murmurs.

"I know. I'm just going to miss this stage. I've really enjoyed it."

"Then maybe it's time to work on a sibling for her."

"You might be right."

A slow smile spreads across his lips as heat ignites in his eyes. "We can start tonight if you'd like."

One hand slips around the nape of my neck as he pulls me to him until I'm close enough for his mouth to cover mine. As soon as his tongue sweeps across the seam of my lips, I open. The deep, languid strokes he uses leave me breathless and hungry for more.

His other hand settles at the hem of my tank top before he drags the stretchy material up my torso and over my head until I'm just as bare chested as he is. His gaze drops to my breasts to palm the softness.

"Have I mentioned how much I love these? Especially when you're pregnant?"

With Avery, I was horny all the time. And Colby was just as turned on by my changing body.

"Mmm...maybe."

"Then let me remind you."

With that, he brings one stiffened bud to his lips before drawing it inside the warmth of his mouth. I can't help but arch, loving his touch. It's one I'll never grow tired of. He releases the tip with a soft pop before focusing his attention on the other. My fingers tunnel through his thick blond strands to hold him in place.

When he finally releases me, his eyelids are heavy and at half-mast as he straightens to his full height. His arms band around my ribcage before hoisting me off my feet until my legs can tangle around his waist. I can't help grinding against his thick erection, needing so much more.

Everything he's willing to give.

As much as I love the flannel pants, I want them gone.

He swings us around before placing me in the middle of the mattress and then following me down. A groan escapes from him as his lips find mine again. He adores my mouth for a few breathless minutes before he sinks lower, kissing a fiery trail along my jawline, throat, and collarbone. He rains sweet kisses on my chest before drifting down my ribcage and belly to the band of my panties.

He glances up until our gazes can catch. "These need to go."

"Please."

A devilish smile quirks his lips. "Oh, sweet girl...you know how much I love when you beg."

He hooks his fingers beneath the elastic and draws the silky material down my hips and thighs before dropping them to the floor beside the bed. His hands press against my inner thighs to spread me wide.

"So fucking beautiful," he growls.

Unable to help myself, I shift, only wanting to feel the heat of his mouth lapping at my softness. It's something I dream about.

When he taps my clit with the tips of his fingers, sensation explodes within me.

"You're always so damn greedy, aren't you?"

My spine arches in answer. "Only for you."

With that, his mouth settles over me. Already I know it won't take much to make me come. When his velvety softness dances around my clit for a second time, it's all I can do not to scream out my orgasm. His fingers, tongue, and lips continue to love me until my muscles turn slack and I melt into the mattress. Only then does he press a kiss against my soaked pussy and crawl up my body until the head of his thick cock is nestled against my entrance.

His eyes lock on mine as he holds himself perfectly still. "I love you, firecracker."

"I love you, too."

With that, he slides deep inside the heat of my body, filling me to the brim.

Giving me every piece of himself.

Holding nothing back.

And just like always, I tumble head over heels in love with him all over again.

Because this man is my everything.

And that will never change.

No matter what life throws at us.

The End

Thank you so much for reading Never Say Never! I hope you enjoyed Britt and Colby's story as much as I loved writing it!

Did you know that Whitney and Gray have their own story?

Turn the page for an excerpt of The Breakup Plan...

THE BREAKUP PLAN
WHITNEY

Out of nowhere, a brawny arm slides around my shoulders and hauls me close, anchoring me against a muscular body. Without looking, I know exactly who the culprit pinning me in place is. The woodsy scent is a dead giveaway.

The deep voice confirms my sinking suspicions.

Grayson McNichols.

"Miss me, baby?" he growls against my ear as his warm breath sends shivers skittering down my spine.

There's an edge of humor simmering in his voice that thankfully kills the unwanted attraction that has leapt to life at his proximity. No matter how much I fight against it, he affects me like this every time. It's why I've made it my mission in life to steer clear of Mr. Hellcat Hockey himself.

Needing to create distance between us before I get sucked any further into his orbit, I ram my elbow into his ribs. It's not nearly hard enough to do any real damage, or even to separate myself from him so I can make a quick getaway.

Gray sticks to me like glue.

"Sure did. Almost as much as I'd miss a particularly nasty case of herpes." I brace myself before flicking my eyes in his direction. "No matter what I do, you keep making an unsightly appearance at the worst possible time, just like an incurable STI." I bare my teeth so he won't think I'm being flirty.

He smirks.

My acidic comments are like water off a duck's back.

It's annoying.

Just like him.

"So, what you're really trying to say is that I'm persistent," he waggles his dark brows in a comical manner, "and you find that oddly appealing."

Please...

As if...

Nothing could be further from the truth. Gray McNichols could eat shit and die, as far as I'm concerned.

He flashes me his trademark smile.

Dimples and all.

Ugh.

Those dimples are a real killer. If I have one weakness, it's for a guy with Eddie Cibrian dimples. And Gray has them in spades. Now that I think about it, he kind of resembles Eddie Cibrian, circa early 2000's. I try not to let the smile or—God help me—the dimples affect me, but it's no easy feat.

I've spent years trying to steel myself against his magnetism and charm. To this day, I'm just barely able to hold on to my composure. Most of my behavior is sheer bravado. If he ever pushed me hard enough, the straw house I've built around myself for protection would collapse.

Not only is Gray ridiculously handsome, but he's captain of the Hillsdale Hellcat hockey team, which only ups his hotness factor around campus. My guess is that he's slept his way through half the female population at Hillsdale. All he has to do is smile and girls drop their panties before falling on their backs and spreading their legs wide.

How do I know this?

Here comes the embarrassing part...

Once upon a time, *I* was one of those girls.

Yup, it's sad but true.

I know exactly what it's like to have all that charismatic attention aimed in my direction. It happened second semester of freshman year. I'd seen Gray around campus and was a smitten kitten. And then, one night at a party, we hooked up.

Needless to say, it was a fuck-and-flee situation—the kind that's chock-full of regret in the morning. I blame alcohol for my poor judgment.

Surprise surprise, I never heard a peep from Gray again.

Was I stupid enough to expect more?

Guilty as charged.

He fed me all the lines that are hot guy kryptonite to stupid girls like me, and I fell for it. Hook, line, and sinker.

I know, I know...

Total.

Idiot.

Trust me, I won't dispute the title. It may have taken a while, but I've come to a place of acceptance. Now, does that mean I'm dumb enough to fall for his easy breezy charm for a second time?

Hell to the no.

Those memories are all it takes to strengthen my resolve.

"What do you want, McNichols?" I hasten my step as we navigate the path that cuts through the heart of campus, but it does no good. I can't separate myself from him. He keeps me trapped at his side.

People wave and shout Gray's name, trying to capture his attention. His celebrity status is irritating. I seem to be one of the few students at Hillsdale who wants no part of him. Like a man who's at ease with his station in life, he acknowledges his clamoring fanbase with a chin lift and a practiced wave of his hand.

What a pompous jerk.

Hillsdale is a Division I hockey school. Every year there are a handful of players drafted to the NHL. There's no question that the muscular defenseman will get snapped up by the pros.

How could he not?

He's the lead scorer three years running.

And yeah, that would be off the ice as well as on it.

Everyone at this school loves him.

Hell, the whole town worships him.

It's nauseating.

He could have accepted a full ride from any top-notch university in the United States—everyone was vying for him—but he chose Hillsdale.

Lucky us.

You'd assume with over ten thousand students on campus, the chances of running into him on a nearly daily basis would be astronomically low.

Think again.

I wasn't joking when I likened Gray to an incurable STI. Every time I turn around, there he is, in my face, acting like we're BFF's.

We don't live near each other.

We're not in the same major or in any classes together.

I make it a habit to avoid parties that I suspect he'll be gracing with his esteemed presence. There are a ton of puck bunnies around these parts, but I'm not one of them.

And yet, I can't get away from this guy to save my life.

Thank God this is our senior year. Once we graduate in May, I'll never see Gray again. It's that knowledge that makes it possible for me to get through moments like this.

"Just checking to see if you've changed your mind about us getting together."

I snort at that little bit of ridiculousness. "Umm, I'm sorry. Did Hell happen to freeze over, and I'm the last one to find out?"

He squeezes my shoulder and a jolt of unwanted electricity zips through me. I gnash my teeth against my body's natural response to him.

"You know how much I love it when you play hard to get." He punctuates that sentiment by nipping at my neck.

My heart flutters, and it takes everything I have inside to keep my voice level and not betray the attraction roaring violently through my veins. "I'm not playing hard to get. What I'm playing is *I-don't-want-to-talk-to-you-ever-again*. If you weren't such a meathead, you'd realize the difference and act accordingly." Before he can sweet-talk me into a situation I'll end up regretting, I fire off a pertinent question. "And when was the last time you actually took a girl out on a date?"

I'm not a moron. I know the answer, but I want to hear him say it. It's my ace in the hole, so to speak. Which is a far cry from the ace in the hole *he's* hoping to get.

That won't be happening.

"Never," he admits cheerfully, "but I'd be willing to make an exception for you, Winters."

See what I'm talking about?

Hot guy kryptonite for sure.

But I'm way too smart for him. Plus, I'd like to think that I learn from my mistakes, which is a far cry from some of the other girls around here.

We're about a block away from Thorson Hall, the business building on campus where I'm headed. At this point, I'm practically speed walking. The sooner we get there, the faster I can ditch Gray.

"It's a tempting offer," I lie, "but I'll be taking a hard pass."

His face falls as he presses his hand against his chest.

And what a magnificent chest it is.

With gritted teeth, I shove that errant thought away before it can worm its way into my psyche and do permanent damage.

"You wound me, Winters. All I want is one date and you're shooting me down without even considering the offer. Aren't you the least bit curious where I'd take you?"

Nope.

Not even a little.

"Sure," I snicker. "Let me guess." I tap a finger thoughtfully against my chin. "Would it be a little place called Bonetown? I'm willing to bet it is." I force my voice to fill with boredom. "Been there, done that, have the T-shirt to prove it."

His laugh is rich and low. It strums something deep inside me.

He tugs me closer. "Have I mentioned how much I love your sense of humor?"

"Please," I scoff, uncomfortable with the physical intimacy. My left breast is squashed against his side. The last thing I need is for my nip to pebble and him to feel the physical evidence of my desire. That would only encourage him to pursue me more fervently than he already is.

And that, I couldn't withstand.

I hold my breath, not wanting to inhale anymore of his decadent scent. I need to get away from him before I melt into a puddle. This flirtation is nothing more than a game. It's what Gray is known for.

Why does he insist on messing with me when I've gone out of my way to make my disinterest clear?

Doesn't he realize that there's no shortage of puck bunnies who would be more than happy to shower him with adoration? He could easily score with any number of them. Probably at the same time.

I glance around, noticing quite a number of girls staring in our direction.

It's enough to make me shake my head in disgust.

Get a grip, ladies! This guy is toxic to the female population!

"Have you ever considered," he says, breaking into my thoughts, "that what I need is the love of a good woman to change me for the better?"

Laughter wells in my throat before bursting free. "You're so full of shit!"

The love of a good woman, indeed.

Ha!

As if...

Gray grins and his dimples pop in tandem. "Maybe."

"Oh, there's no *maybe* about it, McNichols. You're *definitely* full of shit."

I didn't think it was possible for him to tug me closer, but he manages to do it before whispering, "Don't you remember how good it felt when I was buried deep inside you? Come on, Winters. Admit it, you want me."

And there you have it...

The extent of his interest doesn't go any further than him dipping his wick.

I need to get away from Gray before he destroys every shred of my resolve. Deep down, I know he's the worst possible guy for me, but my lady parts are clamoring for his attention.

And that, my friends, would be my cue to leave.

Without warning, I stop and jerk out of his arms. People grumble as they're forced to walk around us.

"Let me make this perfectly clear." I harden my voice, refusing to be taken in by his good looks and easy charm. When it comes down to it, this guy is a predator. If he senses a moment of weakness, he'll take me down before I realize I was being hunted in the first place. And then I'll be lost. "You're the last guy on campus I would sleep with. Your stroke game was mediocre at best, and our encounter was entirely forgettable."

Instead of taking offense, he tilts his head and rubs his chin with his fingers. "Is that so?" He steps closer, his muscular body invading my space yet again, and my body sizzles with the contact. "I find that hard to believe. I've never had any complaints about my," he smirks, "*stroke game*." His finger finds its way to the curve of my cheek. "But I'd be more than happy to give you an encore performance so you can reevaluate your verdict."

I gulp and step away until his hand falls to his side and I can breathe again.

Oxygen rushes to my deprived brain.

Seriously?

How am I supposed to get through to this guy when he refuses to listen to a single word I say?

Unwilling to waste another moment on him, I throw my hands up and stalk toward my one o'clock class.

"So," he shouts at my retreating figure, "you're going to think about it and get back to me, right?"

I flip him the bird and keep walking.

One-click The Breakup Plan now!

CAMPUS HEARTTHROB

BRAYDEN

"Yo, Kendricks, grab me a cold one when you come back," Asher Stevens yells as I walk into the kitchen.

I give him a one-fingered salute to let him know that I heard him loud and clear. That guy drinks like it's his sole mission in life. By the time he graduates college this spring, he'll be in desperate need of a liver transplant. Although, I've got to give him credit—he's at the top of his game on the field. I have no idea how he does it. It's one of the great mysteries in life that I've stopped trying to unravel.

With a yank, I open the refrigerator door and scan the shelves. What I find is a depressing sight. Other than a shit ton of beer and Gatorade, it looks more like a barren wasteland.

Bunch of fuckers.

Don't these guys realize that we live half a mile from the nearest grocery store? Hell, with a few taps on their phone, groceries would magically appear outside the front door.

We're all supposed to be pitching in with the domestic chores. One look around this place will tell you that isn't happening. The toilet on the first floor resembles a sketchy Chia Pet. Plus, it smells like the penguin house at the zoo.

I avoid it at all costs.

With a grumble, I pull out one of the last bottles of water and twist off the top before guzzling down a quarter of it. Then I grab a Miller Lite for Stevens. I've tried broaching the subject of his alcohol consumption a few times, but it's not like I'm his mom. The dude is twenty-one years old; he can do whatever the hell he wants.

Carson, one of the other guys who lives here, saunters in as I slam the refrigerator door closed.

Carson Roberts and I go way back. We're talking elementary school. He's practically part of the family. The brother I never had but always wanted. He was there when I needed him and got me through one of the toughest times in my life. Even at twenty-one years old, I realize that friends like that aren't easy to come by.

Football is what we originally bonded over. We've been playing together since second grade. First, flag football before moving on to a middle school team and then high school. Luckily, we both ended up at the same college and roomed together freshman and sophomore years before finding a house with a couple of teammates. Like me, Carson will enter the draft in the spring. He's one of the best tight ends in the conference and was an All-American last year. The guy is one smart motherfucker.

Before I can open my mouth, he says, "Heads up, Kira just walked in."

Goddamn it.

A groan escapes from me.

That girl takes crazy, psycho stalker to a whole new level. It's almost as impressive as it is frightening.

Scratch that. It's just plain frightening. There have been numerous times when I've come home, afraid I'd find our pet rabbit boiling away on the stove.

Just kidding, we don't have a bunny.

But still...

You get the point I'm trying to make. It's fucking scary. And she won't leave me alone. I've tried everything, going so far as to tell her that it's never going to happen between us.

I mean, come on. Of course it's not going to happen!

I've never even locked lips with this chick, and she shadows me around campus and turns up in my classes. I'm *this* close to taking out a restraining order. The girl needs to move on. Or move away.

Preferably the latter.

For the most part, I've enjoyed my time at Western University, but it'll be a relief to get the hell out of here after graduation. There's only so much of this crazy behavior I can put up with.

Carson's shoulders shake with undisguised mirth. "That's what you get for being so damn pretty."

"Fuck off," I mutter. Just because he's a good friend, doesn't mean he won't give me shit.

He shrugs. "Hey, I've got an idea. Take her to bed and show her that you're not as amazing as she thinks you are. Aren't you notorious for your starfish impersonation?"

Again...

"Up yours."

Not offended in the least, a smile breaks out across his face. "You know what you need?"

I'm almost afraid to ask.

My stoic silence doesn't stop him from continuing. "A girlfriend."

Is he nuts?

"No, thanks," I snort.

I have zero interest in one of those. Especially right now. I've got enough going on with school and football. This is a big year for me. The season is underway, and, so far, we're number one in the conference. The goal is to take home a championship and win a bowl game. That would be an amazing way to end my four years with the Wildcats. Then I can turn my attention to the NFL with the combine and draft in the spring.

"I'm serious," he says, pushing the subject.

Yeah, that's the scary part.

I shake my head, ready to put an end to this conversation.

Over the years, there have been a few girlfriends. What I've discovered is that they're more of a hassle than they're worth. Division I football is more like a job, and my schedule is packed tight. My life revolves around practice, lifting, film review, travel, and games. Most of the chicks I've dated get bent out of shape when they aren't moved to the top of my priority list and end up forcing me to choose.

Want to guess what gets downsized?

I'll give you a hint...it's not football.

After the first couple of times it happened, I decided having a permanent girl in my life wasn't worth the price of admission. Sure, it would be nice to find someone to spend time with, but that's just not in the cards. And quite frankly, I'm not sure it will be in the near future. Not with wrapping up my last year of school and hopefully getting picked up by the pros. It's just easier to screw around with the jersey chasers on campus. For the most part, they understand that sex is nothing more than an hour or so of mindless pleasure. They get to brag about banging guys on the team, and I get a little stress relief to take the edge off.

"Then Kira would have no choice but to leave you alone," he continues as if I haven't already nixed the idea.

Like I need to get myself entangled in one bad situation just to get out of another... What the hell would be the point of that?

"She should have backed off when I flat-out told her that nothing was ever going to happen between us," I mutter.

"Again, if you weren't so pretty, girls wouldn't lose their damn minds over you." His lips curl around the edges before he tacks on slyly, "*Mr. Campus Heartthrob.*"

I wince at the title I've won three years in a row.

Talk about embarrassing.

Sure, I'll admit it—I was flattered at first. Who wouldn't be? I got a ton of pussy by winning that stupid competition. My teammates were jealous, and I didn't mind rubbing it in their faces. As difficult as it is to imagine, screwing your way through all the girls vying to sleep with you gets old after a while. Now the damn thing is just a nuisance. Like I need these chicks trailing after me, following me around all over the place.

Nope. I'm over it.

Last year, I didn't enter the contest and *still* managed to win. How is that even possible?

My lips flatten before I grumble, "I prefer to think of it as ruggedly handsome. No dude wants to be called pretty."

"Please," he snorts, "your face could be plastered on a billboard. I'm surprised there aren't more crazies coming out of the woodwork just to sleep with you."

"Bite your tongue," I grunt. I don't even want to imagine that. I've got my hands full as it is. The last thing I need is to add more bullshit into the mix.

"I don't know, man. I think the girlfriend idea is worth considering. It could be the solution to all your problems."

"Or just give me more headaches." I shift my weight and take another drink from my bottle. "There's only one flaw with your plan. There aren't any girls I'm even remotely interested in."

His brows jerk together. "Who said anything about this being a real situation? I'm talking about finding a friend who could pretend to like your ass for a couple of weeks. Someone who wouldn't mind doing you a solid." He tilts his head. "Don't you know anyone like that who fits the bill?"

Hmm. I suppose a ploy like that could work. Except...there aren't any females who I'm strictly friends with. Even the ones who pretend to be platonic end up throwing themselves at me at some point. And the ones who get all drunk at parties and start sobbing about how much they love me are the absolute worst.

"Not really." I shake my head. "Any other bright ideas?"

He nods toward the backdoor. "I guess you could always try to make a run for it. Lay low at Rowan's girl's place for a couple of hours until Kira gets bored and finally takes off."

Yeah, the last time I did that, she waited around for five hours. Let that sink in.

Five.

Full.

Hours.

The woman is seriously tenacious. Must be part of the stalker job description.

I turn the suggestion over in my head. Heading over to Demi's would give me a chance to see Sydney. And I rarely pass up an opportunity to do that. There's something about the blonde-haired, green-eyed soccer player that has gotten under my skin. Kind of like an itch that is impossible to scratch. And steroids haven't done the trick to cure it, either. If she's anywhere in the vicinity, my attention is locked on her.

My guess is that it's because she refuses to give me the time of day. There's definitely something to that old adage about wanting what you can't have. And what I can't have is Sydney. That girl wants nothing to do with me, which is precisely why I never miss an opportunity to mess with her.

Trust me, I'm more than aware that I'm not doing myself any favors. But still, I get perverse satisfaction in provoking her ire. All I have to do is open my mouth and she goes off the deep end. The girl has a real temper. I've seen it rear its head on more than one occasion. My guess is that she would be a real wildcat in the sack. Not that I'll be finding out anytime soon.

Or, more than likely, ever.

As tempting as it is to flee our house for the next couple of hours, I have a test to study for. I might have every intention of taking my game to the next level by getting drafted to the NFL, but it's still important I do well in school and leave with a degree in hand. Even the most talented players are only one career-ending injury away from being let go. I'm taking every precaution to make sure that my future goes off without a hitch. Even if that means doing something other than playing professional football.

So, ducking out of here isn't really a choice. I drag a hand through my hair and consider my options before blowing out a steady breath. "All right, I'm going to need you to create a distraction so I can sneak upstairs without her noticing."

A smirk curves Carson's lips as he folds his arms across his chest and leans against the counter. "How am I supposed to do that? She's sitting in the living room with the perfect view of the front door and staircase."

Christ...this girl.

I shouldn't have to sneak around my own damn house. "I don't know," I snap in frustration, "just think of something. I need about twenty seconds to get upstairs."

It doesn't escape me that I'm taking out my aggravation on someone who doesn't deserve it, which isn't like me, but I'm over this situation. I want this girl to leave me alone. If I honestly thought sitting down and having yet another conversation with her would put an end to this infatuation, I'd do it in a heartbeat. But I've done that several times and she refuses to move on. It doesn't seem to matter that I'm not interested.

He shakes his head as if I'm the crazy one for going to such lengths to avoid her, and I'll tell you what—I'm beginning to feel like it. "I'll do my best, but I'm not making any promises."

As soon as Carson exits the kitchen, I realize that we didn't come up with a code word. I almost leap after him but stop myself at the last moment.

Damnit! How am I supposed to know that the coast is clear without a code word?

I seriously can't believe this is what my life has come to. I'm skulking around my own house to avoid some chick.

But what else can I do?

Waste the next hour or so fighting off her unwanted advances?

No way. I don't have time for that.

Grumbling under my breath, I tiptoe across the kitchen like it's boobytrapped before arriving at the wide entryway that leads to the dining room. The only furniture in the space is a scarred table that has seen better days—more like better decades—and four chairs. Everyone is crammed together, chilling in the living room. The loud, rowdy babble of voices fills my ears.

Just as I work up the courage to peek around the corner, Carson materializes on the other side. We both startle, and my heart slams against my ribcage.

"Fuck, dude...you nearly gave me a heart attack." I point to the living room. If he's with me, then who the hell is occupying Kira? Even more frighteningly, he might be drawing her attention in this direction. That's exactly what I don't need. "What are you doing in here?"

"It's not necessary," he says with a shrug. "She's gone."

No way.

My brows shoot up at that unexpected bit of good news. "Really?" Well, hot damn! Looks like I've lucked out for once.

"Yeah. I did a total sweep of the first floor. She's not in the living room, and I checked both bathrooms. They're empty. She must have gotten bored and taken off."

Huh. That was way easier than anticipated.

All of my muscles loosen with relief. Until now, I hadn't realized how tense I'd become. "Thanks, man." I slap Carson on the back. "I owe you one."

"No worries." He shoots me a grin. "I'll think of some way for you to repay me." Before I can respond, he swings around and strolls into the living room.

I grab my bottle of water along with Asher's beer before following him. Once the beverage has been passed off, I do a cursory inspection of the immediate vicinity just to make sure Carson isn't fucking with me. Although, it's doubtful he would do that. We've been friends for way too long for that kind of bullshit. If there's one guy I trust, it's him. Rowan Michaels would be a close second.

A quick scan of the room as I beeline to the staircase solidifies that Carson wasn't yanking my chain. Kira is nowhere to be seen.

Carson is right about one thing—I need to do something about this situation before it spirals any further out of control. I refuse to spend the rest of senior year looking over my shoulder and avoiding my own house. I need that chick to understand that we are never getting together. At this point, there's no way we can even be friends.

"Kendricks, where you going?" Crosby Rhodes shouts from his sprawled-out position in an armchair.

I flick my gaze at him. Like most of the other guys, he's

surrounded by a handful of females. Being on the football team will get you all the chicks you could ask for. Having a lip ring and a sullen attitude will get you twice as many.

Go figure.

"Got a test to study for," I call back, trudging up the steps.

"Come on, Kendricks, let me kick your ass in a little GTA," Easton adds from the couch he's stretched out on.

It's a tempting offer, but still...

"If memory serves, aren't I the one who kicked yours the last time we played?" I shoot back.

Easton smirks before shoving his chestnut-colored hair out of his bright blue eyes. If I'm not mistaken, a few girls in the room sigh. "Maybe. How about a rematch, then?"

"Sorry, not tonight."

It might not seem like it, but I've never been a slouch in the partying department. Freshman year is nothing more than a blur. I spent most of it shitfaced, attempting to drown the grief that had been my constant companion.

Big surprise—it didn't work.

What did end up happening is that I almost flunked out of college and got my ass kicked off the football team. Coach Richards pulled me aside at the end of the season and told me that I had a choice to make—either pull myself together or get the hell out of his program.

I could do one or the other, but not both.

That conversation had been a rude awakening, and it had been exactly what I needed to hear. The year before, I'd lost one of the most important people in my life. Losing football on top of it wasn't a choice I was willing to make. I returned home and dried out over the summer. I focused on working out in the gym and getting stronger so I could prove to Coach that he hadn't made a mistake in recruiting me. When I returned to Western for my sophomore year, I swapped out the alcohol for pussy. I guess if you can't drown your sorrows in beer, girls are a close second. Except...it doesn't actually solve anything or make your problems disappear. You just run the risk of an STI.

"Lame ass," Easton shouts after me.

Knowing that I don't have anything to prove, the taunt slides easily off my back. My accomplishments and the records I've broken over the years speak for themselves. "Yup."

As I disappear onto the second floor, I swing right and pass by two doors before arriving at mine. Now that Kira is no longer a concern, my mind gravitates to the exam I need to cram for. I grab hold of the handle and push open the thick wood before crossing over the threshold. I probably have three solid hours of work ahead of me. After doing my damnedest to flunk out freshman year, it's taken a lot of focus and determination to raise my GPA. The fact that, two years later, it's over a three point zero is a source of pride for me.

I'm jerked out of those thoughts by a noise as my gaze cuts to the queen-sized bed at the far end of the room.

And the naked girl lying on top of it.

"Hey, Brayden," Kira coos, shifting on the comforter as she spreads her legs wide. "I've been waiting for you."

Well, hell.

One-click Campus Heartthrob now!

MORE BOOKS BY JENNIFER SUCEVIC

ABOUT JENNIFER

Jennifer Sucevic is a USA Today bestselling author who has published twenty-four new adult novels. Her work has been translated into German, Dutch, Italian, and French. She has a bachelor's degree in History and a master's in Educational Psychology from the University of Wisconsin-Milwaukee. Jen started out her career as a high school counselor before relocating with her family and focusing on her passion for writing. When she's not tapping away on the keyboard and dreaming up swoonworthy heroes to fall in love with, you can find her bike riding or at the beach. She lives in Michigan with her family.

If you would like to receive regular updates regarding new releases, please subscribe to her newsletter here-
Jennifer Sucevic Newsletter (subscribepage.com)

Or contact Jen through email, at her website, or on Facebook.
sucevicjennifer@gmail.com

Want to join her reader group? Do it here -)
J Sucevic's Book Boyfriends | Facebook

Social media links-
https://www.tiktok.com/@jennifersucevicauthor
www.jennifersucevic.com
https://www.instagram.com/jennifersucevicauthor

https://www.facebook.com/jennifer.sucevic
Amazon.com: Jennifer Sucevic: Books, Biography, Blog, Audiobooks, Kindle
Jennifer Sucevic Books - BookBub

Made in the USA
Monee, IL
12 September 2024

65545128R00215